A HANDBOOK FOR BEAUTIFUL PEOPLE

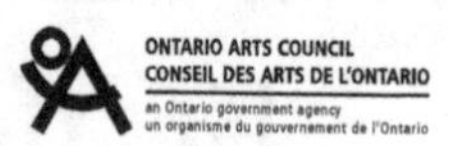

We gratefully acknowledge the support of the Canada Council for the Arts and the Ontario Arts Council for our publishing program. We also acknowledge the financial support of the Government of Canada.

Cover design: Val Fullard

Library and Archives Canada Cataloguing in Publication

Spruit, Jennifer, 1982-, author
A handbook for beautiful people / a novel by Jennifer Spruit.

(Inanna poetry & fiction series)
Issued in print and electronic formats.
ISBN 978-1-77133-441-9 (softcover).-- ISBN 978-1-77133-442-6 (epub).--
ISBN 978-1-77133-443-3 (Kindle).-- ISBN 978-1-77133-444-0 (pdf)

I. Title. II. Series: Inanna poetry and fiction series

PS8637.P778H36 2017 C813'.6 C2017-905379-5
C2017-905380-9

Printed and bound in Canada

Inanna Publications and Education Inc.
210 Founders College, York University
4700 Keele Street, Toronto, Ontario, Canada M3J 1P3
Telephone: (416) 736-5356 Fax: (416) 736-5765
Email: inanna.publications@inanna.ca Website: www.inanna.ca

A HANDBOOK FOR BEAUTIFUL PEOPLE

a novel

JENNIFER SPRUIT

INANNA PUBLICATIONS AND EDUCATION INC.
TORONTO, CANADA

In memory of Angel Buggins,
who laughed louder than the rest.

TABLE OF CONTENTS

PROLOGUE: **FROM A GREAT HEIGHT**

GAVIN CLIMBS with his bare hands on the cold cement, the nobility of the stone lions forgotten, and drops down on the wrong side. Headlights flash, and he worries someone will stop now that he's here and it's almost over, so he backs his heels against the hard certainty of the bridge, trying to be invisible. Under his foot, a rock skitters and disappears, but Gavin can't hear it land. The Bow River below is glacial, rushing and wide, cutting into the sandstone bedrock like it has for centuries. It is thick with spring runoff, surging like a returning hero who is both majestic and dangerous. This is when he should try to find grounds big enough to overcome what has been done, but he has no reason. Only a chest filled with rage.

Gavin unbuttons his pocket to get the wad of bills. He takes the elastic band off and fans them out, seeing the look she gave, then deals them into the river, stalling until the last flimsy flutter. Then he reaches behind himself, tentative, feeling with his fingers until he can hold on tight and lean out over the water and really see the blackness of it.

Until tonight he's always been afraid.

1. FIRST: APPLE SEED

WELL PAST DARK, Marla shakes the tree branch she waits under, thinking snowflakes will fall on her hair and make her look like she walked out of a snow globe. Instead, a hump of wet snow thumps on her head and drifts under her collar. She scoops it out because she is not going to look slushy in front of her man. Tonight she is a lady.

"Where are we going?" Liam matches his steps over the snow bank with the old footprints of others because he's wearing alligator shoes that he cares about, and gives his car a wide berth to avoid the caked-on road salt. Just the way he adjusts his scarf makes her sure she is right about him.

"Surprise," she says.

The wind whistles between the downtown office towers, swinging the streetlights and blowing dried-out snow and frozen garbage back and forth. Foggy lights and bass lines filter out of downtown clubs, and the C-train rattles past in fluorescent glow, carrying teenagers, drunks, minimum wage earners, hockey gamers. Several sidewalks are blocked off because falling ice has been letting go all day, slipping down glass buildings to shatter on cars and hot dog stands. Against the barriers, bands of tittering girls without coats smoke and pretend they don't feel frozen. Marla remembers that.

It's warm inside. Liam holds the door for her, and she purposely walks slowly to create a real Marla moment as she enters the lobby of the concert hall, sliding her coat from her shoulders. She twirls for the clavicle-baring women who stand with their arms held just so while they laugh in a tinkly way at men with generous amounts of grey. Marla grins, thinking she's probably the youngest, tightest woman here. "I love the orchestra," Liam says, squeezing her hand. "Thank you."

Marla knew it. She's been planning this for weeks, saving her diner tips in a spaghetti sauce jar on the stove to buy the best tickets left.

Liam treats her to a glass of wine. She likes the feel of its delicate stem between her fingers, its crystal perfection. It feels like a good omen, and she toasts him. "To me and you."

It's then that a gentleman walking by nods to Liam, causing Liam to pause in mid-toast and stand straighter. "Liam! You're not playing tonight, are you?" The man has one of those goosy accents Marla is into.

"No, I, not tonight. A Russian cellist." Liam fingers his tie and talks with his hands when the gentleman commends him on his performance of Fauré's *Elegy* during a youth talent showcase a decade ago: "Such subtlety and complexity, an incredible range of emotion."

Marla has seen Liam's cello, of course, but she has only ever heard him play it when he's teaching lessons. She remembers peeking around the open door to see him hold it the way one would hold a lover, swaying and confident like the two of them were dancing. She feels suddenly flushed, and sips her wine so no one will notice. It tastes heavy and dark and beautiful, just like this night around her.

The goosy gentleman has his hand on Liam's shoulder. "You're a teacher, right? The University of Calgary Music Department is looking for a cellist. You should apply."

"I haven't played like that for years." Liam smooths his tie, looking down, which is too much for Marla.

"Oh, you should," she says, thinking about him on stage in a tux with tails, bow in hand. Or at a bar, everyone forgetting to breathe because of him.

The gentleman grins in a grandpa way. "And who is this? A student?"

Liam leans close to him. "This is Marla. My girlfriend."

"Oh, I'm sorry—" He turns to Liam. "I heard you swore off women?"

Liam pulls on his earlobe, looking around at no one in particular. He keeps his voice low. "Marla's different." Liam catches Marla's eye, and she wonders if it's an apology.

"What do you do, Marla?"

Marla doesn't answer for a moment, listening to couples behind her make educated little quips about nothing she could ever care about. She looks down at her thrift store shoes and fishnet stockings, which are both really awesome. "I'm a waitress at a diner. I serve coffee."

Liam puts his arm around her. "She's an excellent waitress."

The man, who hasn't introduced himself, *hmmms*. "At least you're not another artist, right?" When he finally leaves, Marla rolls her eyes and tugs Liam towards the entrance to the theatre.

Liam checks his phone. "Sorry. I know him. He's a violinist."

"They know you everywhere."

He nuzzles her neck. "Not the way you do."

Marla traces the outline of his ear, down his jawline. "No, I shouldn't think so."

Liam laughs. "Are you affecting a British accent?"

"Indeed I am."

The orchestra plays the best part first, a wave of sound that grows and swoons and then falls to pieces, all arising from the oboe. They do it for each group of instruments, and each time Marla cheers.

Liam winces at the older couple beside them. "No one cheers for tuning, Marla. No one cheers here at all."

Marla sits very straight. "I always cheer for what I love."

For the rest of the night, the orchestra makes nosedives and roaring animals out of valves and wood and horsetails. Marla watches the string players, admiring how they saw together like a line of lumberjacks. This is fine for several minutes, but the music is nonstop, rushing to a climax only to wallow in several minutes of fluty fluff. A tease.

Marla steals a glance at Liam, who has his eyes on the soloist, a man who is solid of purpose the way Liam is, arching his neck like he's in the throes of indescribable passion. Liam is almost completely at peace: his hands gentle in his lap, eyes soft, nostrils flared in the hint of a smile coming. Marla feels the sound fall away, even the bonging big tub drums and the cymbals (how pale and silly to be a cymbal player, she thinks), as she reaches for her man's hand.

After the concert, Marla can't bear to be out in the black, cold night and slips off her heels. She runs past the other concert-goers through still corridors to try the doors to the plus fifteens, the covered walkways that connect buildings fifteen feet above ground.

Liam doesn't want to chase her at first, but she calls him on, lightened by the energy of the orchestra. He has no choice but to follow her through a maze of little passages—past art exhibits and parking garage pay stations, over traffic, up and down stairs, and around corners to create an impossibly convoluted route to his car. Marla knows all the plus fifteens; she has them memorized like a map she holds in her hand. But she's not homeless now.

When they finally emerge in a concrete stairway with metal railings, Marla kisses him under the glowing EXIT sign. "Liam, take me to Nose Hill."

He laughs, holding her slender hands in his. "It's minus twenty-five."

"I want to see the pony."

He smiles, fond. "That was a deer."

"You didn't see it. When will we go?"

"When it is spring."

Liam carries her the half block to his car, where she puts on her shoes. Marla turns on dance music just to hear something thump along with her heart. She loses herself as she sings, badly, and realizes too late that they're at his house.

Liam's neighbourhood was rough and worth little when his still-together parents bought here decades ago, but has been well tended for years by hedge-growing senior citizens who trusted its proximity to downtown would be valuable in the end. Now Liam's mother is gone, and the house is his, at least in name. Inside there are traces of him, like the upright bass he won in a duelling banjos kind of thing or the musical score from some opera taped to the wall, but they are intruders compared to his mother's period furniture or the paintings by his ex-wife.

"I can't stay tonight." She catches Liam's eyes just long enough to see he is all wounded. "It's not that I don't want to."

"I get it. You have a child."

Marla turns the dance volume off. "Hey, that's mean."

"What am I supposed to say? It's not right, whatever you two have."

Marla sighs audibly because it's totally exhausting to explain her roommate to him every day. "Dani's life is complicated."

"She's a drug addict."

"She's my friend. Come to my place, Liam. You don't work until lunch."

Liam considers it, his face tight. He flips his keys back and forth with his fingers. "Okay. But I want to show you something first."

He leads her down. In the basement corner with the best natural light are framed walls for a little room. The floor is tiled, which causes Marla to feel kind of astounded. "Didn't this used to be concrete?"

"It's for you, for when you finish massage school. You'll need a place to work until you can get your own office." He stands aside so she can really admire the two-by-fours, how straight they stand.

Marla bites her bottom lip. "I'm not even in massage school."

"But you should be."

Marla shakes her head and strokes Liam's chest, gentle. "Let's talk about it later." She slides her hand down, parting the folds of her handkerchief dress. He watches her, shivering.

She kisses him softly, pulling him into her until her back rests against the naked frame.

While Liam's neighbourhood is full of people all tucked in for the night, Marla's is alive: teens posturing in front of the liquor store, grizzled guys and trashy women at the pool hall, future oilfield workers wheeling their hockey bags out of the arena. On the corner, the bus lets people off, and they walk, their breath steaming in the cold. Bowness is rough and ready, full of people who use the street to holler at pretty girls or work together to push a stalled pickup out of the intersection.

Marla lives in the big house beside the church, and the downstairs belongs to Dani. The light is still on in the basement, and Marla can hear music: big band again.

Liam pauses at the door. "She hates me."

"You hate each other equally. I just need to know she's not starting fires or something." Marla shoves a pile of newspapers and boots over to open the door all the way, and leaves her jacket hung over a chair. Marla can't tell if Liam is afraid of Dani or jealous. Maybe both.

Dani's in her bathrobe eating pizza, picking the mushrooms off and flicking them into the box. She hums with the music, breaking into song between bites.

Marla lifts the lid of the record player, but before she can move the arm thingy, Dani is in her face. "Don't touch the vinyl, please." She wipes the lid with her sleeve like Marla soiled it, leaving it loud. "I didn't hear your ass coming in. You could have been a rapist."

"Expecting someone?"

Dani tucks the tag in on Marla's dress. "E's coming by. You know E."

"I don't want drug dealers here."

"He's fine. How was your date? Did you fall asleep?"

"Liam's upstairs. We're going to—"

"Oh, I know what you'll be doing." Dani arches her back as she runs a hand over her breasts and down her side. She moans, and it turns into a dog howling. She barks, grinning at Marla. "Liam!" Dani hollers, "when you get tired of Marla, come give me a ride!"

"Gross." Marla hears the clank of metal on metal upstairs—Liam has dropped something in the sink. Marla takes a piece of pizza from Dani's box and nibbles it. "Don't knock it just because you've never made love."

Dani closes the lid and puts the box in her mini fridge. "The things you don't know."

Marla saves the crust for last and munches it, savouring the crunchiness. "I have to go."

"It's been a slice. You have that forty bucks?"

Marla forgot. All she has left is a ten. "Don't do it."

Dani unwinds Marla's scarf, close enough for Marla to feel her breath. Dani wraps the end of the scarf around her own neck, slowly, so they're joined together for a moment. Her arms move in the kind of arc that encapsulates her femininity: showing vulnerability but completely in charge. Dani's voice tickles, but her eyes are hard. "Hustling isn't something I do. It's who I am."

Marla shakes her head, takes the scarf back. "I want you safe." She helps Dani dig under the couch cushions and through the coffee cans in the cupboard, but they don't find anything. "Turn it down, Dani. I'll get your money."

Marla checks her messages—two missed texts, both from her foster mom. *How was your big night? Just checking in.* Trying to be involved.

Upstairs, Liam has finished the dishes, wiped each one, and put them in the cupboard. "I don't like your pet," he tells her. "When is she leaving?"

Marla shrugs, shutting the door to the basement so Dani

won't hear. "She's getting clean so she can get her son back." Marla hasn't told him the rest.

"I doubt that. Look." E. saunters past the window wearing yellow denim. He has witchy hair, coloured and primped into planned cowlicks and angles. He purses his lips in an O at them, and then bangs on the back door. Dani yodels from downstairs, and the door bumps open and shut.

Liam crosses his arms. "Predictable."

Marla fusses with her fingernails and reminds herself to smile. "I know what you're thinking. He's not a pimp—he's a beauty school dropout." She feels under the table where she leaves all the produce stickers, peeling them off with her fingernails, nervous.

Liam doesn't laugh. "He's a drug dealer, Marla."

Okay, it's not funny. "Give her a chance. She's going through some shit." Liam raises his eyebrows, and Marla realizes she's angry. "Sorry, stuff. It's hard for her." Marla mentally shakes it off, smoothing her hands over her dress. "Come."

Marla leads Liam to her bedroom with its yellow paint and sunflower curtains. She pushes some laundry off the mattress and removes his jacket, loosens his tie, leaves his wallet on the windowsill. Marla holds his hands, pulling slightly on each joint and squeezing negative energy out of his fingers. "Is it bad?"

"Worse than yesterday, but not the worst." Liam's hands are beautiful, with long fingers and delicate bones. He opens and closes a gentle fist with a slight tremor.

"Could you still play?"

"Maybe. Not like before." She knows his parents moved him here from northern Saskatchewan when he was six to make more money to pay better music teachers. This was the big city, and he travelled it like a champion, consistently adjudicated one of the best young cellists in the country.

Marla lays him down, her hand on his beating heart. "You have to try." She undresses above him, draping her dress briefly over his face. He leans his head back in pleasure, and, as he does, she slips two bills out of his wallet before she clicks off the light. Like he's someone else.

They are interrupted by Dani's shrieks from downstairs. "Oh! Making love! So good! So fucking good!" The wheels on Dani's bedframe roll back and forth as the headboard hits the wall.

"That's enough." Liam pushes Marla up and rips the covers from them both. He stomps on the floor until it's quiet, but Marla knows what's coming. As Liam sinks into bed, Dani does a high-pitched *ariba* with rolled r's: The Mexican.

Marla turns away, Liam's money crumpled in her fist.

Gavin leaves his work at the care home as dusk grows into dark. Old snow sits heavy against concrete dividers, and cars flash by. He walks tall and quick, going over his plan. If he sees them, he's ready.

Near the bus stop, Gavin takes the stairs to the pedestrian overpass two at a time, glancing behind every few steps. There he is.

"Hey, retard!" Same flashy red hoody, black cap with straight brim: the guy that mugged him. No friends this time.

Gavin takes the stairs sideways now. He reaches into his pocket, making sure they're alone. He feels the hard plastic, the soft circle.

"Say something...."

Gavin squeezes the air horn repeatedly until Black Cap backs away, hands on his ears. It must be awful, but Gavin can't hear it. He takes a moment to congratulate himself—victory at last! —smiling at how simple it was until he feels something raining down on him from the pedestrian overpass. Each warm drop marks him with defeat. Piss.

Black Cap is laughing at him, shouting up to his friend. Gavin can make out only one word—retard. This is exactly how it wasn't supposed to be. He could scramble under the stairs, go home stinking, and add another check to the list of times he stopped himself from hurting someone—but he rounds the corner, through the piss, wanting to feel his hands on someone real and warm and laughing at him. Gavin grabs Black Cap by the collar and cocks his fist, his movements precise, measured, and serious, because as soon as he can deal with this kid, Gavin will feel calm again. But that's the thing: Black Cap's a kid, maybe fourteen, fifteen at most, with his fuzzy upper lip and the expensive shoes his parents bought him. Gavin hesitates, trying to maintain an expression that might intimidate the kid, but letting go of his collar, remembering the rules. He forces his hands down by his sides, thinking about that list.

Black Cap grins and shoves Gavin, his mouth moving. Gavin grabs at the railing to steady himself, but it's slick with urine. He comes down hard, and when he gets up, the kid is already up the stairs under the security camera, taunting him. Gavin throws the air horn to the ground and stomps on it until the plastic breaks, his heartbeat banging in his useless ears.

People give Gavin lots of room at the bus stop. He wipes his face with a tissue from his bag and sees blood, smells piss in his hair. Gavin forces his feelings down, holds back while the suited commuters exit, and boards last. He straightens his spine, telling himself it could have been worse. A little niggling thought flashes in his mind: the principal's office, the social worker, and the slow certainty that he was never going home. Hitting a teacher, pushing other kids. That time. Gavin bites his lip, harder than he should, and the feelings stop.

He sits down gently, wrapping his coat around himself. That's when he first notices the handbook.

same guys last night
what'd they think of the air horn?
worked for second
bad?

pissed on
fuckers. we'll get them.

Marla rolls over and tries to go back to sleep, but Liam's side of the bed is cold. She pads into the kitchen because it smells like coffee and something involving flour, but he's gone.

He left a note—*going to practise before work*—and fresh pancakes on the counter. Awesome! Marla didn't even know she had the ingredients. She brings a plateful to Dani, who reclines in her chair with the duct-taped arms, watching a talk show in the morning dark.

"Thanks for the cash last night."

It was easy for Marla to slip it under Dani's door after she was sure Liam was asleep, but it's harder to justify anything down here during the day, when the angle of the winter sun keeps everything grey: Dani's tiny fridge and her neat records and her pills. "I'm not doing that again."

"I'm not asking you to."

But Marla knows what the alternative is. "What about rehab?"

Dani wraps two pancakes in plastic and puts them in the fridge. "No. Don't worry about me. Where's your man?"

Marla shrugs. It's best not to say.

"He's gone again? I told you, there's a reason the wife didn't want him."

Marla hears a scratching from the bathroom. "What's that?" She sniffs.

"Got a dog. You didn't notice him last night?"

"No."

"Yeah. He's not very noisy." Dani opens the bathroom door to reveal a yellow lab that jumps up on her and Marla alternately.

"Where'd you get him?"

"Followed me home yesterday." Dani snaps her fingers in the air for the puppy to jump at. "It's for Kamon."

Marla rubs his fur, lets him gnaw her fingers. She doesn't consider the logistics of Dani giving her son a puppy. Kamon is almost five years old, but Dani hasn't had custody for two or three years. Dani sees Kamon once a month, if her mom lets her.

The puppy licks her bare feet, making it easy to forget. "He's gonna love this."

Dani rolls a pancake and eats it like a slice of bologna. "Well, yeah. Are you going to drive me?"

"When is it again?"

"Christmas Day. Set a reminder so you're not off bonking Liam."

"Got it. Christmas Day."

The puppy puts his paws on the table and knocks the pancakes down, then pees on the floor in excitement.

"Shit." Dani moves him to the bathroom. "Fucking animal."

Marla looks around, settling on an old flyer to sop up the wet. She is down on the floor when something about the yellow linoleum with dog urine slopped about makes her shudder. It's definitely the smell.

She runs for the bathroom, pushing open the door Dani's trying to stuff the dog behind. He leaps up, pissing a bit more. Marla harfs into the sink.

"Oh, shit, Marla. Too much party again?"

Marla takes a deep breath, spits, wipes her mouth, and hangs over the counter. She runs the faucet, but a miserable puddle of stringy puke clogs the drain. "I only had one glass of wine."

Dani leans against the sliding shower door. "Too much cock, then."

Marla laughs so hard she almost heaves again. "That happened one time, Dani. One time." Marla closes her eyes and catches her breath.

Dani ignores the jumping dog and swats Marla on the rear. "You know, you are one sexy lady. You keep working it. Work that right into the toilet for me."

Marla has to turn her head to scoop the chunks into the toilet. They plop down. The sound makes her wobbly.

Dani notices and sits her on the edge of the tub. "Leave it." She squints at Marla. "Take your shirt off."

Marla does. "Why, is there puke on it?"

"No." Dani looks at her carefully, then pinches Marla's nipple.

"Ow! Fuck!" Marla wraps her arms around her sensitive breasts.

Dani shakes her head. "Call Liam."

"Why?"

"You are one hundred percent knocked up."

2. BIGGER: RAVIOLI

MARLA DOESN'T BELIEVE DANI—thinks it's indigestion or bad Indian takeout from the other night—but she does the test anyway, in secret the next morning before work. The pee stick blinks at her from the floor with its two eyes. This is the same as all the high school math Marla failed to understand, like infinity is actually right here in this bathroom, her life suddenly wide open with incalculable geometry. She stares at this plastic gossip on the cracked linoleum, and then checks the box to confirm that two lines means what she thinks it does. Pregnant. Of course.

Marla shakes a bit, but reminds herself not to be stupid: one has to go about these things properly. She pulls her pants up and buttons them. Dani's right—she is bigger. Marla mimes an oversized womb unfolding out of her front, curving her fingers like she's holding a skirt full of peaches. That's a happy image.

First things first: Marla grabs the Calgary Flames schedule magnet from the fridge for easier counting. If she's sick and testing positive, then she's what, six weeks into this? Maybe more with a size increase. She thought it was just the winter blahs. Marla counts thirty-four weeks from now and runs out of season. Next summer. June? July?

This is what she knows: a baby means a family. It means making scrambled eggs for breakfast, holding the baby on her hip. It means birthday cakes for little friends at the Riley Park wading pool in summer. Car seats and storybooks and playschool. It means all the things she never had.

Marla looks in the mirror and tells herself to snap out of it. A baby is forever. She bites her lip. But this would be her baby. Her very own.

She pictures Liam holding a baby, cuddling her while she claps her pudgy hands, but cuts it before the fantasy baby can grab Liam's wire-rim glasses and spit up all over his crisp shirt. She wants to call him, but all this extra preening has made Marla nearly late for work.

Last: closing her eyes, she can believe in herself. A baby. She doesn't deserve such richness.

Today no one knows. She is righteous, a miracle, the property of humanity, because she has gone and done what her foster parents told her she would. She breathes fast, her heartbeat like a rabbit's. At quarter to eight it's still dark, but there are lights on down the block and cars idling on the street. Marla doesn't mind this time of year, finding it reassuring that neither night nor weather gets in the way of the movement of the city.

Her car starts on the second try. Today more than ever, Marla drives with old lady tension due to the terrifying brakes on her shit-heap car: they are right spongy, sopping wet, and full of holes. She inches along 16th Avenue, relieved for the traffic pileup that guarantees no sudden stops. There was no time to bleed the brake lines, and besides, she needs two people: one to push the brake, Liam's job.

She dials Liam. "Guess what?"

Liam's voice sounds fuzzy, like it's coming through a plastic pipe. "Marla, what is it?" He seems concerned. Busy.

"I have something to tell you."

"What happens before eight?" Marla can hear Liam's espresso machine beeping.

"Lots of things. I got a prize in my cereal, I used a new toothbrush, and I found out I'm pregnant."

"No, you didn't. Well, maybe you did get a prize."

In truth, Marla has used pregnancy as a conversation starter in the past, but also outrageous things that are true, like being pulled onstage at a punk concert, and rescuing a baby rabbit from a scraggly dog. Liam's so rhythmic in his schedule that Marla finds herself accentuating her whimsy and packaging it in stories about her lovability. She wants everyone to love her, but especially him. Marla thinks about it, reconfiguring. Most women probably do this over celebratory dessert. "I got a pair of 3D glasses. I can take them to the movies."

"You can't try something like that on, Marla. A baby isn't a joke."

"You're right. Hey, let's get together tonight. Supper?"

"I'm working, but come by later."

"'Kay." He hangs up, and she holds the warm phone in her hand at the stoplight. Liam, the father of her baby. She pictures him wearing a baby carrier and giggles.

Gavin holds the spoon level and waits for Stephen to open his lips before he slides it in. Stephen's tongue is pointy and patchy-white. It knocks the spoon around, causing a dribble to run down Stephen's chin to the napkin Gavin pinned to Stephen's shirt. Stephen shrugs, sorry, and Gavin shakes off his momentary disgust. It's not Stephen's fault. Gavin thinks of his own first teacher and how she sat with him, patiently signing the same words over and over, showing him pictures and moving his hands for him. Gavin dabs at Stephen's face with a warm wet cloth and tries again.

After lunch, Gavin wheels Stephen through an early eighties suburb to get a real coffee and people-watch, their guilty pleasure. Stephen types on his computer, and his software reads it aloud in a robot voice Gavin can't hear. Gavin reads it on the screen. "Look at her."

Gavin sees her, a girl just out of high school with straight black hair and yoga pants. His age. Gavin turns off Stephen's volume and writes on his notepad. PERV. CLD BE DAUGHTER.

"For you, Casanova."

DON'T TALK HEARING GIRL.

Stephen cocks his head more than usual, his body spasming. Compared to Stephen, Gavin knows he's being precious, but he can't help it. Since he finished high school, Gavin hasn't kept up with his friends, all of whom are deaf. Most of them left for university, one to backpack Europe. He doesn't know anyone else who signs.

"Get a life," Stephen types.

Gavin's heart beats faster. This is his safe, easy life with no surprises. It's true he was accepted to U. of T. for January, when they will have a translator available, but he's been telling himself this job is too important. There's no need to take a risk. NOT GO ANYWHERE.

"You're amazing, don't get me wrong, but there's more to life than wiping my ass."

Gavin chokes on his coffee, he's laughing so hard. Stephen too, flapping his good hand against his knee. People are staring.

Gavin glances at his watch. NEED GO. ART THERAPY.

"Think about it."

Gavin accidentally bumps Stephen's wheel into a table as he tries to navigate the narrow space of the café, and feels several people watching. The yoga pants girl moves her chair to clear a path, calling to him, but Gavin doesn't notice. He won't feel better until he's wheeled Stephen back through the entrance of the care home, where everyone is used to him and art therapy is at the same time every day.

Marla uses her foot to open the clinic door, juggling her bag and the two coffees she had to ask the barista next door if she could pay for later.

"Hey, Katelynn," Marla says, leaving one on the ledge for the receptionist, who's on the phone, her usual arrangement. Marla suddenly remembers she should probably pour her own coffee out. Is that a thing?

Katelynn loosens her phone face for a second to sip coffee

with exaggerated bliss. Then it's back to business. "I understand that, but I can't squeeze you in until tomorrow."

Three mornings a week, Marla is the file clerk here. She creates new patient files and sorts paperwork on pull-out trays between rows of shelves. The shelving units have twisting plastic handles, like ship's wheels. Each bank lumbers over: port, starboard. There aren't any windows, so Marla distracts herself in other ways, swaying and whispering the good last names. It's impossible not to read about the people who come here.

Julie Goodman suffers from frequent thirst, fainting, and yeast infection. She's thirty-three years old and heavy. Marla checks the lab results to see if they tested her A1C levels. Poor gal: diabetes.

Marla scans the year of birth on lab requisition forms, looking for grandparents. She pulls several files, reading the doctor's notes until she finds what she's looking for. EPA and DHA. Isn't that fish oil?

Someone's coming. Marla slaps a stack of files on the one she was reading and pretends to be sorting by date.

"Marla, hey. This is Alex." Katelynn indicates a hipster university girl with a plush vest and ironed pants. "Alex has a nursing practicum here this semester."

Alex nods and shakes Marla's hand before Marla knows it's happening. "Pleased to meet you, Marla."

Marla stands taller and reconsiders the black stockings she wore for Liam's benefit, wanting to say something about them to lighten the super-professional mood, but Katelynn catches her eye and interrupts. "Marla helps with filing. She's a friend of Dr. Leal's."

"My foster parents. They're his friends." Marla clears her throat. "Maybe we can all get lunch later," she adds, but Alex and Katelynn are already continuing their tour.

Marla eavesdrops as Katelynn lists Alex's duties: filling out patient intake forms, weighing children for the doctor, dipping urine. As if it's so complicated to fill out forms they need Alex and her vest.

Marla's phone vibrates but she can't answer it here. She waits until the caller leaves a message, then goes to the bathroom to check it.

Three short whistles, then a flutter from loud to soft. Two low rolls at the end. Gavin is like a bird, a loon in late summer.

She texts him that he is her favourite. That his voice is the sweetest.

She usually ignores the Employees Must Wash Hands poster out of spite, with all its ninny rules like using paper towel as some kind of barrier between her hand and the taps. Any other day it would be ridiculous.

Pregnant. Marla tickles her tummy, her little creature. She wants to be fabulously big, right now, in this pastel public washroom! Marla fantasizes about her belly button ballooning out like it could be pinched. When she tells Liam, he's probably going to start bawling and tell her he's the luckiest man ever.

After work, Marla heads to her other job, the one she got all by herself. The falling snow is heavy and sticky, the kind that makes commuters nervous. Marla suspects she'll leave the car at work overnight. The diner is in Motel Village, which is a strip mall of concrete bunkers stacked between the university and a McDonalds on the highway, bordered by the football stadium. Some of the motels have windows too small to climb out of, all barred. The diner's open twenty-four hours.

The pay at the diner is better, somewhat in spite of the clientele. Coffee-drinking seniors are good tippers, but it takes quite a few of them to make any money—they come in the morning and fill the seats for hours. Drunk university students come after eight, and half of them tip fabulously on giant meals and endless refills. The rest eyeball girls and barf in the dirty bathrooms. Marla covets the evening shift, but her prissy manager isn't keen yet. Marla's still on afternoons, proving herself.

After lunch, when the restaurant is asleep, Marla makes her move. "Naomi, I need you to cover for me," she says. Naomi is a wrestler at the university, all long muscles. She once did the worm in the diner's entrance.

"Yeah, what for?" She's filling ketchup bottles, dancing with them.

"I have to go to the walk-in clinic to renew my birth control."

Naomi shakes her head. "You need a physical for that. It'll take forever."

"I always tell them I'm just on break and I'll do the exam next time."

"Really? That works?"

"Every time." Marla is always so happy when university kids with their brand-new phones look up to her. She could teach them a thing or two.

"But Bettina's coming on soon." Bettina is stick thin and gets mani-pedis and hates when Marla forgets to stack the menus face-up. She's the manager.

"Tell her I'm taking the grease out or I'm making a call from the can. I'll be back in a half hour."

Marla is positive she's pregnant. She went through the checklist twice: no period, sore breasts, a new tendency towards napping, and a positive pregnancy test. This is for confirmation, to find out what to do next.

Marla takes the C-train two stops with university students and grandmothers with wheeled carts. It's not cold now, and she looks forward to riding the bus to Liam's because there's a bus stop at the Vietnamese noodle place. She wades through the snow piling in the parking lot, past the banks and fast food joints with their drive thru lines idling, the sagging grocery store and the pub with the dark wood panelling, to the walk-in clinic. She answers no to everything on the medical history form except for "Female Only: Pregnant Not Pregnant". She circles Pregnant and then writes beside it, "Yes, I am knocked up," for emphasis. She's always liked the sound of that phrase.

Marla scans the other questions and stops at "Other," with its stack of blank lines. She should probably write it, in case it's important for the baby, so she does. Marla hands her form in, feeling good, like the first girl to finish her test. She flips through magazines, stuffing one in her purse for Dani.

When the nurse calls her, Marla fills the pee cup and leaves it in the hole in the wall, then waits in the examination room. The walls are covered with posters and pamphlets about how the inside of a person should be behaving: bodies cross-sectioned and full of plasticine-like parts. Marla wishes she had someone to bring with her to this appointment, someone who could tell her it's normal to be excited in a heart-in-your-throat way. Her foster parents, Dave and Elise, will be disappointed because they think she can't do anything right. She hasn't told Dani yet in case it makes her sad about Kamon. She wants to be sure.

The doctor taps on the door as he opens it. "Marla?" he says. He is mid-forties with lush hair, wearing dress-for-success socks. Marla likes that even down to his feet he is a prepster. He reads a paper, the one she filled out. "You are definitely pregnant."

Marla congratulates herself and her tiny stowaway. What a feat!

"What was the date of your last menstrual period?"

Oh. "I'm not sure, exactly." He's looking at her over the rims of his glasses like she's an insolent twelve-year old instead of twenty-two. "It's probably been almost two months."

"You should narrow down the date," he reprimands. "I take it you will be terminating?"

"Pardon?" This man must have the wrong person.

"The pregnancy. You will be terminating it?"

Marla shakes her head slowly. She hadn't considered abortion. "No, I don't think so. I mean, I don't know how far along I am."

"The D and C can be performed up to thirteen weeks gestation. An ultrasound will confirm the dates."

Marla thinks about it, trying to hurry because the doctor is tapping his foot. It's the logical thing to do, she supposes. Get this taken care of and maybe have another baby sometime. Marla pictures herself lying on the table for the procedure. Would Liam come? Dani would, but she would say harsh things maybe, sad things, and Marla would cry.

The doctor is not fazed. "Well?"

"I don't know, I mean, I just thought about keeping it." She brushes a hair from her face and accidentally knocks the vagina light awkwardly close to her ear.

The doctor repositions it without looking up. "It says here you have fetal alcohol syndrome. What kind of support network do you have?"

It's partial FAS, but she doesn't correct him. He should be able to read. "I have my boyfriend, and some other people."

He takes off his glasses to level with her. "You know, this is a decision you want to be really sure about." The way he's looking at her gives her such a horrible mix of self-pity and shame that it feels like hatred. "I'll write you a requisition for an ultrasound, and you can go from there."

"I'm not an idiot," she says.

The doctor pulls pamphlets off the wall as he talks. "Of course not. If you decide to carry the baby, absolutely no drinking. Also: no smoking; eat nutritious foods, there is no need to binge; take prenatal vitamins with folic acid; some bleeding is normal; if you are going to miscarry, don't go to the hospital, there is really nothing we can do at this stage. After the first three months, you should have regular prenatal care. Do you have a family physician?"

She shakes her head, a bad mom already, holding government-sponsored literature on quitting smoking. Isn't he going to do an exam? "I don't smoke anymore," she says.

He's not listening. "Where will you deliver?"

Marla hadn't thought of that. "The Foothills, I guess. It's the closest." She might be able to see the mountains from her room.

"I'll refer you to a doctor who delivers there. Their office will call you to set up an appointment."

Marla presses her hand on her lower belly right where she gets menstrual cramps. That's where her baby is. "What about the heartbeat?"

"Your doctor will check the heartbeat once you are at twelve weeks. Is there anything else?" he asks, hand on the doorknob.

"No."

"Great. Have a nice day."

Marla gathers all the pamphlets and reads them as she walks to the train. Snowflakes melt on her hands, their tiny perfection repeated endlessly like even the air is heavy with possibility. The pamphlets are written in two-syllable words for tween moms. One is about healthy eating during pregnancy, and Marla circles foods to avoid: albacore tuna, unpasteurized cheeses and milk, raw eggs. These people care about her baby. The pregnant women in the pictures aren't feeling stupid or unsure; they're bulging with happiness.

There are more: domestic abuse, common pregnancy complaints, how to recognize a miscarriage, what to know about your newborn. Hemorrhoids, jaundice, colic. What if the baby cries all night and needs to be driven around in the car to fall asleep? Or put in a mechanical swing? Marla wonders how much those cost. Probably fifty bucks. At least twenty-five, even if it's used. Marla closes her eyes, worried, and then laughs at herself. She doesn't need that garbage. She can figure it out.

She tucks all the pamphlets into her sack, thinking about making a special file. She will steal a folder from the clinic and use their stickers to write "My Kickass Baby."

Need a new idea?
Stay late instead
why? did you fight them?
not like that now.

The snow has turned to slush, which means it's safe to drive, so after work, Marla stuffs the baby pamphlets in her glove box. Seeing no other cars in front of Liam's house, and peering in his window to be sure there are no little students still standing around, she lifts the brass knocker and lets it fall.

"Marla," Liam says when he opens the door, "you are radiant. Come in."

"Hello, mister," she says. She's going to tell him right now. As a prelude, Marla jumps into his arms, knocking over his cello-shaped umbrella stand.

"Hey, that was—"

"Don't worry about it," she whispers. She wiggles out of her heavy coat and presses her breasts into Liam's face. "I have a secret."

He reaches down to right the umbrella stand, holding her awkwardly with one arm. "Me too. You want to do the car now or later?"

Marla slides to the floor. He has a secret too? "I think the brakes are getting better," she says, lying. She doesn't want to be the mom-to-be driving a car without brakes. That's irresponsible.

Liam pulls on a suede jacket and leather kid gloves. "Marla, you know how I feel about that car."

"Yeah. She must be stopped. Get it?" He gives her a half smile. She reaches into his closet for the overalls and work boots she kept from her parks and rec city job, another gig her foster parents got her. She hands Liam the keys. "Let's go."

Marla waits until Liam has angled the rear wheel up on the curb so she can see. There's a little nipple under there, and she takes it off and puts it in her pocket, then wiggles under to wrap a rag around the opening. Slush gets under her collar.

"Hit it," she says.

Liam pumps the brake and nothing much comes out for a bit. When the rag gets oily, she tells him to stop. "I don't have any more brake fluid."

He steps out and gets down on one knee beside her. "Hardly a concern for a girl who drives around with almost no braking capacity. How much is in your car fund?"

Marla thinks about it. "Dave and Elise gave me five hundred for my birthday last month. So, five fifty. Besides, the brakes are probably at sixty percent now." She puts the nipple back on so they can do the other side. When both brake lines have been bled, she throws the rag in the back seat.

"Have you thought about taking the bus?"

"Yeah. It's expensive."

"Not more than the car."

"I'd still need the car for work. The clinic isn't on a bus route."

"You need a plan. What if you took the bus more often, not all the time, and put fifty dollars a week into your car fund? Your car would last longer, and you could buy a new one sooner."

"That sounds complicated." Marla doesn't want to tell him that she usually runs out of money before the end of the month and ends up living on peanut butter and frozen perogies, or that Dani arranges the bills so nothing gets cut off. It's not like her foster parents didn't make calendars and send text reminders, but there were so many it got overwhelming.

His phone beeps, and he reads intently, then types with his thumbs for almost a minute. Marla stands under the streetlamp, waiting, thinking. She makes a hole in the slush to scuff at the hard snow with her boot. "Liam, what if we moved in together? Then I could walk to the clinic."

He stops, slips his phone into his pocket. The streetlamp glows orange on his face, and for a second she's not sure he heard her. But he did. "I can't live with Dani. Plus, I don't think we're ready. I'm still getting over everything."

She knows about his cheating ex-wife. Marla's not that kind of see you next Tuesday, but she was a bad person the other night. She takes her tip money for the week from inside her coat, quarters and loonies in an envelope, and hands it to Liam. "This is yours. I took money for Dani the other night."

Liam folds the envelope, smoothing it. The creases around his eyes bunch up, but he's not angry like the first time, just sad. "I'm not an enabler. This doesn't help her."

Marla stuffs her fingers in her pockets, cold. Of course she's helping Dani. Who else will? But that doesn't matter now. "I'm sorry. I won't do it again."

He stares down the road as if her words are tiring. "Dani should be paying rent."

"I want to live with you, not Dani."

Liam holds the door open. "Come."

Inside, Liam puts on classical music that he'll tell her about and she'll never remember. He plates two pieces of baklava and slides them down the counter. "Marla, I'm going to tell you something," he says, his fork pointing at her a bit.

"Okay," she says, ready for a lecture.

"I thought about what you said, and I talked to someone about that university job."

His secret! "Yes, you have to do it!"

Liam leaves his fork in the air. "The audition's really serious. I have the teaching experience, but I just don't see how I'd be able to practise for hours every day with my hands like this." He opens and closes his fists, his knuckles red and swollen.

Marla reaches in her purse for two plastic pill bottles. "I did some research at work, and the doctors said take loads of fish oil, more than recommended. It's supposed to really help. And vitamin D."

"Really? Thanks." He reads the labels, frowning. "Even if that works, it's probably temporary. It's not going to slow the disease."

"There's also pot." Liam frowns at her, but she keeps going. "Look, I know you won't see a doctor, and I know why—you don't want to hear a time limit on your genius hands. How long can you play for now?"

"Forty-five minutes max."

"Maybe with the pills you can play long enough to practise

for your audition." Marla wants to work the baby thing in, but she can't without deflating him in his moment of bigness. How could she have forgotten the job thingy? "You're totally going to nail it," she says, trying to mean it.

"Maybe. Thank you for thinking of me." Liam wipes his mouth with a napkin and scoops all the crumbs into his hand. "How's the diner going?" he asks, being polite.

"Well, Bobby Love seated a pile of es in my section on purpose and they didn't tip."

"You shouldn't have to deal with that, especially for that pay."

"It's fine. Plus, I sent him into the men's room to break up some sex."

"You need a different job."

Marla remembers doing resumés with Elise and getting exactly one call. It's not like she's not trying, but her job experience is patchy, and there was that fussy KFC manager who only wanted the chicken at one special temperature. "You and my foster parents will really hit it off, you know? That's what they're always saying." Marla stands up too fast to take her plate to the dishwasher and gets dizzy. She has to hold onto the counter to steady herself.

Liam stands behind her, his hand on her back. His voice is gentle in her ear. "See, it's taking too much out of you. Please sit."

"It's fine. I'm fine." She smooths her hands over her stomach, ready to tell him, but his mouth gets softer in that way she likes when he lets down his guard.

Marla refuses to load her dinnerware into the dishwasher, and pulls him into her against the kitchen wall, taking his glasses off. "I love you," she tells him. She draws spider webs on his back, ten fingers at a time, and kisses him with an open mouth. He is warm and calm, and he is the father of her baby. She squeezes his hands.

Liam pushes away, then shakes his hands out between them. "It's really bad. I think it's the weather."

And just like that the energy fizzles into the sound of fluorescent lights buzzing. "I'm sorry," she says, and follows Liam to his mother's couch. She massages his hands, squeezing each finger and paying special attention to each nail bed until he closes his eyes. She thinks of her baby, of little chubby hands.

"There's this thing," she says.

He raises one finger. "Shhhh. The song."

She waits, trying to think of adjectives to describe the music in case he asks her later. Broken-dollish, oom pah-y, painfully slow. "What are we listening to?" she asks.

"Satie," he tells her, his voice heavy. "A drunk."

"He seems playful."

"You know he's dead, right?"

"I suspected."

Marla pulls on each finger, making a snapping sound. The music has softened, gone mournful. Liam's fingertips are calloused with little sandpaper stones. She knows she won't tell him tonight, because Liam's asleep.

3. TORTILLA CHIP

MARLA PUTS IT OFF, getting right into torrid little work dramas and keeping Dani happy. She thinks of the baby as her special secret, seeing how that feels. It's mostly good and easy, unless she smells meat, which tends to make her gag. And her breasts look great. It's almost as if no one would ever have to know. She plans to tell Liam at Christmas, which is still a month away.

On her day off, Marla leaves early to drive through fancy riverfront neighbourhoods in the Southwest for an ultrasound, something her new doctor wants to see before they meet. Here the houses stand proudly with vinyl siding never needing paint and sidewalks beautifully shovelled and salted. The medical building faces a park full of dads shovelling off a skating rink and tying skates. A pack of kids slides down the hill on toboggans and racing sleds, hollering.

Marla takes one last swig of water despite her bursting bladder and slams the car door.

"It's going to be a while," the receptionist tells her. "Wanna come back in forty-five?"

"Can I pee?"

The receptionist directs her down the hall to the bathroom, where Marla half pees, which is so far the weirdest feeling ever.

She cruises the library next door. On a whim, she takes the elevator to the second-floor children's section. Books are layered on the table in tidy mom stacks, and there are several piles of winter kid gear on the floor. Marla sits in a child-sized chair and thumbs through some books, thinking she'd take her baby here all the time: it's free.

There are three other moms. One has two big blond kids who are on the computer having a book read to them. Marla would never do that, parent electronically. Another mom with three children leaves her baby strapped into a car seat while she reads to the others.

The third mom is young, with night makeup and highlights, dragging a toddler of indeterminate sex in a snowsuit. She says, "We're leaving in one minute." She tosses books at random into a red bag: "Here's one on dinosaurs, and this one's about a grandma. You'll like them." She picks one more, and the kid whines, pulled along by the sleeve. When the kid's arm disappears inside the suit in a sit-down protest, the mom hisses in the kid's face. "Don't make a scene in here or we won't come back!" She pulls the kid roughly, and it yelps until she leaves the books on a table and uses both hands to haul her child away.

What a hag. Marla follows her with the books. "You could do better, you know."

The mom eyes Marla and hits the button for the elevator. "Excuse me?"

"Your kid is probably just tired or something." Marla holds the books out, but the mom doesn't take them. The kid, now quiet, is put down. It looks up at Marla and moves closer to its mother in solidarity.

"Are you telling me how to parent? Where are your kids?"

Marla starts to feel like this is a bad idea. The other moms are staring. "Just be nicer, that's all," Marla says.

"That's all?" She gets right in Marla's face, like Dani would. "You want to come down where I live, clean the shit out of the sheets, and be awake every morning at 5:30?"

Marla shakes her head.

"Then mind your own business."

Marla watches the elevator door close. With her baby, Marla would lie on a beanbag chair all snugly, but there are no fantasy moms here. It's this realization that causes Marla to feel something horrible in her gut. She trips over the wheel of a jogging stroller she could never afford and catches herself before anyone can ask if she's okay. Marla wants to throw up and heads for the bathroom. She walks around the bank of elevators looking for it, past the librarians at the desk who are gabbling like turkeys. Wait. They probably know.

She asks them where they keep the mom books, pushing nausea back down her throat.

"What kind of books, hon?"

"You know. Having a baby and keeping it alive." Marla digs a piece of hardened gum from underneath the lip of the desk and slips it in her pocket.

The librarian writes down a call number. "Best of luck." She has a big doughy face. Sincere.

Marla grabs several birth manuals and parenting encyclopedias, because how hard could it seriously be? Okay, so all the moms in the books have husbands and money and expensive jogging strollers and don't look at all like the woman hauling her kid by its suit. But really, everyone has kids eventually, pretty much, unless they can't or something.

Marla sits down in a carrel to read some things, flipping from newborn fevers to choosing diapers and removing cradle cap, but she finds the books annoying. They remind her of the checklists Elise used to make for her: "Marla's Decision-Making Process," "Marla's Summer Job Plan," "Marla's Transition from High School to Adult Life." Marla doesn't consult a textbook to feed herself and have fun. If everyone has kids, this stuff is probably easy.

She checks her phone, but it's not time for her ultrasound yet, so Marla sits at a computer, clicking aimlessly. If only there was someone she could talk to. Marla phones Liam, but he doesn't answer. Dani won't be up yet, and Marla hasn't told Dave and Elise. She texts Gavin: *wanna be an uncle?*

Marla looks up plane tickets just to punish herself. Too much money. She could drive to his place in Ontario, or take the bus if she had a week, but she can't miss that much work. Still, it would be great to see him, and he's done school now. She should make sure he's doing okay. Marla checks bus tickets, surprised they are only $170 one way. That's doable—maybe he could come stay awhile. She could dip into her car fund for that.

She texts again: *I'm buying you a bus ticket. come visit!* Marla smiles. Suddenly even the covers of the parenting books don't look so scary. She opens a day-by-day pregnancy guide and decides she's on day fifty-six or so. The magnified picture of nubby little limbs fills her heart and makes her smile.

Gavin runs in the park, his feet soft and his knees ready in case he slips, hair tied back. He runs here every day, through the trees and up the hills. In many places, his tracks have pushed down to the raw ground under the snow. Frozen mud. He breathes in and out, measured, calm. Here the whole world feels open, unthreatening.

He dreams about running across the country like Terry Fox, but raising money for deaf kids. Watching videos of Terry makes him cry every time. That's the kind of guy Gavin wants to be.

Back in his apartment, Gavin jots down his post-run pulse in his training log and checks his phone. He sucks in a breath. *having a baby? When?*

He feels deflated, a bit, because his sister has this perfect life. She's always so excited about anything at all, like a concert or a breakfast. He tells himself to stop it, that he's not being generous. Then he reads her other text: a trip.

Gavin's never been back to Calgary, though his old social worker said they could probably apply for funding for a visit. He's never told Marla that.

He consults his to-do list on the fridge. It's a life list, several pages taped together so three-quarters of the fridge is papered over. Many items are crossed off, like "Recreate Antique Inlaid Wardrobe" and "Run in a Marathon," but he still has lots to do: "Paddle Lake Ontario" and "Find My Father," although that would be hard considering even his mom probably doesn't know where his father is. Maybe it's stupid.

Gavin writes "Talk to Mom." She's in Calgary, last he heard. He should see her, or at least try. But that's just an excuse. If he's honest, it's more about what Stephen said: safe isn't satisfying.

Gavin paces. Everything's been harder for him, which is what he likes to think when he considers all the work he's done to get to this, the person he is right now. But everything is controlled: get up, go here, do this. No negative emotions, or almost none. Sure, he could start university with an interpreter and a deaf student society. He'd have his classes signed to him, eat alone, and cross more inconsequential items off his list while other people have adventures and fall in love. On impulse, he texts Marla that he'd love to come. *Maybe for Christmas. Can build you a crib.* He has lots of savings. He shivers, although he's not cold.

Gavin opens the handbook from the bus. The interior is totally blank. He takes his to-do list from the fridge and his university acceptance letter and tapes them page-by-page into the handbook. Now it doesn't feel so empty. He closes it and runs his fingers over the title written on the cover. He'd like to be a beautiful person too.

Marla buys groceries for Dani on the way home because that's what she's been doing for months. She carts the bags downstairs, feeling the bass line vibrating the walls.

There's a rig pig in Dani's chair, flipping through the records in her milk crates, taking them out of their sleeves with his dirty fingers and dumping them on the coffee table. Even his neck is beefy.

Dani has always told her never to waste time; always do the plan. Marla drops the bags and slides her hand under the table, searching. "Who are you?" she says.

He spits on the floor. "A friend. You the roommate?"

"Where's Dani?"

He stands up, wrapping an arm around her. "Working."

Marla finds Dani's bear spray and points it at him. "Fuck off."

He raises his arms, grinning in mock submission. "I don't need you, sugar. I already had mine."

The puppy barks from Dani's room as Marla pushes the door open. Dani's counting cash in her panties while an acne-ridden fat guy smokes in her bed. "Hey, the boss is here. Time to go." She hands Marla several bills and stands in the doorway to watch them leave. "Did he bother you?"

"Not really."

"Good job, babe. You knew what to do."

Marla fingers the money, knowing she's going to take it and hating herself for it. "What's this for?"

"Paying you back. I'm not a freeloader." Dani wads the rest of it up and wiggles off a baseboard to hide the money.

"There's a lot in there."

"Yeah. I'm making a comeback."

Marla pulls her ultrasound picture out of her coat pocket and realizes she's afraid. This isn't her life anymore. She sits on the concrete block that is Dani's other piece of furniture and says, "You were right."

Dani steps into her jeans and buttons them. "How far along?"

"The ultrasound lady said eleven weeks." Marla pictures lying in bed with Liam on a sunny September afternoon, a breeze in the curtain. She hands the photo to Dani.

"Nice baby! You told Liam? It's his, right?"

"Of course it is."

"Just saying, Marla. You gotta have your answers down when you get into these things." She crushes some pills and snorts them.

Marla shakes her head. "I'm straight now. Stop doing that."

Dani comes closer, still topless, unsmiling. "So you get pregnant and now you're better than me?"

Marla takes a step back. Years ago at Jim's photo lounge, Dani was different: she had long hair, soft arms, and full lips. Jim and Marla had something he called sex, and then he set her up with Dani or some other girl to film.

"No, like you're fucking," he said, in a different scummy basement.

Marla bent her boy-body towards Dani, arching into her.

"Like you want it."

Marla, taking her cue from Dani, tried to make her face sellable.

Jim set his jaw and knocked a chair over. Marla fake-moaned, shaky.

"Hush, you," Dani said. She let go of Marla and said, "Dim the fucking lights already. She's a kid."

Being filmed was much easier than working the street—Jim's next idea.

Now Dani takes another step closer, but Marla stands her ground. "You've been here a long time."

"A couple months."

"Eight. You got kicked out of the last place in April." Marla made Dani sleep in her car because Marla thought Dani would steal if she were in the house. Marla didn't have much to take, though, and it was cold, with wet, slushy snow falling. The kind of weather that made Marla remember bouncing around and running away. "This needs to be a safe place for the baby."

Dani fastens her bra. "Look at you, keeping a man and having a baby."

"Don't be a bitch."

"Shut up. You're so full of luck I could puke."

Dead stop. "I know that." Lots of girls didn't make it.

Dani is a wolverine. "You don't know. You were part of all that for what, a summer?" She waves her arms to indicate *all that*.

"Yeah, I guess."

"Tragedy. I've got a kid I can't see and this fucking dead body. Look at me—look me in the eye."

Marla does and tries to remember that the shirtless woman yelling at her is a friend. Her drug-addicted, once beautiful, thrown out friend. Dani would never cry.

"Dani," she says, with fingertip carefulness. "I want you safe. Better." Marla shakes an old film canister from Dani's dresser. It rattles, full of Dilaudid that Dani's been addicted to since she hurt her back in a car accident years ago.

Dani slides bangles on her arms. "Didn't I get it together when I had my kid?"

"Yeah, you did. For a bit."

"Here's the more pressing concern. If I'm not here, who's going to make sure you put gas in your car, turn the stove off, and get up for work? Not your fancy-boy."

"Don't say that about him. I can handle my life."

Dani sniffs a shirt and hucks it in the wash. "Nope. I know what that looks like. Remember all those total shitbags you owed money to, how they came around here? The fire department lecture about taking the food out before you prance off somewhere? The broken water heater that was pissing all over the basement for days?

"No one's perfect. Look who's talking."

"I'm talking, babe, because it keeps you listening. What does Liam say about the baby?"

Marla shrugs. She can't tell Dani too much.

Dani softens. She gets it. "You haven't told him. Marla, all I'm saying is that he isn't ready."

"I think I want this baby, Dani."

Dani takes off her bra and replaces it with a tube top. "Of course you do, but you'll need help."

"From you?"

Dani looks around. "There's no one else here. Who's going to remind you about her appointments? What's the baby going to do while you're at work?"

Marla sees Dani playing with her baby, leaving it in a playpen while she hustles. "Dani, let's go to Sev, get a treat."

Dani shrugs. "Why the fuck not? I'll buy."

While Dani works on herself in the bathroom, Marla rolls tobacco for her. She licks the papers and makes them real tight, the way she used to while she waited for Dani to get home from blowing johns. She sat on Dani's bed and listened to the patrons of the Shamrock Hotel bottle each other on Saturday nights.

Marla lived with Dani for two months because Jim wasn't going to bother looking for her once he realized she couldn't make him any money. There was a new girl anyway. Jim was a problem, a long-haired, initially perfect problem. Dani told Marla that it's always the same. She had a boyfriend of her own, a fabulous older guy with a car who bought her clothes and jewellery, whatever she wanted. Marla remembered that. There was something delicious about Jim, the way he knew everyone and could take her anywhere. The cigarettes he bought tasted better, and the bars she smoked them in didn't look sketchy at the time. Or desperate. Then the guy says you gotta help me, you kinda owe me, I'm in a jam, I love you and I wish it didn't have to be like this. Or whatever. He has friends who back him up. With Dani it was, you have to leave town with me, he says, the cops are after me, I don't know, for jack shit, let's get out of here. Oh, and you owe me all this cash for those drugs. Teenaged Dani, locked in a van, then a room. She never finished high school.

In the end Jim was hard and angry, threatening Marla and punching her up, always over money.

"You're getting out there tonight."

"I can't, Jim, I got my—"

Jim got up close to her, his gelled hair on her face. "Figure it the fuck out. You owe me."

"But I gave you that money yesterday," Marla whispered.

His fingers closed around her throat. "Yesterday's money means shit to me."

And there was Dani standing over him, naked except for the scarf on her head. "Enough," she said, solid as a stone, the bravest woman in the world.

She's ready. Dani emerges from the bathroom with her hair tousled and her breasts corralled but not quite concealed in her tube top. She throws a men's duster riding coat over the ensemble, leaving it unbuttoned.

Marla *tsk tsks* her. "You know it's freezing, right?"

"Whatever." Dani ties a leash on the puppy and thumps up the stairs and outside.

The snow blown against the concrete foundation is going grey with the wind and the endlessness that Marla feels about living here. The entire street seems wary, leaning away from the river as if in defiance of those who would judge the peeling paint of its houses and the kicked-down stop sign. Marla can feel all the moisture in her skin getting sucked out. "Dani, I need you to keep a secret for me."

"Yeah? Like what?"

"My brother's coming next week, and you can't tell him I used to work the street."

"Funny. That's the same secret I've been keeping from your man."

"Gavin's different. I haven't seen him in years."

Dani snorts like a horse. "You have to face who you are, Marla. Stop keeping secrets."

"I'm not a prostitute."

"Having a job and a man and a car does not erase your past."

Marla says nothing.

"Don't cry about it. It happened."

"No one can know."

"Or what? They won't like you anymore?" Dani pulls a cigarette pack out of her pocket and, finding it empty, hurls it to the ground, dismissing the idea. "I don't hide who I am or what I do." She kicks a clump of snow down the sidewalk. "I won't."

Marla hands her a rollie. "Drama queen. You should do spoken word with me."

"Spit my shit? I don't think so."

"Just keep your hands off him. Gavin's nineteen."

Dani flares her nostrils. "You think I would take your baby brother to bed?"

"Just promise you won't start anything."

"Fuck off, Marla. Don't order me around." She's already jaywalking across Bowness Road.

The high school boys in front of the Sev are hyenas who feast on Dani. They lean with bravado, trying to set her off while she ties up the puppy.

"Hey, lady, you got some crack?"

"Maybe we can smoke a fatty together."

"Yeah, and then you can smoke this."

Dani fingers them, unfazed, but Marla lingers with her hand on the door, trying to think of the mom response to punks like that. And the guys in the basement.

Once inside, Dani abandons Marla immediately and straightens her back for the cashier. "Hey, sugar," she says to him. He looks fifteen. A kid. Dani opens a pack of gum under his nose and takes care to show her mouth as she puts it in to chew. She licks her lips.

"Uh," he says, looking alarmed. His voice is horrible, anxious and afraid. He's responsible for the gum. For Dani in the store.

"We'll pay for it," Marla says, putting her hand on the counter. "It's okay." Only it's not.

Dani does her usual move and manipulates the fear she creates into something else, something she can work with. Marla's seen it before. Walking around the counter behind him, Dani says, "You know, your Slurpee machine trays are just disgusting." She draws the word out, her mouth lolling over it as if it were candy. She fills a big mug with pop, his eyes on her.

The kid stammers, and Marla pulls Dani away. "Babe, stop it."

Dani winks at the kid, lifting her hips up and down and all

around as she walks past, away from Marla.

Marla counts out candies, Coke bottles, and sour soothers, listening. Some of the boys from outside have come in. They're at the magazine rack, stuffing skateboarding magazines in their pants every time the cashier turns around to stock the cigarettes, talking about Dani. They see her sunken eyes and her braless cleavage hanging out of her tube top. Marla tells herself that Dani's a good person, that she deserves respect. She's lived in the bowels of this city her entire adult life, working nights with the most desperate people in the most dangerous job. Yes, what's left is hardened, unsocialized. Of course it is. It's Marla's fault for thinking Dani was like a real friend.

Dani's busy taking the hot dogs out of the grill and lining them up on the dirty counter, the boys eyeing her from the magazine rack. She didn't even put a napkin down first. Marla counts the hot dogs: eleven.

"What is wrong with you?" Marla pinches Dani on the arm and apologizes to the cashier with her eyes, but Dani pushes Marla away and puts a single hotdog in a bun, leaving the kid to throw the rest in the garbage. "Dani, you're going to get in shit."

"*C'est la vie*. Let's go." While Dani pays, she chats up the cashier. "I could give you my number, you know."

The kid scrunches his nose, and the boys holler, which makes a door bang open somewhere in the back. A man with a pinched nose and a huge body joins the kid behind the till, his eyes on Dani. The manager.

"I told you not to be here," he says. He looks at the kid. "Did she take the hotdogs out again?"

He nods miserably.

The manager points to the door. "Get out."

Dani stands a little taller, and Marla feels a bunch of pressure in her ears like the room is shrinking. "Am I a problem for you?" Dani pours her pop on the floor, real slow. It would be funny except that it's awful.

Marla grabs the cup out of Dani's hand but it's empty. "Don't do this."

Dani laughs. "Look who's telling me what to do again."

"I'm calling the police," the manager says, his face a red bubble of anger. The boys slink outside.

"We're just leaving," Marla says.

"But I'm so clumsy." Dani kicks a promotional endcap of beef jerky right over and makes like she's going to sweep the counter clear. The kid is gripping the lotto display case, white-knuckled.

The manager reaches across the counter and then thinks better of it. He points at Dani, his finger an arrow. "Go."

Marla grabs the bag and pushes Dani to the door, waving away the receipt. She can see the boys outside looking in under cupped hands. They'll be talking about this for days. She knows how they feel.

"*Au revoir, mon chéri*," Dani calls to the cashier, blowing a kiss.

Marla reaches for Dani's hand, her humid skin, and tries to pull her out the door, but Dani yanks her hand away and slaps Marla with an awkward backhand that lands on Marla's ear. It rings, and the door dingles as Dani kicks her way outside.

Marla stands there, shaking for a second, feeling her ear throb. The kid behind the counter looks intentional, like he wants to say something. Marla waits for him, gives him the space. "Have a good day," he says slowly. They must teach that in training. The door makes its chirpy little ding-dong when Marla opens it.

The boys outside fan away from the door and flatten to the glass. They have a heavy air of feigned nonchalance going on while Dani bends over to untie the puppy.

"Have a nice fucking day, hey?" one calls out, a brave one. "And give me your number!"

Dani turns around and smiles like she's naked. "You couldn't handle me," she says, cupping her breasts and biting her lower lip. The boys hoot, asking for her panties. She flips them the double bird. Marla stomps past her, refusing to make eye contact.

Dani keeps up easily. "I probably fucked at least one of their dads," she says, all confidential. "Little dipshits."

Marla doesn't laugh. "Dani, you sucked in there."

"Look, I'm sorry I smacked you."

Marla throws the bag of candy at her and keeps walking. "I don't want you in my house anymore."

Dani stops to pick the candy out of the snow and put some in her mouth. "Oh, Marla, come on. It's not like you're perfect."

A piece of cardboard blows down the street, getting run over by cars and sucked back into the air in their wake. "You always have to fuck up the nice shit."

Dani gives a theatrical bow. "Fine. I'll be docile and chaste and quiet so you can pretend. Sound good?"

"Do whatever you want. I'm done."

"Don't kid yourself. No one does it on their own." Dani links arms with Marla and skips. Their breath puffs out in little clouds.

"What are you doing?" Marla yanks her arm, trying to get free.

"You're so concerned with how everything looks that you don't know what's important."

"The people in the store, they don't matter?"

Dani faces her, holds Marla's belly with her red, chapped hands. "Nope. Not really. You're who I care about. You and your baby."

Marla feels like she always does around Dani—like she's being sucked up by some giant vacuum cleaner. "What about your kid?"

Dani hugs her and Marla can smell Dani's unwashed smell. "That's what the money's for. I almost have enough for my own place."

It sounds good. So good that Marla doesn't think to say it takes more than money. Dani would be so happy living with

Kamon in their own apartment, probably across the street from a park, or maybe a school. Besides, something about the dingy late-afternoon light makes Marla feel tired of this battle. Traffic rumbles by them, exhaust hanging in the air, and Marla decides to stop acting like she knows everything, because she certainly never has. "I didn't like those guys downstairs."

"Easy. They won't be back. Regulars only."

Marla holds Dani at arm's length. "Promise me."

"I promise."

"And we're going to keep looking out for each other."

"Always."

4. CHRISTMAS ORANGE

Picking up my brother!
That's wonderful, honey. Maybe you can bring him to dinner. We'd love to meet him. How long is he staying?
don't know. he's kinda shy.
Tell him he's welcome here anytime.

GAVIN GETS OFF the Greyhound after two days, seven hours, and forty-five minutes of driving across the wind-blasted prairies to the mountains. Now, foothills in the distance, he disembarks in a place he hasn't been since before he could read. Calgary, December 23.

He's been thinking about this city: its dry air, its shape like rolled out dough, growing each year, its coulees and jackrabbits, and the two rivers that anchor it. It's a meeting place, where the rivers join, and people have been coming together here for centuries to share and build and make a living. He's just one of hundreds of thousands to arrive here: First Nations, farmers, steelworkers, recent newcomers, and Maritimers, and in that moment, he feels the enormity of everyone's desire to succeed. And the vastness of the space all around. He wants his hometown to be a hopeful place, and it will be once he gets to know it. He can do this.

Marla is standing alone under fluorescent lights, buying tea from a window in the wall, and he sees her first. He taps her on the shoulder, waving. "... glad ... see you!" She makes their sign for love, both hands clasped over her heart, tears in her eyes. "How ... bus?"

She speaks so quickly he wants to turn back, stop this experiment. He's not used to thinking in English. Gavin holds his notepad out with GOOD TO SEE YOU pre-written on it. He holds his hands to say *long*, then hugs her, picks her up. He feels her bones, holds on tight.

She pulls back to say, "Just love ... your hair so long ... face ... haven't seen ..." She's crying.

He struggles to keep up, reminds himself to be strong. He can fake it if he has to. LOVE YOU. MISSED YOU BAD. Gavin takes in her woman body. She's right. He can't tell she's pregnant.

She stares at his notepad. "Why ... you talking?"

He knew this would happen. EASIER THIS. He doesn't want to tell her he doesn't know what to do with the way people look at him, that it's unrealistic to expect everyone around him to learn to sign. That what he would hate most of all is being a burden.

Nothing bothers Marla. She smiles and puts on her coat, brown wool that is cut to fit, her movements long and slow. When she gets the tea, even the way she holds her cup is sort of agonizing, wrapping her hands around and stroking it, bringing it to her mouth to softly blow the steam away, then tucking it against her chest, finally raising it to drink.

She holds herself tall, though she can't be more than five and a half feet without the shoes. She has stunning features, with her oval face and black hair, but if Gavin didn't know better he would think she was much younger than twenty-two. It's her easy smile and thrift store clothes, the way she's not carrying a bag or in a hurry. Because he worries, he looks more carefully, the way he looks at himself, and finds more. The stitching is coming undone under the right arm of her coat, and the part in her hair isn't straight. She twirls with the teacup, noticing him staring. "... what ... you think ...?"

Gavin gives her two thumbs up.

Marla kisses his cheek. "… get bag … car's running."

Gavin nods to his toolbox, the sack on his back. THIS IT.

"Gavin … you mean? I didn't … return ticket."

NO? He's only booked a week off. Does she want him to stay past Christmas? He's making a mental list of the steps he'll need to take because that's what he's supposed to do when he's feeling worked up—clarify dates with Marla, call work, use some savings to buy a plane ticket—and feeling proud of himself when he remembers something more important. NEPHEW-FATHER OUTSIDE?

Marla's face crinkles. "Who?" Then she gets it. She says a name Gavin can't understand.

He has to tell her to slow down. SPELL HIM.

Marla writes: L I A M.

NOT HERE? WHERE? WANT MEET.

Marla's expression is wilting. Gavin sees sadness in her eye corners. "No, he's not … maybe we can …"

YOU TELL? He holds her hand.

"Not yet." She pulls his arm. "Come."

The car is idling smoky, blue oil burning. No one would steal it. Inside, he sits in the back, because there's no passenger seat. GOT DEAL THIS?

She leans over to face him. "Did I. Listen … roommate … Danny."

Gavin nods okay—wait. GUY?

Marla takes his notepad and writes, DANI. GIRL. She crunches her eyebrows. "… takes getting used to."

Gavin knows all about that. As they drive, he reviews the rules for meeting hearing people.

- Don't sign with mouth open: people think that's gross.
- Ignore stares.
- Use eye contact when writing.
- Listen without ears for other people's needs—soothe their fear of you.

- Write in complete sentences for people who don't know you, even though it takes much longer.
- Touch carefully for attention, because it scares most people.
- Don't try to speak, because the sound is all wrong. If you speak, people think you're retarded.
- Show the card or people will think you're a bum. "Hello. My name is Gavin and I am deaf-mute. I write and read lips to communicate. Please speak slowly without covering your mouth." Hate that phrase deaf-mute.

At a long light, Marla turns around. "Almost there ... have fun ... promise." She's pleading.

Does she think he's nervous? He hastens to reassure her. COURSE. MUCH CATCH UP. She reads while she drives, nods. Gavin sits back, imagining Marla's roommate. Probably a sweet girl who will pity him or try too hard. Hate that.

They drive for half an hour, and Gavin concludes that the entire city is made of single family dwellings with garage faces and fenced yards, put up in succession so the houses get larger the further from downtown they go. Marla's neighbourhood is older, tucked in against the river and anchored by a main street with a variety of businesses targeting all income levels. It's full of people: men in work boots, older ladies with wheeled carts, and kids without hats on a playground, tearing around. There is division here: million dollar homes along the river and the fancy organic eateries they come with—and two blocks away, a sagging school and dilapidated cookie cutter houses from the sixties. Bowness has a good feeling to it, like everyone might be allowed to fit in here. Marla's house is number 111. "Please come in," she says. Formal. Nervous.

The house smells yeasty, like bread. Gavin steps out of his boots and, not seeing a mat, sets them on a newspaper to avoid getting the hardwood wet. When he looks up he notices the blonde woman on the couch, her long legs bare under her skirt.

She turns off the TV and comes right up, surprisingly tall and really close. Her body is firm but thick, like that of someone who swims in open water. Shapely. She holds him by the shoulders, her breasts rising and falling with her breath. She smiles as she sees him noticing, baring her teeth, then puts her hand over her mouth and blinks like a fawny little girl. He can't tell whether she's threatening or sweet. Her posture projects an aura of strength, an unflinching steadiness that makes him think of a jungle cat, and yet she waits with a soft jaw, her lips barely touching.

When he doesn't say anything, Dani talks over his shoulder to Marla. "... brother ... yummy ..." Then she's yawning, and he can't figure out what she's saying.

Gavin waves and reaches out a card. He studies her face as she reads. Did Marla not tell her?

"What ... you mean deaf?" Her nostrils flare. Marla is shaking her head and saying something.

Gavin's feeling crowded. He writes, CAN'T HEAR.

Dani laughs and laughs. She wraps her arms around him, her hair on his cheek soft, tickly. She's saying something, but he's not watching her mouth. He's looking her in the eye.

SAY AGAIN?

"You're hilarious!" She talks slow for Gavin. "I like you already."

Gavin reminds himself to write about this moment, check it off on a list. Add it to his list, even. LIKEWISE.

Dani holds his arm, clearly enunciating. "Tell me if you don't understand. I'll work on it."

Gavin allows the tension in his shoulders to smooth out, a feeling he'd like to savour. K.

Marla takes his arm. "Come ... show ... room."

Marla's walls are blood red, and the baseboards are stained walnut. They pass a room with a broken door—inside is an armchair and a toilet. Is that the bathroom? How's he going to pee there?

"This way," Marla says, pulling him along. The bedroom is full of odds and ends: a coffee table, stacks of papers, extra bowls, and flippers. It has a big closet with steps up.

Gavin puts his toolbox in there and clears some clothes off the bed to set his bag down. WHEN GO HOME?

Marla gets campy, full of false cheer. "Why ... you ... leave already?"

HAVE JOB.

She's confused, her mouth too still. "You don't ... stay?"

He immediately feels bad. He didn't want her to be upset. COUPLE WEEKS? Gavin looks at her face. MORE?

She is small, her elbows tucked like folded wings. "I ... love you ... stay as long ... want. I'm sorry ... ticket. I'll get ... just can't ... now."

This is the Marla he knows, the girl who can't manage details. It's an old story. WHERE YOU GET $$?

"Borrowed." She folds her lips under her teeth.

FROM?

"My car ..."

HOW?

"I'm supposed ... new car ... Dave and Elise ... putting money."

Not good. The relationship there is tenuous at best. NEPHEW NEED NEW CAR. I BUY TICKET LATER + PAY YOU BACK.

"Gavin ... necessary ... you have ..."

MONEY? NO WORRY ME.

"I'm sorry, you know ... dump this ... you I need ..." Marla hangs her head and he lifts her chin with one finger, kisses her cheek. Gavin is needed here, much more than he expected. He feels a rush of opportunity, a moment for pride: he can help Marla, his only real family, and he'll see more of Dani. He must call work tomorrow. STAY AWHILE.

She hugs him tight. "Come ... celebrate with me."

He points to the bathroom to indicate he'll be with her in a minute. The bathroom door lacks a knob and hinges. He leans it against the frame but he can still see the living room: Dani on the couch, the TV. He sits on the toilet and can still see her, so Gavin pulls a red bathrobe off the armchair (Marla's house!), and hangs it over the corner of the door. It almost covers everything.

He gives himself a pep talk in the mirror, signing, *you can do this*. Gavin pees looking over his shoulder. No one comes in.

Marla's waiting in the kitchen eating cookies. Dani puts them in her mouth whole while Marla offers the box to him. NO THANKS, he writes. He sits on patio furniture, staring at his legs through the slats in the plastic tabletop before he realizes Marla's talking to him.

"... not hungry? ... used to ... your ..."

DON'T EAT SUGAR NOW.

Dani reads lots of the last page over Gavin's shoulder as he writes, saying something to Marla. "... gorgeous ..." Gavin reviews the whole page just in case: baby, money, car. She would know that, right? He flips over a new sheet anyway.

Dani taps him on the arm. "Why don't you eat sugar?"

MAKES FREAK OUT.

She licks her fingers. "I'd love to see that."

NOT. HEART RACE, OVERWHELMED.

"Honey, that's anxiety. Not sugar." Dani cracks a beer.

Gavin shrugs, not wanting to get into rules and research. Marla offers him a beer, but he declines.

He points to himself. GLUTEN FREE. Marla shoves the bottle back in the fridge.

"... how ... not starve?" Dani looks like she wants to laugh but feels it might be rude.

Gavin raises an eyebrow. EAT UNLIMITED RHUBARB.

Dani laughs so hard beer sprays out of her nose, which makes Marla stamp her feet under the table. For a heartbeat, Gavin wonders why he's wasted so much time if it's this easy. Then Dani leans forward and grins, her nostrils flaring. "What are you really here for?"

She's figured him out, knows he's a fake. Gavin nods at Marla, but Dani shakes her head. She holds his eyes steady, reaching for his hands from across the table, anchoring him with her touch, waiting patiently. Gavin sees in her the desire to understand that so few people have, and he tells her the truth. WANT FIND MY MOM.

"... you ..." Marla's frowning at him, looking disappointed. "... how she is."

Gavin used to pretend all his friends at deaf school were just like him until their moms and dads arrived on weekends to pick them up. The day program kids had parents too, ones that took signing classes while Gavin stared at a computer screen doing speech drills: *dee da deh do du tee ta teh to tu bee ba beh bo bu pee pa peh po pu.* SOMETHING NEED DO.

Marla rolls her eyes, about to say more, but Dani cuts her off. "No, I totally get that. I know exactly what you mean."

"... your funeral," Marla says.

Gavin squeezes Dani's hands, feeling both awakened and undone. He watches her fingers as she shuffles cards, deals. The way her hands move is precise but elegant, like a magician. Gavin is suddenly sure she can dance, capture a room with only movement. She glances at him, smiles, shows her teeth.

They play Hearts. Dani gets the queen of spades four times and hurls it at the table. Shooting for the moon.

Before he goes to sleep in Marla's spare room, Gavin opens the scrapbook his sister made him years ago. It's full of pictures she cut out of newspapers and magazines she took from the dumpster behind Safeway. Pictures of clothes: hats, socks, and a cowboy costume. Spaghetti, cereal, raspberries, bread. Bath toys, toilet paper, a swing set. It was a dictionary he pointed to every day, before they made up their own signs. All the things he couldn't say. He puts it on his nightstand.

Marla always listened.

Marla gets up early and opens the door to Gavin's room a

crack, excited at how easy everything feels now that he's here. She wishes she'd invited him sooner because he's clearly missed her loads. He's asleep, a hairy foot outside the blankets. Marla should leave, walk out before he wakes up, but she doesn't.

The few pictures he's sent haven't done him justice: first, he's huge, and his face has broadened since she saw him years ago, with a wide, low-slung mouth. His loose hair is long, past his shoulders. She can see glimpses of his six-pack in the mashed-up blankets, the way his waist tapers below his ribs. Gavin's body is that of a track star, she thinks, all muscles and precision power. He has giant quads.

She opens the door further to find Dani reading the scrapbook Marla made Gavin when he was a little boy. The spine is duct-taped, and the pages are falling out. She hisses at Dani. "Are you snooping? Get out!"

Dani thinks about it. She speaks in her regular voice. "Nope. I got here first."

Marla giggles. "We shouldn't be here."

Dani shrugs and points at Gavin. He sleeps with his mouth slightly open.

So, Marla looks around. Gavin's clothes are folded at the foot of his bed like he's in the army or something. Discount jeans that aren't terribly flattering and an oversized plain T-shirt. Marla digs in his bag to see what else he brought: notepads, running clothes, more silly jeans, and super tight underwear. And a fabric-covered book with "A Handbook for Beautiful People" on the cover in someone else's writing. She opens it and reads: "Today bohemian waxwings at park. Bobbing plump bodies, peck rotten apple on snow. Yellow tail feathers, black curve around eyes—terribly fem, old women with fur coats. Noticed me—jerked heads. One open beak for sing.

Want hear my voice. Practise mirror, mouth open, sounds fall, splash in sink. No one hear."

Gavin farts in his sleep and wakes himself. Marla drops the handbook, but he has seen her reading it.

He rises, alarmed, holding the blanket around his bare torso with one hand. On his notepad, he writes, SOMETHING WRONG? I LATE?

Marla scrambles to give Gavin his handbook. "Sorry, I didn't realize it was your journal."

He holds it to his chest and combs his hair with his fingers, his eyes darting to Dani. WHAT U THINK IT BE?

Marla didn't want to make him embarrassed. She hates herself, but just a bit, because she refuses to think she's like all those other people who have taken advantage of his disability. How else will she ever know if there's stuff he's not telling her? She wants to apologize, but Dani interrupts.

"Let me see that." Dani slips the handbook out of Gavin's fingers and skims a few pages. The softness in Dani's voice is unexpected. That's the voice she reserves for Marla.

Gavin shifts his weight from one foot to the other, glancing down at his plaid pyjama pants. NOT ALL DARK, he writes.

Dani nods. "I really like the idea. Romantic." She's over-enunciating her words, making these huge mouth shapes.

"Dani, he's not stupid, he's just deaf," Marla says, but Dani ignores her. She's pressing her hand over a page of writing, drawing an outline, watching Gavin's face.

Marla grabs the handbook away from Dani and points to the cover. "This isn't your writing," Marla says, not sure when Dani and Gavin became so close.

FOUND IT BUS.

"What is it?"

Gavin smiles. WAITED WEEK TO OPEN. PUT POSTERS: FOUND, HANDBOOK. NO RESPONSE.

"And?"

He shrugs. EMPTY.

Marla flips through. "Really? Even with that title?" The covers are worn and soft. Someone must have carried it for a long time. All that time without writing anything.

I USE NOW.

"What do you write?" Dani asks.

MY LIFE. USE AS ALMANAC. HOW TO CHANGE WHEN MOST RELATABLE TO SEASON.

"Wow," Marla says, trying not to be sarcastic, because he is her brother even though he uses words like almanac. "How does it work?"

OBSERVE NATURAL. RELATE TO SELF. TRY BE BETTER, MORE IN HARMONY.

"You're sensitive, hey?" Dani doesn't laugh, which Marla can't quite figure out.

YEAH. Gavin hesitates. YOU CAN USE IT TOO, IF YOU WANT.

Marla imagines Dani crushing pills on it, or using it as a pizza plate while she digs for the remote. Dani and Gavin are staring at each other, and Marla feels weird about it. He's Marla's little brother, a boy she has always looked after, not some man with hairy legs and huge farts.

She waves her hand in front of her brother's face, a plan materializing as she speaks. "Get dressed. We have all day before you get to meet Liam for Christmas dinner. We're going out."

"Come back after so we can party." Dani smiles at Gavin. "You too. It's my birthday tomorrow."

ON XMAS?

"Yep. Just like J.C."

Marla pushes Dani out the door so Gavin can get dressed, but not before she catches them sharing something she didn't know either was capable of unless it was about her. A feeling, she thinks: a big one.

Marla and Gavin each buy a day pass so they can spend the day on a C-train tour of the city. Gavin tries to memorize everything, the way snow is ground into the concrete of the train platforms, how many grocery stores are on the train line, the university with its confident buildings and trails of footprints in the snow, mentally drawing maps so he can make rules and running routes. He's going to need to fill his time here, be productive, and keep busy. Marla shows him the tunnels where the suicides crouch and the backs of supermarkets and furniture stores, the cranes parked everywhere. The river rushes over plates of ice that shift and overlap at the edges, blue and bitter. Downtown is a procession of empty buildings with the lights on, reflections in glass. Homeless kids pass the time in front of the pregnancy care centre, doing drugs. Then the Stampede grounds, naked parking lots and blowing snow, dissolving into miles of residential neighbourhoods: endless sound walls protecting endless communities. Chinook. Anderton. Fish Creek. Half-finished construction resolute throughout.

People crush on with their bags, and the heaters work full blast. The train smells like wet wool. Women glance around as if seeking affirmation, texting and dialling, older men sit with their eyes closed. Here, people are obvious, self-involved: head up, strutting, or head down. More American, as if this city is tied more to Houston by pipeline than the rest of this country. He studies his sister, who is calm like she's outside of the economic machine grinding night and day in this place. Her clothes don't even draw attention to her. Marla draws on the frosty windows with her fingertips, smushed beside him like they've never been apart.

Later, she falls asleep on his shoulder, and his phone buzzes. It's Dani. He doesn't know how she got his number.

Liked your book. Look forward to seeing more of you tonight.

Gavin wants to do some wandering, so Marla drops him off downtown with a map she drew on a napkin before she heads to Liam's. She made lots of labels, and it's not like he's never been in a city. He'll probably be fine.

When Marla arrives, Liam is practising, music spread over the floor as if everything Marla said worked a hundred percent. She's really on a roll, so she pre-warns him about Gavin in case he needs to mentally prepare. "You know how my brother's here now? I invited him to dinner if that's okay." Marla stands on tiptoe to kiss Liam hello.

"You say that like I would tell you not to." He steps around her to lean his cello back onto its stand. "Marla, may I take your coat?"

"Okay." He manipulates it onto a hanger, folding the sleeves over so they don't stick out like a dead person's arms, all akimbo and uncivilized in the closet. Marla steps out of her shoes, and he fits them together like two halves of a broken toy before he slips them into the right-sized shoe cubby.

She doesn't say anything about his crotchety obsessions and how old they make him look. They're all going to have a crazy madhouse time celebrating anyway as soon as she makes her announcement. "Merry Christmas, you."

"Ditto. Come into the bedroom," Liam says, but she knows he doesn't mean sex.

He irons his clothes in silence, tucking the iron into folds and corners and sweeping it out and across his pants like it is a weight he must lift with perfect form. "I'm going to do the audition," he says, but like he's talking himself into it. "The fish oil's really helping."

She clears her throat, feeling like she's interrupting something private. "That's great!" She watches how his body moves, listening to the clock tick. "I like to iron them flat, with the creases on the seams."

He pauses, the iron steaming in midair. "The things you love. They always surprise me." Liam squeezes past her to hang his pants on the top of the door, then again to lay his shirt on the ironing board.

Marla hops out of the way, perching like a bird. "Listen, Gavin's not like me," she announces, thinking she's definitely put him off balance by adding her brother to dinner.

Liam looks up. "Tell me about him."

Okay then. "Well, he can't hear. And lately he doesn't talk either."

"Really," Liam says. Marla can't tell if he's being serious or hilarious. "Does he sign?"

"Yes, but I only know made-up signs, so he writes to talk. I think he feels signing makes him look too deaf."

"Ah." Liam thinks about this, stands the iron up. She sees Liam's jawline relax a bit. "Must have been hard having him away at school. Lonely."

Marla wants to say that everything is so easy for Gavin, and she's not sure how to talk to him now that everyone likes him and he can take buses by himself. But that's off-topic. "I haven't told him this, but it's actually good he went to school. I understood him before, but not many other people tried that hard."

Liam raises his eyebrows as he flips his shirt. That's good. Marla wants him to like Gavin.

She sidles up to Liam and puts her hands around his waist, but he doesn't stop ironing.

"Marla, not now." He finishes his shirt and turns off the iron. He collapses the ironing board with one hand, then unbuttons his shirt to change.

"We have time." She pulls at his sleeves, and the shirt drops to the floor.

"I need to pick up my dry cleaning."

"Do it tomorrow," she suggests, running a finger along his forearm, sucking it in a bit in case he reaches for her.

"I have to get ready."

"You look ready to me." Marla hushes him with her mouth, something he didn't see coming.

He doesn't kiss her at first, his lips hesitating. "I'll have to drop you off to meet Gavin in fifteen minutes."

"You don't have to be worried. Or jealous," she tells him. He confirms the accuracy of this statement, holding her chin in his hand, keeping her perfectly still. Then he relents, his body yielding and yet in charge, swallowing her, baby and all.

5. LEMON

GAVIN GETS OFF at the wrong stop and has to run along the icy river pathway to meet Marla at the Chinese restaurant. The skyscrapers shine black under the soft tones of Christmas lights, sturdy and tall like they've always belonged here. At ground level, downtown is mostly dead, except for prostitutes who puff cigarettes in the cold. They don't wear gloves.

Gavin's late, but he knows he's getting close when he sees the bridge with the lions on it. Marla is getting out of a car, waving. He checks to make sure he didn't get his pants salty, and, when he looks up, the car has pulled away.

"Gavin, hey," Marla says. "Don't ... baby tonight ... haven't told ..."

It's been two weeks since she told Gavin, and Dani definitely knows. Marla should have told Liam by now. Gavin's eyes spell concern, surprise.

She shakes her head, flipping hair off her face. "... wasn't the right ... he ... job ..."

Write: TONIGHT, YES?

"Yeah ... Christmas present ..."

WHERE HE?

Marla's face very serious. "Picking ... dry cleaning ... meet us there."

The Bow River is soft and dark, blanketed in ice: nothing like the roaring animal of daytime. Behind it there seems to be nothing at all, just night and wind. Maybe a hill or a park, he thinks. An island. They cross the street into Chinatown, which is electric red with a gold fringe. Even these businesses are mostly closed—just a few restaurants open on the corners. Gavin pictures Liam: nervous, kind of poor, anemic, perhaps.

"... going to ... super." Marla has a lot of colour in her cheeks. "Unless ... don't think ..."

Gavin shrugs. Does Liam need special handling? No one meeting Gavin would be nervous. Unless they're crazy.

The restaurant is real Chinese, with ducks hanging in the window and that fried dough smell. Gavin scans for a pasty musician while Marla asks the waitress. He's not here.

They sit by the window. Gavin watches flashy Chinese TV, but is trying not to. It's the movement that gets him, and the streamers blowing back and forth on the ceiling. Concentrate. He pours tea for two, keeping his elbows in to let the waitress by. Marla holds her teacup, warming her hands.

Write: YOU LOVE HIM? Watch her face. The answer is yes, but with reservations.

Marla is explaining, as if he might not understand. "... would be fabulous ... could be happy." Who is happy? She is rationalizing. A dangerous, confining thing to do.

HE WANT BABY? People at the next table are having their food delivered, waitresses crowding around. Watch close.

She shrugs. "... romantic the idea ... womb ... child ... don't think ... time ..." Her body sags—she's admitting this to herself for the first time.

Gavin tucks his hair behind his ears. SORRY. NOT MEAN UPSET. WORRIED.

Liam is here. Marla's shoulders go back before she stands. Warm beautiful easy smile for him. Wants it to work. Gavin flips the page over to start fresh, then stands to shake hands.

Liam is thirty or so, tall, masculine even in fitted clothes, but with a longness to him that makes him seem fine-boned. He has the curly brown hair of models and musicians.

As Gavin takes his hand, Liam pulls him in for a hug/handshake combo. Interesting. Up close, Gavin smells expensive cologne and notices that Liam wears cufflinks and a crystal watch. His jaw is angular, and he has high cheekbones. Thin lips, but commanding green eyes. He has a ring on his middle finger, a brassy number that catches the light.

Gavin steps back as Liam embraces Marla and helps her into her chair. Seated, Liam has beautiful posture, not that horrible ramrod straight back that causes people to look constipated, but a shoulders thrown back, tall way of sitting like he's used to being in charge. Liam checks his phone, types on it and places it face-up on the table. Comfortable, but in control. Gavin respects him immediately.

Gavin doesn't want Marla to have to say it, so he writes. I AM DEAF BUT I CAN READ LIPS. PLEASE FACE ME WITHOUT COVERING YOUR MOUTH WHEN YOU SPEAK. More personal than the card.

Liam smiles, disarmed. "... course. Pleased to meet you."

Seems all right, how he is cultured. Natty. Gavin feels good, like he's a normal person out with his family. Behind Liam goldfish pace their tank, their filmy fins moving so slightly as to be beautiful, stoic in their role as decoration.

When he looks back, Marla has blushed some colour into her face, and made her lips fuller somehow, something to do with her teeth. She is stroking Liam's arm, her hands in his to help him unfold his napkin. Saying something just to him with her mouth pointed away from Gavin. Enchanted.

Noticing him staring, Marla talks about Gavin non-stop, obviously excited. "Gavin is fixing ... Gavin ... works with ... Gavin has always ..." Liam's head bobs politely.

Gavin asks, WHAT DO YOU DO?

Liam turns his body to Gavin, careful. Speaks slower. "I teach music ... and ... cook."

CLASSROOM?

"No, private music lessons. I gave up classroom teaching with all the band program cuts."

She grabs Gavin's shoulder. "... audition ... because ... like amazingly ... university ... he's very good." She mimes playing a stringed instrument, grinning at him, teeth mouth.

Neat. Gavin catches Marla legs tangling with Liam legs. Notices how he looks at her, like if he doesn't subdue all her energy she might slip away from him. He needs her soft sweetness like skin.

The waitress comes around. Marla knows better, and lets Gavin order by himself. He uses the back of one of his cards to ask the waitress for steamed vegetables and rice, no sauce. Marla and Liam start apologizing in chorus for bringing him here, but he waves it off, wanting to make sure the waitress gets it right. When it is her turn, Marla points to several different pictures because the menu's in Chinese. Liam orders without pointing. Clever guy.

He says, "Gavin, tell me ... Belleville." Lush hair barely moves.

Write: KNOW LOT DEAF KID.

"How cruel ... separated from your family ... must have suffered tremendously."

Liam doesn't baby Gavin with two-syllable words. He likes that. Write: MISSED MARLA. WORK WITH DISABLED. He thinks about someone else feeding Stephen and feels guilty for a second. But Stephen's right.

Liam still has his ears pulled back like he's thinking, but his mouth stays still. Marla was right. With Liam, one has to wait.

Gavin watches their bodies, ignores mouths. She crosses and uncrosses her legs, laughs with a lilt of her head. Liam keeps his hands folded on the table. Rarely shows his teeth.

A crowd of waitresses bustle up with dinner. The food smells amazing: duck, frog, fish, vegetables, rice. Gavin sniffs his bowl. No soy sauce. Liam puts several pieces of tofu on top. "Try this," he says. "Incredibly flavourful."

Gavin takes a tentative bite to be polite, although who knows what spices are on it? Marla eats slowly, putting her frog bones in her napkin. Is that what one does? Gavin checks. Liam's bones are beside his bowl. Gavin winks at Marla, puts his tofu in his napkin too.

Liam touches Gavin's shoulder. "Gavin, when did you ... here ...?"

Gavin holds up two fingers.

"Two days ago?"

Nod. Smile. He asks Liam, HOW LONG HAVE YOU KNOWN MARLA?"

Liam holds up nine fingers. Ever clever.

MONTHS?

Marla nodding. "... at the diner." She lays her hand on Liam's thigh, as if feeling the wool of his pants for the first time.

Liam doesn't seem to notice. "How long ... staying?"

Gavin doesn't really know. He's been texting back and forth with staff to get shifts covered, ignoring the university's emails. "FEW WEEKS." Catch them looking at each other as he finishes writing—missed something. Marla has jiggle legs.

Liam digs his phone out of his pocket. "Excuse me." He answers walking out the door.

Marla pulls Gavin closer. "What ... you think ..."

LIAM?

"Yeah ... he great?"

Careful. THINK SO. SMART. HOT. Gavin whistles. Must be noisy in here, because no one stares.

Marla laughs. "I'm ... you ... could ... hear." No: here. Glad Gavin's here.

Smile. Liam's coming back.

"Sorry ... student ... Christmas wishes ..."

Gavin waves his hand. NO WORRIES.

Marla is saying something to Liam, very close without touching, like a hummingbird, and Gavin feels his muscles tighten. He waits, catches her attention. Nods.

"Liam, Gavin: I ... announcement ..." Her face is hopeful, but she's looking at Gavin, not Liam.

Liam turns his whole upper body. Alert. "What is it?" Gavin rests his forearm on the table beside Liam. Just in case.

Marla wants Liam to want this. More, she wants to remember this moment, this boisterous and un-Christmassy moment when she gives the best gift ever. She taps her feet, excited. For all her casualness, Marla knows what she says will change everything. "I'm pregnant!"

Liam sits even straighter and folds his lips against his teeth. He moves his jaw around in a weird way like he's trying to keep himself together. Then he pushes his chair out and signals for the waitress. Marla covers her mouth as if she could take it back. She shouldn't have done it this way, put him on the spot. He hates not knowing what to do.

She sees Gavin's pad open on the table, waiting: CONGRATS YOU 2. Gavin beckons her closer, writing under a cupped hand. HE EVER HIT YOU?

Oh, Gavin. She shakes her head. Marla has a blip of her brother being pushed down the stairs as a little boy. Their mom used to get so angry when he couldn't understand, even after she found out he was deaf. Maybe especially then.

Liam leaves his chair where it was, pushed away. An island, then. She will row to him. "Liam, I'm sorry. I should have told you sooner."

"Indeed." Liam gathers himself up and sits tense, eyeing Gavin. "This is neither the time or the place." The end. Marla feels like an afterthought, a goose that waited too long to fly south.

He probably just needs facts. "I'm twelve weeks along. The baby will come in July."

Liam grinds his teeth, but he says nothing. Marla holds his hand, wishing he would lean back and slouch a bit, but his body is made of rebar. She feels a surging momentum, something huge and inevitable, and a sudden hatred for the baby.

TELL MORE, Gavin writes. He places the pad so Liam can read it too. People at the next table rise to make a toast.

Marla rattles on. "I go for a check-up every month. There will be another ultrasound soon, and if we go together you can see the baby." Gavin is nodding at her, encouraging her to get through it. Marla grasps. "We'll be able to hear the heartbeat." Liam sniffs and folds his arms and pretends not to notice the tears in her voice.

She can't do this, not this level of indifference. It hurts more than plain anger, and he knows it. Marla breaks away, sinking lower with each step to the bathroom, feeling rejected and yet wanting to fight for him. Marla tells herself they have something, but perhaps all they have is her silly little girl desire for fairy-tale love. She sees Liam's back reflected in the bathroom mirror before the door closes, and she crumples.

She knows Liam is so much more than what he is out loud.

Gavin's nephew-father can eye spell. There are words all over his face, big ones. Betrayal in block capitals.

NOT SO BAD, Gavin offers. Give him a way out.

Liam's not taking it. Narrow eyes read scorn. Arms crossed on chest. "Saying nothing … typical Marla," he says. That's what he says to Gavin. His voice is a snake, and Gavin hates it. He feels it crawling all over him.

Watch his jaw tighten. Liam wants to blame and Gavin suddenly hates this bastard. He can feel himself winding up, *tickticktickticktick* like a toy, getting tighter. SHE GOOD TO YOU. Gavin makes the period visible from across the table.

Oh shit. Gavin's up, hands ready, his chest heaving because Liam's standing, leaning over the table. "… knew it … when … she … you …" In Liam is a fear that Gavin recognizes. He edges around the table, getting close enough. Gavin probably won't hit Liam here, but it would feel good.

One word now, Liam's saying. "When … when … when?"

Behind him is a crowd of Chinese on the edge of their seats, and the waitress is talking to a man who looks like the manager. Play it safe. Don't give anything away to a guy who gets messed up over his sister. Gavin drops his hands, pushes pad over and pen. Point, WRITE.

He knows what Liam's going to say before he writes it, but he waits just the same: "When did you know about this?"

Gavin can't keep the answer off his face, the answer Liam doesn't want. Why didn't she tell him? Liam makes for the ladies' bathroom, and Gavin moves, one step behind, sure now, because no one is ever going to hulk after his crying sister. A bunch of guys roll their shirt sleeves up, but Gavin gets a hand on Liam's shoulder, turning him before it's too crowded, grabbing him by the collar to pull him in and then other men are putting their bodies between Gavin and Liam, putting their hands on him. He wants to tell them it's fine, but his pad's back on the table and he's shaking. Everyone's staring at him.

Gavin tries to catch his breath, reminds himself not to make deaf sounds. Liam says something, his hands palms up, then lowering to the floor, and the guys with the rolled-up sleeves loosen their grip. Gavin can't help trying to shoulder the other men away. Then he softens.

Behind Liam is Marla. She's come out of the bathroom with her arms outstretched to see Gavin held behind a line of men. She is weeping.

"Marla ... sorry ... handled that all wrong," Liam says, and the men relax a bit. Everyone yielding at the sight of a woman's grief.

Gavin can tell from their embrace that she's not going to leave him. He eye spells, OKAY?

Marla releases Liam, her fingers trailing along his sleeve, and hugs Gavin: in the feel of her arms around him, Gavin disappears back into every one of those moments Marla took on the world for him. She knows how to take care of people.

Gavin just wants to know she can take care of herself.

Marla watches Liam dust Gavin's shoulders off, nod to him, and put his forehead on her brother's. They talk. Liam must know what to say, because Gavin lets go of the tension in his body. Always a fighter. They get into the car, but she doesn't. She licks her lips. It's much colder now, and she hides her face in her scarf. His hazard lights are on: blink-blink, blink-blink. She can see Liam looking in the rear-view mirror, searching for her eyes. She doesn't know what to do.

Marla needs just a minute to think, to figure all of this out and know exactly what the plan should be. She didn't expect him to be upset. He probably thinks she can't look after herself like everyone else. She knows people see her as immature and she looks younger than she is, so she makes an effort to be perceived as a woman. This didn't help. Liam's building a massage studio for me, she tells herself. He has a running car. He's waiting. Marla meets his eyes in the mirror, sees his dry-cleaning hanging in the passenger window and turns away.

She hears the car door open, the ding-ding of the interior bell. "Marla, come home with me."

Marla wants to; nothing would be better than eating homemade tortellini on the couch and watching cheesy Christmas movies together. She closes her eyes and hears him yelling at Gavin like he was the enemy. But Marla's the enemy who made him angry and afraid. Marla and the baby. She turns, resolved.

"Just tell me if you want to have this baby with me."

Liam huddles close to his car, wrapping the open door around him so that other vehicles can pass. He glances at an older couple walking arm in arm on the sidewalk. "Please get in the car."

She can't because she has no grip on where any of this is going. It was a mistake, yes, maybe, and hiding it was bad, but Liam looks more embarrassed than angry or confused. Part of her feels like he should be an adult too: it's not just her baby. "I need to know."

Liam sidesteps the snowdrift at the curb and approaches Marla, puts his arm around her. "I understand. Let me drive you."

She stands there with him, looking for the future. She hates herself for not paying better attention, for complicating things just when they were working. It's often this way. "I'm sorry, Liam."

"Don't be sorry. It can happen to anybody. We can get this taken care of, if that's what you want." He smiles, tentative, trying to pull her in to his warm body.

So, he doesn't think she's an idiot. She should have told him sooner, because he does like her. Marla edges Liam in front of her so Gavin can't read her lips from the car. "An abortion would be scary. And I'd have to get it done soon." It's probably the right thing.

"I'm there for you. This is a big surprise, that's all."

Marla tucks that away and holds onto the feeling of Liam, the way he's looking at her, holding her. That's what she can't afford to lose.

They drive along the river in Bowness on the way to Marla's because the sidewalks are lit with candles in paper bags that no one kicks over. Each one flickers, illuminating families walking around snowplow heaps and an old man smoking. Gavin feels an affinity for this neighbourhood, like it's still its own town separate from Calgary, sunken lower and nestled in the curve of the river. Perhaps it is the scale that makes it feel normal, or the fact that downtown is so far. People understand the difference between aspect and prospect here—looking at and seeing from— the kind of people who have gratitude along with their desires.

Liam has apologized to Gavin, hugged him, and called him brother by the time they get to Dani's birthday party. He has also told Marla he loves her and agreed to stay for a drink. Gavin takes a deep breath, thankful he didn't hit this man tonight. He watches Liam loosen the knot in his tie and wishes he were wearing one so he could do the same.

Gavin hasn't been in the basement. He's surprised by how much cleaner it is than Marla's rooms on the main floor, and he admires Dani's carefully labelled crates of records and how the non-perishables are lined up on the counter. For the party, Dani has decked out her place in cheap department store decorations from twenty years ago: plastic hockey puck Christmas lights around the tiny window, a silver tinsel tree on the counter, and bright blue glittering balls hung on paperclips punched into the stippled ceiling. Her puppy wags its tail manically, jumping on everyone. Liam and Dani stand far apart and do not hug when he wishes her happy birthday. Gavin looks for a place to sit, but there is only the one chair, and it has Dani's tall boots leaning on it.

She has hats for everybody: an elf for Marla, Rudolph for Gavin, Santa for herself, and a green monster for Liam. He wears it, and sings something they are all terribly familiar with, making gestures Gavin doesn't understand. Then Dani sings too, her posture magnificent and her body lithe. He can tell that her voice must be very good by how Liam and Marla look at her when she's done. They all talk at each other, and with the hats hanging in their faces he can't make out a single word.

Gavin's going upstairs to get some tea when Dani takes him by the arm.

"... not leaving, right?"

He shakes his head.

Dani pulls him close. "Is Marla okay?"

Gavin nods. Rounds his hands over his stomach and nods to Liam.

"She told him! Good. He took it okay, then?"

Gavin shrugs, and she gets it.

"It's you that needs the drink. I thought so."

She leads him back, dancing with him to music he can't hear, dancing him right over to her rather elaborate bar area to hand him a drink. It looks okay, a shot of some kind. Something dark. Her hands on his feel warm and it's almost her birthday and for a moment Gavin feels okay. Comfortable, even. He tips his head back to drink and Dani smiles. Whiskey. She pours three more shots, and then Marla's hand is on hers.

"Make it four."

Gavin shakes his head, and Liam and Marla exchange a look. Gavin's missed something.

"... fine ... talked ... not keeping ... baby." She looks decided, but Gavin can tell she hasn't thought it through yet. Her smile is empty.

He blocks her from reaching the shot glass, and it spills on the floor. Marla scowls at him, about to say some things.

Dani picks it up and refills it, keeping the puppy away from the puddle with her foot. "Calm down. There's lots." She holds Marla with her eyes. "Only one for you, Mama."

Marla raises it. "To good friends." She smiles a fake smile and takes the shot. So stupid.

Dani gets into some heated argument with Liam, and Gavin sits on the floor in the corner and writes a list of points to go over with Marla tomorrow. He had forgotten this part, how everything takes so long with her, how she needs to be reminded over and over and yet not babied. He used to help her with her homework, explaining and re-explaining, but after she dropped out of high school he felt relieved, not just for her but for himself. He wonders how much help she needs, and if it's more than he suspects.

Eventually, Marla tells them they should exchange gifts to lighten the tension. Gavin gives Marla blocks he's made from blow downs for the baby, and she doesn't know what to say. She gives him designer jeans, then Dani opens a record of some guy Gavin doesn't recognize and she high fives Liam, puts it on. Everyone dances, which turns into sexy time for Marla and Liam. They grind, their eyes locked on each other.

"She's a goddess," Dani says, sitting beside Gavin.

Gavin considers his sister, her body moving like nothing could ever be wrong. She has an energy that looks confident, alive, alluring even, and a soft sweetness that could cover anything.

But it's a coping mechanism. He should be helping her more. Liam's not used to someone like her, a girl who looks like she knows what she's doing.

"I don't like it either."

Gavin grins, surprised that Dani can see what he's thinking. HAPPY BIRTHDAY.

Dani lays her hand on his thigh, just long enough for Gavin to know she meant to, then he pulls her up to dance.

The next day, Gavin is sick. The skin around his cuticles is peeling away, jumping ship, and there is something terribly clenchy about his stomach. He burps in bed, just to check it out: tastes like dinner last night. Tofu had something on it, something he doesn't allow. It's impossible to eat out, he finds. Everything is suspect.

He wants ginger tea for his stomach. Marla is already in the kitchen eating toast.

"Merry Christmas! ... want ... make ... " She leans back on her chair, and he wants to tell her she's going to hurt herself. She offers him her plate.

Marla doesn't get it. CAN'T

"... won't kill you ... one slice."

MAKE ME SUICIDAL. Her face falls open, and he regrets it immediately.

"When were ... suicidal?" She touches him on the shoulder like he might get away.

Gavin bangs the cupboard door on purpose, looking for a kettle. BEFORE

"... probably depressed."

Gavin looks at her, trying not to make her feel stupid. Of course he was depressed. NOT DRINK, YOU ESP.

Marla roots in the sink to find a saucepan. She rinses it, fills it, and sets it on the stove to boil for him. "... not ..."

She's talking too fast again, not looking at him. Frustrating. Gavin raises his arms in a question, and Marla enunciates like he's two, her face exaggerated. "We're not going to fight again, right?"

She's smiling, but today he can't laugh. And it's not funny. His face is itchy and his joints are aching and he just feels mean. He waves her away, knowing she's trying to talk to him. Marla is like the rest of the world, never having to worry about anything. He takes a cucumber from the fridge and washes it, considers peeling it.

He writes: TRY PROTECT YOU.

"Seriously ... my life."

Gavin thinks about what the right tool would be, how a professional would handle this. WE NEED MAKE LIST.

"... who ... you ... social worker?"

She's right. He's not her social worker. SO TALK THEN.

"... can I do? I don't ... enough for rent ... Liam ... mad."

Gavin cuts her off by waving his hand. He points to himself, shakes his head. Marla should know this. CAN'T QUIT YOUR CHILD. YOU EVERYTHING FOR HIM. This is the only thing Gavin knows for sure.

"You're not—" Marla gets up suddenly, opens the cupboard under the sink, and pukes in the compost bucket. She wipes her mouth and leans over the sink. Gavin watches her shoulders hitch up and down, feeling terrible. Poor Marla.

He gets her a glass of water and leads her back to the table. The water is boiling. TEA?

She smiles in a sad sort of way, shakes her head.

LAST NIGHT HARD. He catches movement from the corner of his eye and flips over a new sheet on his notepad.

"... fuckers are crying?" Dani has her puppy in her arms. She starts to set him down but changes her mind and shoos him downstairs. "On Christmas? What's the deal?"

Gavin considers Dani, evaluating. She's dressed up and genuinely concerned. MARLA BARFED, he writes.

"And you?" Dani sits beside Gavin, eyeing the hunk of cucumber in his fist.

"Gavin ... food ... won't eat." The way Marla says it feels disdainful, or maybe it's just that he's thirsty and sick. Still, Gavin hates her for a second.

ALLERGIES. FEEL SHITTY. UP TOO LATE.

Dani looks confused, like she can't figure out if he's serious or not. Then she shrugs. "You'll be okay, soon, right? No biggie." She goes to the cupboard. "Raisins? Rice crackers?"

Gavin nods okay, and catches Marla rolling her eyes. Dani hands Gavin bags and boxes, then turns to Marla and says something Gavin doesn't see.

Marla closes her eyes and looks at the ceiling. Exasperated? "Totally forgot ... be five minutes."

She throws dishes in the sink and takes off for the bathroom. Dani paces, then calls the puppy, not looking at Gavin, waiting for Marla. She ties a ribbon around the puppy's neck, her hands trembling. Gavin pushes his chair away from the table. He has no idea where they're going.

On her way out, Marla says to Gavin. "Make a shopping list ... go tomorrow."

They're going without him. He watches the door slam, and then he's alone.

6. COOKIE

MARLA GLANCES BACK at Dani while she drives, counting. One puppy on the floor, a box of Timbits on Dani's knees, and a tiny stuffed turtle on the seat beside her. It looks good. Dani's wearing a tailored burgundy jacket, undone, and a stretchy silver skirt of Marla's with come-fuck-me boots. Marla giggles. "Nice boots."

Dani looks at her, surprised. "Should I wear something else? Do you think she'll notice?"

"You can't see the tops."

Dani leans forward to check out Marla's feet, in black flats. "Trade me."

"You won't fit into these, She-ra."

"I don't care. Trade me. I have to get this right."

Marla shimmies out of her shoes at a light and drives in her socks. Dani grabs the shoes while the dog gnaws her boots.

"Little fucker." Dani takes the puppy on her knee and lets it chew her fingers.

"Are you going to ask her today? To sign custody back over to you?"

"Yep." Dani puts the shoes on and strokes the puppy. "Drive, Marla."

"I'm sorry we're late." It's a long way, through the city. Marla thinks about asking Dani for gas money, but doesn't.

Dani crushes pills in a cigarette case and snorts them. "You're lucky you don't have to deal with your parents today."

"Foster parents. Should you be doing that right now?"

Dani ignores the question. "Same shit. Wait until you have a kid."

"Yeah," Marla says, although she hasn't once considered her baby being in a room with Dave and Elise, period. She's been thinking about Gavin, about how he does everything the proper way and knows everything. He would fit right in with her foster parents. They're on their annual trip to Mexico right now, splashing in a hot tub.

Dani's mother lives in High River, a little town with the same twenty-five-year-old houses and vinyl siding as Calgary subdivisions, hemmed in by ranches and emptiness. People film movies there in the summer because it is all cowboy picturesque, but right now it's just cold. "I hate this fucking place," Dani says as Marla pulls into the driveway. Dani straightens the ribbon on the puppy and stuffs the turtle in her pocket. "Wish me luck."

"Should I drive around a bit?"

Dani presses her lips together. "I don't know."

Marla shuts the car off and watches Dani approach the door with a tremor in her leg. Dani knocks, scratches her face, shakes her hair. Marla reaches for Dani's boots. Her feet are cold.

When Marla looks up again, she sees Kamon, who is as she remembers him, sort of. He used to be an accessory of Dani's, a smiley pet in a car seat that Dani unbuckled to put new diapers on. Marla remembers feeding him a bottle while Dani drove them to some party. Then he was a toddler who screamed from his playpen or went right for Dani's meth pipe, fascinated by it, and slept in Dani's bed once he learned to climb out of his crib.

This Kamon is big, jumping, and wearing all new hockey equipment. He darts out in his socks, dropping his stick. Dani sets the Timbits on the ground and bends to hug him. The puppy licks him, and then Kamon gallops back inside.

Sandra, Dani's mom, has a perma-glare. She looks pointedly at her watch and shouts something at Dani, who holds the struggling puppy as its ribbon flutters to the snow. Sandra points to the dog and makes a cutting motion at her neck. Dani says something severe, using her hands. She can't hold onto the dog any longer, and it bursts out of her arms and into the house.

Kamon gets bulldozed by the puppy and turns around to chase it. A big stuffed animal he was carrying lies as if dead in the front entrance.

Dani tries to go in, but Sandra blocks her way. She gives Dani a terrible look, and Marla wants to tell her to stop being such an ugly old bag because it's freakin' Christmas. Sandra disappears into the house, and Dani wiggles her fingers for Kamon. She whispers into his ear, and he nods, very serious. She takes two Timbits out of the box and hands them to him one at a time. He grins, then bends down to hide them in his socks. Dani tucks the turtle into the waistband of his hockey pants, then stands up. Sandra's coming.

Sandra hands Dani the dog like it's been swimming in a shit lagoon, shaking her head, closing the door.

Dani keeps the door from closing with her foot and blows a kiss to Kamon.

"Bye, Mommy!" he shouts. "Happy birthday!"

Merry Christmas. Thought you were coming with me?
Crap. Had to drive Dani to Kamon. Forgot—so sorry.
No prob. My mom's dead, so it's not like she can tell time.
I'll be there soon. An hour, tops.
You know which cemetery?
Yeah. By Confederation Park. Got it. Sorry.

Gavin does a hundred push-ups and a hundred sit-ups and reviews his list to see if there's anything new to check off, but there isn't, so he sits with the phone book and looks for his mom, needing to get back on schedule. There are many Parkers, lots of C. Parkers too. Too many. He looks at a map, circling street names, trying to figure out the closest one, but it's a pathetic thing to do alone on Christmas.

Gavin tackles something easier: going through Marla's cupboards and throwing out impure foods. He keeps the garbage can beside him, hauling it from cupboard to fridge to pantry. In go the chocolate marshmallow sandwiches, orange cream popsicles and expired salad dressing. Away with the monosodium glutamate soups, aspartame pop, frozen chicken nuggets. He feels superior as he scoops hydrogenated sugary peanut butter out of a plastic container so he can wash and recycle it later. So no one like him will later be tempted to reclaim it from the garbage.

He's mid-scoop when Marla appears wearing Dani's black boots that go nearly to her knee. Dani too, and she looks pissed. Marla stares at the spoon in his hand and the peanut butter falling in the garbage and drops her bag on the floor.

He scrambles to write one-handed, his pad against his knee. I BUY NEW. HEALTHY.

She takes the pad and throws it under the table. "Gavin, what the fuck!"

Gavin retrieves it from the peeling linoleum on his hands and knees. Marla is obviously a food addict. He should go slowly with her. NO WORRY. I COOK.

"No." She tips the garbage can towards her to see how full it is and pushes it back so hard it falls on its side, cookie sleeves falling out. "... your deal about food?"

He can't tell her some of it is stuff he can't have in the house: pasta, chocolate bars, ice cream, honey. He envisions himself putting honey in his tea and shudders. BETTER FOR BABY.

"What ... baby ... can't ... rules." She's spitting a bit, speaking fast. Dani's laughing.

He nudges the garbage can with his foot. THIS POISON.

Marla holds him by the shoulders, purposely speaking

slowly. "This is what I can afford."

SAID I BUY.

Marla puts her forehead to the wall, her arms above her head. He can see the shape of her belly now, how there's something there. Someone.

There are still sugary granola bars and kids' fruit snacks in the pantry, but he leaves them for now. I'M SORRY. He places his pad on the wall beside her until she looks at him.

"... don't want your food. Do not throw anything else out." She nods at Dani, who makes her face all serious and salutes. "I have to go."

Shit. Marla bangs out the door, and Gavin sinks into a chair. It feels like the worst Christmas ever.

Dani sits beside him. She takes the peanut butter and eats it off her index finger. "You had a moment here, looks like."

Gavin scans the rifled kitchen, empty boxes stacked in the corner and the mostly bare shelves. YEAH. CRAP.

"Think she's going to send you home?"

Gavin feels panic sliding up his arms and around his throat. Is it really that bad?

"I'm kidding! You kill me." She throws the empty jar in the garbage and picks up the map with the circles on it. "What's this?"

TRY FIND MOM.

"Festive. Want to get high?"

Gavin's not sure if he understood that right. She's waiting for an answer while he runs through alternate possibilities: What a good tie (time?), good eye?

She holds her thumb and forefinger in a circle beside her mouth and puffs an imaginary joint. "Right downstairs, my friend. On the house."

The basement is different during the day with its bright fluorescent lights and the TV on. It looks smaller down here, quieter, like Dani's not putting on a show, but inviting him into where she really lives.

They sit on the table side by side, and he takes the joint every time she offers. He feels mature to be breaking rules, like he's eating cake in bed and no one needs to know about it. He giggles, thinking about cake, and she smiles. "First time?"

He shrugs: *maybe*, then nods. She shows him how to hold the smoke deep inside, teaching him, and then they have a secret: he and his friend Dani.

"Fun, right?" She kills it, and they lean against the wall. "Listen, we have to talk about Marla."

Right. SHE HAS F.A.S. SHE TELL YOU?

"No, but I recognize it. I help with day to day stuff, making plans."

Gavin hasn't lived with Marla since they were small and she was the one looking after him. LIKE WHAT?

"There are three things I have to be strict with: having alarms in her phone so she doesn't miss work, no cooking unless someone is here, and always come straight home."

Gavin had no idea it was like that, that his sister was unable to really grow up. She always told him about her successes, and he never thought to ask if she needed supervision. LOT OF WORK.

Dani shrugs. "That's the kind of support she needs. She can't plan ahead for what might happen, so without help she's always getting into trouble."

Gavin inches closer to Dani until her warm forearm is against his as he writes. They have their love of Marla in common. GLAD YOU HERE FOR HER. YOU TALK HER ABOUT ABORTION?

She shakes her head. "I'll go with her."

BUT IS WHIM—CHOOSE LIAM OVER BABY BECAUSE HE IN FRONT OF HER.

"I know, partner. Listen, be calm. We have to let her go her own speed." Gavin hugs Dani, his face in her hair and neck, feeling her sink into his arms.

Dani insists on coming with Marla to the abortion clinic, citing the fact that she's a woman who's actually had an abortion, which is more than Liam can claim. He's been testy since she was late to the cemetery. It was windy there, and Marla didn't know what to do while Liam cried to his dead mother about how proud she'd be of his practising.

"I'm sorry I can't come today—I have to work," he says, pouring coffee for them.

"It's the only appointment they have. I'm almost thirteen weeks."

"Are you sure this is what you want? I mean, I'm there for you."

"Just not today."

"I'm really sorry." He hands her forty bucks. "Take a cab home, okay? Please?"

He drops Marla and Dani off early, and they drink slushies outside even though it's freezing.

"You scared?"

"Yeah. Were you?"

"I didn't have a choice."

The little room is cold, but they let Dani come in with her. Marla lies in a paper gown waiting for the doctor. She wonders if it will be the same dress for success guy who told her this would happen, doing abortions on the side. "This sucks."

Dani shrugs. "Yeah. But once it's done, you're laughing. No baby, no worry."

Marla thinks about all the rad parenting ideas she had, like pulling the baby in a wooden sled and how she wouldn't mind getting up in the night because she's a light sleeper. "I'm not sure," she says, because she's afraid it really is terribly simple.

"Kids are forever. You have to really want them."

Marla tries to quantify what she wants, hold it in her mind, but she can't pin it down. It doesn't include feeling guilty about this procedure or any inkling she can't be a good parent. It was more about feeling proud of herself for having something in her life that was bigger than just her.

"I'd be a great mom."

Dani tucks Marla's hair behind her ear. "Of course you would. You're a very caring person."

That's true. Marla is caring; she knows it. Look at how she takes care of Gavin. But if Marla's being honest, she knows that she is also impulsive and forgetful and easily bored. People have been telling her that for years. "Tell me, Dani, honestly. Do you think I could do it? I mean, with some help."

"The kind of help you need takes some explaining. Does Liam know how to support you? Do you know how to support him?"

A little flare of understanding flickers in Marla. "He thinks you're staying with me so I can help you, Dani."

"You do, babe."

There's a knock, and the nurse is back, barging into the stream of thoughts about all the ways Marla has been there for people and made their lives better. She sits up and grabs at the side of the bed, holding the panic to savour and understand it: she wants her baby. "No. I can't do this."

Dani frowns. "Run that by me again?"

Marla feels jolted with electricity. Everything is humming, building, locking into place. "I don't know. I'm sorry—I just got it." She puts on her clothes, talking through her shirt. "I need to go home."

In the car, she calls Liam.

this is a sit-down thing, but you guys are away, so:
I'm pregnant
Oh, honey. I'm so sorry.
no, it's good. want you to know
How far along are you? Who is the father? What can we do? We're home in 2 days.
it's going to be fine
Phone us anytime. We need to talk about this.

On New Years' Eve, Elise asks Marla if she's bringing Liam to the annual New Years' party at her gallery. Her foster parents have nagged her about meeting him forever, but Marla's giving them time to cool down first. Instead, she brings Gavin, who's on his best behaviour of late—building shelves for Marla's poetry notebooks and making vegan-boy suppers for everyone.

The cozy purple gallery has pashminas hung over the windows for the big opening and hand-painted signs with heavy weight fonts. The artist is a photographer who takes pictures of people's closets and storerooms—the stuff no one wants you to see. Marla likes the idea of it, but fails the guy for staging everything—filling closets with skinned deer hanging from hooks, or ladies' shoes stacked on jam jars.

KNOW WHO LOVE THIS?

"Liam?"

YEAH. TEXT.

She should, even though she's packing around this baby he doesn't seem to want yet. He told her she was confusing and immature, going one way and then the other and keeping secrets. Which is true, but really. A baby's a big decision. Dani offered to explain the help Marla needs, but Marla doesn't want him to think she's an idiot. And Gavin said he'd stay longer to support her. Anyway, it's New Years' Eve. Marla sends Liam the address and a picture of a coat rack closet. He responds immediately. *Love to.*

Marla and Gavin cruise the exhibit. People look at the photos for too long, and Marla finds herself people-watching instead. It's mostly older men craning their necks to get a better view and their pinched wives clanking around in boxy jewellery.

As Marla and Gavin giggle together, Elise flutters over in a vest with a fringe. She puts a hand to her throat, her eyes wide. "Is this who I think it is?"

Marla leans back so a waiter with a tray of wine glasses can get by. "Mom, Gavin. Gavin, Elise."

Elise plucks glasses of red wine—one for her and one for Gavin. "It's so nice to finally meet you! Will you have a drink?"

Gavin nods and sets the glass on the floor between his feet. He takes out his notepad.

Elise turns to Marla, glancing around. "What is he doing?"

"Talking to you."

Elise leans to see Gavin's message: THANK YOU. PLEASED TO MEET YOU. Her mouth makes little tics only Marla knows to look for, then peels back into a power smile.

"What a charming young man!" She takes a sip of wine and speaks, looking about the room. "How long are you staying?"

Gavin gives a little wave to catch her eye and hands her a card. She reads only part of it before a fat man in thick corduroy taps her on the shoulder.

"Todd, how wonderful to see you!"

Marla shifts her weight, uncomfortable for Gavin's sake, but he doesn't seem bothered. He holds his wine glass steady, not drinking from it.

"An enchanting evening, Elise," Todd says, looking Marla up and down. "And who is this?"

"I'm Marla," she says, holding her hand out. He kisses it like she's from Europe.

"This is my daughter," Elise says, beaming. "And her brother, Gavin."

"Oh." Todd gives Marla and Gavin a "this must be one of those situations" look.

Daughter. Marla's embarrassed when Elise calls her that, like one more person slapping this label on her is going to make everything better. This woman who calls herself Marla's mother is part of Marla's life because she wanted to be—like a whim, Marla thinks. Not like blood. Elise's place and her people are so far from what Marla imagines for herself that her chest feels tight. Marla's family is Gavin, the sturdy man-boy who at least looks like her and can sense how she feels and what she needs without having to be told.

Todd's been saying something or other, and now kisses Elise's cheeks before squeezing through the crowd. Elise turns to Gavin, holding his card like it really matters to her. "My apologies, Gavin. Where were we?"

"You were asking how long he's staying," Marla says.

Gavin shrugs. HAVE A JOB IN O.N.

Elise nods with her mouth open like she couldn't be more amazed. She glances at Marla, nods some more. "Well, good for you!"

Gavin gestures to the crowd, then writes, IS YOUR HUSBAND HERE ALSO?

"No, not tonight." Elise gives Marla a tight smile, one she's seen before. It means Dave's disappointed in her for getting knocked up. Predictable.

I LOOK FORWARD TO MEETING HIM TOO.

Elise reaches around to hug Gavin while he's writing, and he jumps a little. She speaks to Marla, wrapped around Gavin so he can't see her mouth. "I want to see you soon, so we can talk about this baby." Then she's off again, working the room.

Gavin waves to Elise as she floats to another group. NICE MOM.

"She plays her part."

DON'T SAY THAT.

"She wants me to volunteer at a daycare so I can see how awful kids are."

Gavin raises his eyebrows. He leaves his wine on a table and points to a poster advertising for nude models. THIS FIRST. MAKE MONEY.

Marla laughs so loud that upscale old people stop and stare. She doesn't care. She puts her arms around Gavin so they are nose to nose. "Let's get out of here."

They meet Liam outside, parking the car. He checks the time. "It's not over yet, is it?"

Marla had forgotten all about him.

Liam is a man in his element in the gallery, Gavin thinks. He shakes hands and seems to know people. Marla relaxes on his arm, and people treat Gavin like he's important by association.

Even Elise is impressed, although she is careful not to mention Marla's baby. Gavin respects her for that, giving Marla time to work things out on her own. They eat cheese and Liam leads a toast—to the promise of the future.

As the party winds down, Gavin and Liam collapse tables and carry containers of leftover food to Elise's SUV. Marla stands in the doorway folding tablecloths. The whole time, Elise lingers beside Marla, tucking and re-tucking her blonde hair behind her ears, but neither of them says anything. Gavin hates that. He didn't even get foster parents. He remembers his first days at the deaf school, wanting someone just for him but knowing no one, clutching Marla's book to his chest. Everyone flapping their fingers in front of them like he should know what they meant.

After they've said goodbye and Elise has thanked them several times, Marla says, "... downtown?"

Gavin shrugs. Liam stops at what Gavin assumes to be his house to pick up a large instrument in a black case, then drives like he knows where they're going. The streets pass on a predictable and relentless grid laid over rivers and escarpments—the influence of the Canadian Pacific Railway—but downtown bears little homage to the company that changed Calgary from a fort to a city over a century ago. Now glass-panelled oil and gas office towers create downdrafts on the streets instead, the old CPR station buried and replaced by the spaceship-looking Calgary Tower. Gavin is delighted by how the past disappears here, challenged by new opportunity. He'd like to reinvent himself too.

They park and enter the deserted lobby of an office tower, taking the unmoving escalator to the second floor with its little cafés and jewellery stores. Everything is closed. Marla leads them through a set of double doors into a covered walkway above the street, something Gavin had admired as necessary for a winter city until now. This is why the streets lack human scale and instead sport private plazas and cheap little businesses.

Everyone with money and mobility is rushing around up here, breathing recycled air, and stopping for sandwiches encased in plastic triangular prisms. They follow Marla through so many buildings that Gavin loses count.

When they do get outside, the neighbourhood is decidedly more alive. The bar is called Soap. There's a line, but Marla takes them to the front and gets them in, no cover. Inside, a little jazz group plays something to people who lean close together at round tables and shout, their mouths wide. The room is pulsing with bass, sweaty. Gavin remembers Dani, the way her arm pressed against his, and his heart beats faster.

He watches Marla talk to the bartender and write on a paper taped to the bar. She comes back with pop for herself, a boozy coffee for Liam, and mineral water for Gavin. The jazz group finishes, and someone else gets up. It's a comedian, Gavin thinks, although he can't follow what the guy's saying because he squishes his face in different ways to talk. Doing voices, maybe.

More people take the stage, singers and poets, and Gavin feels the evening is wasted on him. Why would Marla bring him here? Then it's Liam's turn. He sits on a stool with a cello, his bow slow and steady, his head up, eyes closed, using vibrato on the strings. Gavin watches the people around him, impressed by their wonder.

Next is Marla.

"I call this High River Christmas," she says, speaking right to Gavin, and rips into a lilting rhythm, her words fast, then slow. She raises her eyebrows and speaks with her hands, putting on a show—spoken word. Gavin follows her actions: Marla smooths her hair, looks forlornly at her clothes, puts on pretend lipstick. Holds a nostril and snorts something, her eyes going wide.

The crowd snaps their fingers, nodding, leaning forward. It seems to Gavin like Marla doesn't even stop to breathe, that the whole thing is one long exhalation. She holds her arms against her chest, struggling to hold onto something, letting it go. Getting down on her knees and blowing a kiss, tears in her eyes. Gavin can see sweat on her brow, but, when she looks up, she's smiling. The crowd roars applause that Gavin can feel.

Scrabble with Marla:

M	G	
~~10~~	~~18~~	mauve
~~29~~	~~38~~	voodoo
~~43~~	~~54~~	yep – double word score
~~66~~	~~61~~	blank letter
~~74~~	~~101~~	jeez – double word score
~~99~~	~~110~~	jo
~~113~~	~~120~~	barrio
~~155~~	~~132~~	dope
~~179~~	~~138~~	four a's and a b!
~~203~~	~~149~~	grab
~~212~~	~~156~~	ink
~~230~~	~~174~~	direct
~~239~~	~~184~~	wedge
~~247~~	~~191~~	immun_
~~249~~	~~196~~	no more vowels, stuck with a b
~~256~~	~~193~~	Marla has all the y's and s's
258		

One frigid day in January, Marla learns Gavin's extended leave has been approved, which is rad, except it means he thinks she's unable to manage her own life. He cooks, cleans, shops, and reminds her to go to work, just like Elise did. She's ready to pour herself a bag of chips to wallow with when she gets a call from her landlord telling her he's raising the rent by a hundred bucks. She needs a distraction from all this reality, so she drives off to sneak into Liam's house.

She closes the door like a spy, turning the handle slowly so it doesn't click. She creeps down the hall, choosing which floorboards to step on from experience. From his bedroom, Marla can hear Liam counting patiently in the next room for a student: "ONE, two, three, four, ONE, two, three, four."

Liam has this beautiful brass bed with a plush foam top that is irresistible. Marla slides under the covers. She likes the smell on his pillow, his sleep smell. It's kinda turning her on, except she can hear the kid talking, and now Liam too, in his teacher voice. Sort of even hotter, maybe.

Marla makes the bed up nice and waits on the down quilt, arranging herself sensually on the pillows, but she gets bored. She examines the items on his bedside table, opens the drawer. Then Marla removes the lid from this old tin she's curious about.

Inside are letters, of course, neatly folded love notes with ribbons and drawings and tiny trinkets: bubble-gum, photos, chopsticks, a wallet calendar. Marla is hungry, insatiable. The letters are addressed to Liam's ex-wife.

"Leila,

I have this dream: when I see you coming around the corner to meet me, I run to you, arms and fingers and legs all straining. I can never have enough of your embrace: you are a symphony. Meet me tonight: I have something for you."

Silence. "Marla," Liam spits, "what are you doing here?"

"I brought you cinnamon buns." Marla replaces the letters into the tin with bird's egg carefulness and closes the lid. "Why do you keep these?"

Liam pushes her back after this two-second-old-grandma-non-hug and ekes past her to smooth the rumples she made in his bed. "Don't be in my private stuff."

"Sorry." She doesn't mean it to come out harsh, but she can't help it. She was just trying to do something nice. And it's not a secret he has an ex who cheated on him right after they got married. Marla watches him tucking the corners of the bed sheets in like a hospital bed and feels sorry for him. He wants everything to be just so. "I think all kinds of things about you might be hidden in little tins throughout the house. I like your stuff, the way it feels and looks. It reminds me of you."

"It belongs to me."

She follows him into the kitchen, where she reaches beside him to open the cupboard for plates. Marla shimmies her girl-boy hips into Liam's side, hoping some part of her jiggles satisfactorily.

Liam smooths his beard. He looks at the Styrofoam boxes on the table, the crumpled napkins.

"Come on." Marla trails her thumb down his spine. Nothing, not even a lean-in from Liam. She uses her rummaging mouse hand to tickle him, even though she knows him to be impervious to it.

Liam jumps, his hand waving in the air. He knocks Marla's head hard into the corner of the open cupboard door. She drops the plates and they smash on the floor.

"Ow!" Marla feels in her hair with her fingertips. Blood. She can feel it running over her scalp. She cups her hand over the cut and reaches for the dishtowel hanging on the stove.

"Wait." Liam steps around the broken plates to get her a paper towel. Marla wipes her bloody fingers on it, trying not to worry about the size of the dent she just made in his floor.

"It's bad."

"I'm sorry. Jesus."

Marla holds the paper towel to her head, but it soaks through. "Do you think I need stitches?"

He peers over the top of her head, puts his fingers in her hair. His touch is so gentle. "I don't think so. You don't feel woozy, do you?"

She strokes his hip, thinking getting hurt made him less mad and more concerned. "Maybe a little. But that's mostly the nausea."

Liam carries Marla over the shards on the floor to his boxy couch. "Sit here for a bit." It's quieter in his living room full of fabric and drapery. Softer. His cello guards the room from its stand, his music filed neatly on a shelf behind it. She can hear him sweeping up the mess, and then he brings her an ice pack wrapped in an old burgundy towel.

"Thanks."

He sits on the coffee table facing her, puts her feet on his legs. "Look, we should probably make a plan."

Here it is. It's exactly now that Liam's going to give her the whole story about why he can't have a baby. Maybe his evil ex had a miscarriage or Liam dropped a baby brother on his head. "Did you have a brother?" she interrupts.

Liam exhales like he's trying to blow out a birthday candle. "What does that have to do with anything?"

"I just thought maybe you had a little brother."

"That's you, Marla." He stares at her like he forgot he started this whole conversation. "This isn't working."

So, there is nothing, just Liam with his important job interview and his expensive furniture. That she's probably bleeding on. She checks the back of the couch. Good. No blood. "So, you've had another plan all along."

"Well, I know I'm not ready to be a dad." Liam puts her legs down and starts pacing the room. "I feel like we should just work on us—see how that goes."

Marla pictures the fishy little creature growing inside her and tries to decide if she will look like her or Liam. "We'll be good parents."

Liam ticks items off on his fingers: "We could break up, we'd need more money coming in, I'd have to find a new place to do lessons—"

"You think we're going to break up?" Marla takes herself back to when she first met Liam, who drank bottomless cups of coffee that she refilled as he marked up music, smudged in graphite. Of him driving her home after her shift, talking about being abandoned by his dad and caring for his mom after she train-wrecked. And now, lazing around while he practises, feeling the low notes reverberate in her chest and wishing there was something about her that could be that generous and true. Without Liam, Marla would end up with the kind of boyfriends she used to have, mostly skateboarders she met at raves who were into punk music and drinking beer for lunch.

"Look, I need to trust you."

"That's easy!"

"No, it isn't. You can't sneak in here. You can't take money from me and give it to Dani."

He doesn't get it. When she doesn't respond, Liam lifts his cello by the neck and flips the page on his sheet music. He plays the same brooding thing he's been sawing at for months: quick notes with sharp edges, and the part that sounds like a rollercoaster—up, then down and looping around. He runs one ten-second clip on repeat, his upper lip sweating. It's for his audition.

Most guys, she gets tired of. But Liam is different. She worries he'll get tired of her. "Listen, I won't do that again. I promise. What if we went on a trip to the mountains, to celebrate your audition? Spend some time together just you and me."

Liam pauses with his fingers waggling back and forth on the string. "Okay. I mean, we have to give this a chance—so, yes." Liam strokes her hair. "Is your head still bleeding?"

She holds the towel out, moving it back and forth slightly as if it's a hologram. Red on red. "I can't tell."

7. POP CAN

MARLA AT WORK, so good time to help her organize. Dealt with these items from Marla's spare room:

- vacuum cleaner, nonworking: garbage
- toaster oven, nonworking: garbage
- iron, nonworking: garbage
- miscellaneous paperwork that shouldn't be recycled; Marla to look through
- extra kitchenware: give away
- old school projects of Marla's: box in the closet
- clothes that need mending: sewn
- cans of baked beans, expired: garbage
- newspapers and magazines: recycling
- gift bags: saved three in the closet, rest in garbage

Dani sitting on the floor, watching me clean, smiling at me. Playing with her puppy, named him Zigzag. Not lonely now.

The days get longer, but it is still grey in the late afternoon, and the snow sits in hard crusts in the cold. Marla swallows prenatal vitamins and wears stretchy pants and focuses her thoughts on Liam.

He's been so happy these last few weeks, calling her after work to say good night and asking her if there's anything he can do, which is weird, because she hasn't been seeing him much with all his practising. Everyone's been happy. Marla thinks it's because of Gavin, who spends all his time making people feel good. He's been building shelves for Dani's records and eating with her when Marla's at work; and cleaning up Marla's house for her, room by room, boxing up donations and filling the recycling bin. He somehow had time to make Liam a kind of glockenspiel for his birthday and then took everyone bowling, even Dani. He's quiet and good and Marla doesn't want him to ever leave.

The Friday before Valentines' Day, Dani's on Marla's bed when Marla gets out of the shower. "Hey. What are you doing?"

"Waiting for you." Dani is flipping through one of the pregnancy books Marla keeps forgetting to return to the library.

Marla shakes her towel off and steps into her panties. She has to get ready, because Liam will be here any minute.

Dani gestures towards a picture of a swelling body. "I remember all this shit. You had a pregnant orgasm yet?"

"No. Why?"

"Get familiar with yourself, Marla. It's like a thousand times more powerful. Wait until you get big."

"Yeah? What else?"

"Your hair gets thicker. Sometimes your pee smells."

Marla laughs, throws a pillow at her. "No, that's just you, Dani."

"You'll grow tons of butt hair, and by eight months you'll be too big to run or walk, just waddle."

"As if!" Shirtless Marla tackles Dani and pushes the pillow over her face. It's an old game.

"Okay, okay," Dani says from under the pillow. Marla lets her up. "You'll still be a waif, but you'll have a basketball belly that will make it impossible for you to drive."

"Maybe," Marla says.

"Let's measure." Dani sits behind her and holds her arms around Marla's waist in an approximation of a womb at capacity.

"Really? That big?"

"Massive. I was out to here." Dani holds her arms wide

enough to put several watermelons inside. "Pretty soon you'll need new clothes."

Expensive. Marla's already had to get a new bra. Her breasts used to be so nice and small, something she could run with, but not anymore. "Liam's going to be here soon," Marla says.

"Lucky you, going away for a romp or two."

So that's why she's here. Marla slows down, inching around the subject. "Should be fun."

Dani takes a prescription bottle out of her pocket and pours several pills. "I see what he did to your face."

Marla touches the scab at her hairline. "What are you talking about? I walked right into it."

Dani throws her head back, swallowing five pills at once. "Did you?"

"Well, no. I tickled him, and he bumped the cupboard door and it hit me." Marla pulls on a long button-up dress, leaving the top button undone. The dress is tight across her belly.

"He whipped a cupboard door into your head. You want me to believe he didn't know you were right there, at that exact height?"

There's a part of Marla that's been pushing this very thought down for weeks. "You want me to be afraid of him, but it's not like that."

"Just saying. I don't trust him."

Marla piles clothes in an old suitcase of Elise's. "Tell me what you're going to do while I'm gone."

"Nothing much. Eat me some vegan."

Marla has gotten used to Dani and Gavin spending so much time together, but she still doesn't like it. She wonders what they could possibly have in common. "Do you think Gavin's depressed?" Marla slaps the suitcase shut and zips around it, but the zipper gets stuck.

"Why—because he doesn't dance and sing?" Dani grins.

Marla pulls on the zipper. "No, because he has so many food rules."

"He's a monk, a delicious monk."

"I'm serious. I'm worried about him."

"Don't smother the guy. You're not his mom."

Marla stops Dani with a look. She absolutely was his mom, in a way, back when their mother used to take off. Back when she made Gavin Marla's responsibility.

"Either way, you do it smart this weekend. Don't let Liam surprise you," Dani says, sitting on the suitcase.

"He doesn't hit me." The zipper's not budging.

"He's a twat, a finger up his ass know-it-all." Dani bounces, grinning.

If Dani would shut up, Marla could think. Marla feels herself losing control, an almost-sick feeling. She closes her eyes and counts to ten.

"Telling you what to do all the time, making you feel dumb—"

Marla opens her eyes and screams. "Dani, so do you!"

Dani nods, the smile growing on her face. She reaches over to pull the zipper back, and then zips the suitcase shut. "I knew you could stand up for yourself, Marla. I think you really are ready for a fuckfest with your man."

Liam is here to pick up Marla. Wave hi, embrace. Gavin tries to allow Liam more space in this house where he is nervous, be generous with love for him.

"Gavin, hello."

Write, MARLA DANI GETTING READY.

Liam gives Gavin a look that says exactly how he feels about Dani. Takes Gavin aside. "... don't care for ... you know ... her?"

M. SAID KNOWN FOR YEARS.

"... Dani is older ... didn't ... school together."

Liam's doing that thing that happens when people forget Gavin's deaf—have to remind him to slow down. NO, DON'T THINK SO. MAYBE WORK?

Liam flexes his fingers, then squeezes each joint. "I can't see ... working ... junkie."

Gavin shakes his head. SHE SICK. Marla told him that, about Dani's car accident.

"... own fault, Gavin ... Marla shouldn't ... clean up ... mess."

Gavin thinks Liam's jealous, like Dani might be a lesbian with all the hair-brushing and clothes-trading she and Marla do. GOOD FRIEND.

"Of yours?"

Gavin's about to say no, which makes him feel guilty. Why shouldn't she be his friend? Is she dangerous? Unworthy? Surely not. He nods, but his hesitation has given him away.

"There's something going on with her." Liam nods to Dani coming down the hall, and Gavin realizes Liam mouthed the words. Clever.

Liam slides a flask out of his coat pocket and offers it to Gavin. "Vodka," he says. "Gluten free."

Gavin laughs and takes a pretend hit to be sociable, hands it back.

"Come on, you fucker," Dani says. "Not gonna offer me any?"

Liam is suddenly wooden. "Dani, I refuse ... any more profanity."

"Just a taste." She's looking at Liam with her head turned slightly. Something about her posture is really promoting her breasts.

Liam hands her the flask, wordless, and she downs quite a bit. Looks at him while she exhales a deep breath that softens every part of her.

"... going, Dani," Marla says, gentle, coming up behind her with a suitcase.

"You two have a nice time." Dani hands the flask back to Liam, turning her body away from Marla and into his. "Keep your fucking hands off her this weekend," she says to Liam, sliding her hand around his neck to flip his collar up. She lingers, slipping her fingers down his jawline and leaning in close like she will kiss him.

Liam steps back and into Gavin, his crisply ironed shirt wrinkled at the waist. "What did you say?"

"You heard me."

Marla pats Dani. "... big girl ... leave him ..." She and Dani hug, then Marla kisses Gavin on the cheek. "Look after ... other," she says, and then Gavin and Dani are alone.

Dani stares at Gavin, flares her nostrils. He suddenly feels very hungry. "I'm having a bath," she says, her look trailing over her shoulder like she wants him to come too.

Instead, Gavin lies in bed with the phone book list of C. Parkers, his heart thumping. To distract himself, Gavin looks at the map he and Dani put together on the several afternoons while Marla was at work. Marla didn't want to be a part of finding Candace, which Gavin thinks is typical Marla. Once he finds his mom, he can go home. Or not.

Gavin imagines Dani in the bath: she is no doubt very elegant as a naked woman, without all her layers of roughness. She has secrets, which he allows her. Sometimes he leans against her kitchen wall downstairs and watches her boil perogies on her little burner, and sometimes the door to the basement is locked all day. He thinks about what it would be like to watch her soap herself, how she might lift her leg high out of the water to run a razor from ankle to thigh. She's a woman who knows how to love her body.

Gavin rises so he can see the bathroom door from bed. She's hung her clothes over the crack between the door and the frame (something he hasn't bothered to fix), blocking the top two-thirds of the view. He waits for her to leave the tub, and when she does he can see her hand reach for something on the floor, then her feet stepping into panties. He lies back in bed, knocking the map to the floor. He clutches his notepad and writes gibberish until she appears in his doorway.

Dani is fully dressed, all bangles and beads. "Come with me."

Gavin flips the pad closed. He can feel himself sweating. Have to remember to throw that page out later.

"I'll make you something," she says, walking her fingers down the doorframe.

Nod yes. Gavin has the feeling this might never happen again if he doesn't go downstairs with this woman right now.

The fluorescent lights are on, making the whole place less shadowy. She pours a bowl of salsa and a plate of nachos and eats with passion, unafraid to chew in front of him. She offers him the bowl.

Gavin takes a single chip, has a bite. Dips it in the salsa. Salty, but good. ROUGH WORDS WITH LIAM.

"Liam's a knob. I don't take him seriously." Dani takes a plastic tube from her pocket and shakes out several pills. Pops them.

WHAT THAT FOR?

Dani shrugs. "Pain pills. You know."

Gavin reaches for the tube, resting his hand on hers until she lets him take it. The label says it's homeopathic, but the pills are much too big for that. YOU TAKE EVERY DAY?

She nods, crossing her arms, but keeping her eyes on his. "Yeah."

LOT OF PAIN, THEN. He watches her eyes, not wanting her to take it the wrong way. She reads it twice.

"You could say that. Look, it's not a secret."

DON'T NEED HIDE FROM ME.

She stands the tube up on its end, her fingers long and strong and sweaty. "I have this problem. I've had it for a long time."

MARLA KNOW?

She nods.

I STILL LIKE YOU.

She smiles at him, flicks the plastic tube over. "Me too. But I don't like Liam."

WHY? HE TRYING.

"How can you say that? It's your sister he's the worst with."

WHAT YOU MEAN?

"He hit her."

For a moment, Gavin is almost unhinged, but he pushes it down. Marla told him that was an accident. Dani must seem like complete chaos to Liam, but Marla is calmer. Pacifist eyes. He doesn't think Liam would hurt her, but maybe he should check. YOU BATED HIM TODAY.

She pushes the plate away. "He deserved it. He treats me like shit."

HE DIDN'T SNAP.

"He's afraid of me."

YOU LIKE THAT. He sneaks a look at her while she's reading his words, and her eyes meet his. FEELS GOOD FOR YOU.

Dani runs her hand through her hair, pulling it over her shoulder. "How do you know what feels good for me?" She tickles his arm, just gentle. Her touch starts something in him, a sliding sensation like the room is tipping. There is the taste of pennies in his mouth.

He scratches his thighs just to feel something. TELL ME ABOUT YOU.

"I ran away from home when I was fourteen. Stole from my family and went to jail."

WHY?

Dani doesn't look away. "I was stupid. Took years of lessons and threw away everything."

SINGING?

Dani puts his hand on her throat, and he feels sound rise and fall. She breathes from her diaphragm, her eyes on his. It's beautiful.

Gavin feels something inside him let go, or maybe click together, he's not sure. What he does know is that Dani is the type of person who really hears him. HELD BACK IN SCHOOL. TOOK YEARS LEARN TO READ.

"Doesn't mean you're not smart. What else?"

OUR MOTHER TRIED SUICIDE—O.D. THEY WOULDN'T LET ME

COME SEE HER. TOO YOUNG.

"Oh, crap. Marla didn't tell me any of that shit." Dani's face is open and soft like he's never seen. He doesn't intend this reaction with his story. Or maybe he does.

WHAT DID M. TELL?

"That you can speak but you don't."

EASIER.

"She said you're a suicider too."

LONG TIME AGO. Gavin stares at his feet.

She brushes her fingers along his cheek, down his neck. "You seem to be doing okay now."

He nods, not sure what he's agreeing with.

"Come here," Dani says, her eyes melted chocolate, her skin like pastry. When he kisses her, Dani's lips are cold like stepping outside in winter. She feels smooth and heavy and intoxicating.

In his throat was a lump, but it's gone now.

Marla sleeps in the car through the foothills and mountains to Banff, soothed by the dark and Liam's edifying jazz playlist. She awakens at their hotel, a wooden palace; the snow is so much deeper here, so much more like a Christmas card. Elk nose in the snow outside the lobby window, and the banister under her hand is shiny with use. Even the lights make Marla feel beautiful, but something about the air reminds Marla of a different trip to Banff, with another man Liam's age. A curled lip and a hard, ugly body. But that was ages ago.

They eat in a jolly pub with candles and mounted antlers on the walls. There are probably a hundred people in this tiny place, but it doesn't feel too noisy. Just warm.

Liam puts his hands on hers. "You told her I hit you?"

"No. She's looking out for me. I'm sorry about before."

Liam brings out a little box. "Listen, I don't think we'll need her help. Marla," he says, and stands only to bend down on one knee, "I want to marry you."

She jumps up and knocks her plate onto the floor. "Yes!" she shrieks, holding her hand out for him to put the ring on. She's kind of shaking. It's like everything she imagined it would be and more.

A waiter stoops to collect her upended plate. "I'm getting married," Marla tells him. People at tables near them applaud until Marla feels like the queen of the universe.

Liam grips her hand. "We can get married in the summer, after the baby's born."

"Are you saying you want the baby?"

Liam does not look at her the way a man in a movie would, with passion fogging up his eyes. He sits, smoothing his napkin on his lap. "Marla, it's my child. If you're set on having the baby, I should be a part of it." He swallows and corrects himself. "I want to be a family. I want you to move in with me."

Marla is sorting this out, reconfiguring her mental image of being a mommy onto Liam's house, with his bed and his instruments and his students, which would totally be cleaner and quieter but completely without Dani. Marla remembers the last time Dani was on her own. "Sure, as soon as Dani can get her own place, I'm in."

"Why do you owe her? What is she about?"

"It's ugly, okay? You know her story."

Liam sets his jaw and leans on his elbows. "I don't know your part in it."

Marla can't get into that, so she focuses on the edge in his voice and how it bangs into the warm space of the restaurant. "She helps me."

"She's dragging you down."

No one should be insulting Dani, especially not someone who is also supposed to be looking out for Marla. "Why did you hit me with that cupboard door? Because I read your letters?"

Liam speaks in a low voice. "You're accusing me of beating my pregnant girlfriend. That's the sort of man you think I am?"

"I didn't deserve that."

"You know it was an accident." Liam snaps the ring box closed and grips the edge of the table, his voice an angry whisper. "Let me get this straight: you're twenty-three and you work at a diner and you're saying no to a father for your baby because of your junkie friend? And you think I hit you?" People at the next table erupt in totally unrelated laughter.

"Twenty-two. I'm twenty-two."

A waitress brings them a floating candle while someone else dims the lights. Marla tries to collect all the thoughts in her head, but Liam is totally bent on whisper-fighting with her. "I want to know—did you do it on purpose?"

Marla scrapes her nails under the table, scratching off grains of wood. "Get pregnant? No!"

"I thought it was so you could unload Dani and live with me, but now I think you did it to punish me. Talking you out of an abortion. You'll be rolling in child support, laughing it up together." He has a hurt look on his face like he actually believes that.

"You didn't even want the baby until an hour ago."

"You're right."

"Listen: Dani's not my girlfriend, and she's got her own money—"

"How? Is she a drug dealer too?"

Liam doesn't understand that it is Dani who gives Marla the courage to do everything difficult, Dani who told her it would be hard, but manageable. Dani who doesn't talk in riddles and so obviously loves Marla that it scares her a bit. "You don't get it at all!" People murmur and stare, and now Marla is the trashy girl at the nice restaurant again.

"No. And I won't." The waiter edges by, and Liam pulls on his earlobe. "Don't do this here."

"Do what—figure it out? That's what everyone's doing." She makes her voice calm and looks him in the eye.

He looks around the room to see if anyone is looking at them, but they're trying not to. She waits, which is what she should have done in the other restaurant when she told him about the baby. He's off balance, but if she can be confident, he'll feel her strength and meet her halfway. His face moves, and she lets him work it out, practising her patience.

It's true. He leans closer, embarrassed. "I'm sorry. I'm under a lot of stress," he says, like he's apologizing that she has to see him this way. "Look. I believe you, and I shouldn't have said all that, especially about the baby. But you need to know I'd never hurt you. Otherwise this can't work."

Marla pushes her new plate away. The smell of ketchup is making her nauseous. "Fair enough. I like you, Liam, but you have to like me too."

"Good. Then we're engaged." He leans back in his chair and signals for the bill.

"I'm talking about all of me."

Liam pauses with his arm in the air. "Marla, I love you, and I will marry you and raise our child. But, just to be clear, I'm not marrying Dani too." He stands up, thin and beautiful and impossible. "You have to make a choice—the sooner, the better."

It's like something he will check off his list, at first: an experience to have. But the way she takes her shirt off, and the paleness of the skin at her throat changes everything, sharpens it until there is nothing but flesh and pleasure and hunger.

Gavin has never been with a woman, and yet Dani makes it so easy he's not even nervous. She is gentle first, taking time to admire his body, feel each part and pleasure it with such care and attention that he feels flawless. When he embraces her, he understands that his body has been made for this work; it knows this song, and so does Dani's. He holds onto her, her weight like an anchor, a reminder that she is real and has asked this of him, something he can do without hearing. He looks in her eyes and feels that delicious sense of inevitability that lets him know he can stop worrying and just be. Just do.

It's late when they wake up. The dog's whining, so Gavin

pulls his T-shirt and underwear on and lets him out, then grabs his notepad, knowing he needs to see himself think. But what should he say?

Dani crushes pills and snorts them. "Did you put your panties on because you want me to go?"

It's hard to write sense with a naked woman doing drugs in his bed. He looks around for her clothes, a bra at least, but she pulls him closer before he can find anything. MARLA CAN'T KNOW.

Dani traces his nipple. "She told me not to get involved with you. Said you were a child."

Gavin is forced to hesitate. YOU KNOW I'M NOT.

Dani runs a finger up his thigh. "Not now, anyway. We're lovers."

He's been telling himself this was a one-time thing—that Dani was just bored and lonely— because being so uncovered and present is inviting judgment he can't handle. Love is something else entirely. She reaches her hand under his waistband. He steps back. WAIT, PLS.

"There's nothing wrong with us fucking."

BUT DON'T KNOW YOU V. WELL. That is the nicest way he can put it. He's a little bit afraid of Dani—her violent anger towards Liam, her secretive thing with Marla, the seamless way she has enveloped him.

"I won't bite you, I don't think." She pulls him down and kisses him instead.

In that kiss is the certainty that Gavin's old life with his little apartment in Belleville and his job looking after Stephen at the care home are so far away as to be another, lesser reality. The thought is puzzling yet liberating. He belongs in this hearing world that he was yanked out of so long ago. These people are his people. This person.

MARLA HERE TOMORROW.

"So, love me until then." He lies with her, and she traces his collarbone with her index finger. "Love me."

8. BURGER

POEM FOR DANI

Without sound you'd be like me: stretching
in the morning curled toes flexed arms reaching
for the headboard to pull against, eyes closed
keeping it in, this moment all body bliss
just the right tension and the air so still,
then opening to sneeze in the sunshine
blink
now look to see if the door is open, if someone is there, talking
and you've missed everything

After their scene in the restaurant the night before, Marla decides to make the most of her and Liam's Dani-free vacation. There's no need to tell him now that of course Dani's always going to be in her life. She'll get her own place soon, and everything will be fine.

Marla doesn't mind the wind and the swirling snow on the mountain—it makes the nausea less noticeable. She balances against the car to step into her rented snowshoes, and Liam straps her feet in. They walk slowly up the trail, Liam behind.

"Keep your feet further apart," he calls to her after she almost trips herself.

"What, like this?" Marla assumes a sumo stance and hulks

forward until she does fall over. Liam reaches his pole out to pull her up, laughing. When she rights herself, she swats him and says, "Catch me if you can."

Liam gives her a head start, but even so, it takes him no time to reach her. He tags her on the butt. "You're sticking your rear end out too far."

"Only because you like it."

At noon, Liam spreads a blanket on the snow for her, and they eat sandwiches wrapped in wax paper that he made in the morning—ham with red onions, mustard, and that crumbly cheese he likes. "Did you buy all this stuff before I got up?" she asks with her mouth full.

He smiles at her, shy.

As the afternoon fades into winter grey, Marla worries about how far they've gone, but Liam has it all plotted out. "We're actually going in a circle," he tells her, showing her on his laminated map.

"So, we're almost there?"

"Exactly."

Once they get in the car Marla is too tired to keep her eyes open, so she doesn't realize Liam has brought her to the hot springs until they've parked. "I have your suit packed," he says, opening the car door for her.

"Liam, I can't go in a hot spring. I'm pregnant."

"Of course you can. Don't be ridiculous." He walks purposefully up the hill without looking back, and Marla jogs to catch up.

It's really crowded because the ski hills have just closed for the day. Marla changes next to several other women with braided hair and tanned skin. Hollering kids. She hurries to the pool deck.

The thing is, Marla doesn't exactly look pregnant yet, just puffy. Her middle has been pushed out, but it could easily be a liver disorder instead of a baby. She sucks it in and looks for Liam in the crowd.

He's sitting away from the children jumping in the water. Marla smiles to herself: Liam showered without getting his hair wet, so he is the only person here with a perfect do. She sits beside him on the ledge and dribbles water into his curls.

"Marla!"

A mom glares at them, and Marla wipes her hands dry on her bathing suit. "It's only water."

"Will you get in?"

She stops herself from pointing out that all kinds of people are sitting on the ledge who might also be at the beginning of an invisible pregnancy when you can't cook the baby and expect it to come out the same, never mind that there are a hundred people in the water, so Liam is certainly not sitting alone. So, the problem isn't really Dani at all. She stays on the ledge. "I'm comfortable here."

Liam raises himself out of the water. "We should go. It was a stupid idea."

"No, stay. It'll be fine." She lifts her toes out of the water and lets them drip near his hand on the ledge. He looks at her, this animal look that breaks her heart, then moves his hand so the drips splash on it. "See?"

He slides back in and pours water from his cupped hand onto her knee. "That's the difference between you and me: you like chaos and mess."

"No. I just accept them."

I'm wonder woman now.
What does that mean, honey?
getting married to superman.
Liam? Congratulations. That's a great first step.
who else?

Gavin and Dani get off the C-train at Marlborough and can't take a bus because Dani jumped the train and so doesn't have a transfer, won't let him pay. Across the street a mid-level mall slumps against a tired neighbourhood: duplex after duplex, each the same rectangular shape with a lattice separating the front doors. A couple of the nicer ones have balconies with enough room for a couple of bikes to be chained to them. They walk to Penbrooke Meadows, passing a man who taps ice from his parking spot, while inside his living room a huge dog chews the blinds and snaps its jaws in big doggy woofs.

This morning, Dani called all the C. Parker and plain Parker numbers for him until she heard the right name on the voicemail. The spare and high-density complex that matches the address he wrote down is done up with peeling blue trim. There is no balcony, and the basement windows have security bars.

Gavin knocks on the door. He is afraid that it really is this easy, that his mom might be here and living in a house with a phone but unwilling to talk to him. That he'll find her and hug her and go home.

No one answers. Dani cruises the perimeter, peering in the stuffed mailbox and kicking the rusty mini trampoline standing sideways in a snow bank. "I used to live a few blocks over," she tells him.

Gavin sits on the steps to write a note, angry with the way his writing looks calm on the page. DEAR MOM. WHERE ARE YOU? He scratches it out and tries over. CANDACE. THIS IS GAVIN, YOUR SON. He writes his number, and then crumples it up. He punches a can of butts, and it rolls on the ground, dirty water spilling out.

"Whoa, there, tiger."

Gavin peers in the window, looking at the ragged curtain, the dried-up hydrangea on the table. HATE THIS. Dani nods and helps him pick up the butts. He puts the jar back and leaves his name and number tucked inside the door.

As they go, a neighbour in a housecoat waves in his face. "What ... deaf?" She's exasperated.

Dani smirks. Gavin pulls out a card and lets the neighbour woman read it. He writes, DO YOU KNOW CANDACE PARKER?

"... watching her place. You are?"

HER SON. GAVIN.

She takes a step back, looks at him, distrusting. "Never said nothing about no son."

WHERE IS SHE?

The housecoat woman looks at Gavin like he is an imbecile. "Rehab. Where else?"

Shopping list:
kale
garlic
olive oil
Cayenne pepper
hemp seeds
ginger
honey
eggs
flowers

Gavin sets the table pretty for Marla because he feels guilty: tablecloth he bought at the thrift store, matching plates. Tea with honey for the ladies.

He scrambles eggs and steams kale with garlic. Arms around his waist, Dani's hand on his groin. He jumps back, spatula in hand. MARLA CD SEE.

"So?" Dani licks her lips. "What's for breakie?"

She already has her plate so he serves her, sprinkling hemp seeds on her kale. She gives him a bemused grin and eats her eggs standing up, wedged in the corner by the stove.

Gavin glances at the flowers on the table, the teapot in its tea cozy, the cutlery just so. SHD WAIT?

Dani says something with her mouth full that Gavin can't understand, especially with her looking over his shoulder. He turns and beams at Marla. He flips his notepad back to his prewritten greeting. WELCOME HOME. I MADE YOU BREAKFAST.

Marla squeals, her face all scrunched up, and jumps into Gavin's arms. He drops the spatula on the floor, and little pieces of scrambled egg glob here and there. "You are so amazing!"

He sets her down to write. WANTED DO NICE THING.

"... so perfect ... because ... getting married!" She turns to Dani and nods, talking with her hands, then back to Gavin. "Liam asked ... our trip!"

Gavin hugs Marla. This is big news, adult stuff. He'll probably be in the wedding party, maybe even the man who gives Marla away. He wonders when that will be, and how many hours it will take at the care home to earn enough to come back out here next year. Probably next year. Which reminds him to check his bank balance. Out the corner of his eye he sees Dani sliding her half-finished plate along the counter, slouchy and snarly.

GOOD NEWS. He holds it up, but Marla is busy interrupting Dani. He catches only pieces of the conversation.

"... asshole ..."

"... seriously ..."

"... make ..."

"... about him ..."

Gavin pushes his way between them with one arm on Dani's shoulder and the other on Marla's. He does a deaf-mute pantomime: hands over ears, headshake, hands over mouth, headshake.

"Sorry, Gavin," Dani says. She tries a bite of kale and makes a bitter face. "What is this shit?"

KALE. HIGH IRON.

Marla tries some too. "Gavin, this is low on taste."

He turns the stove burners off, not looking at her or Dani. Sometimes you can't help people. And sometimes they make you feel like shit. He collects himself in the hallway, and when he joins them at the table with his own eggless plate they've finished and pushed their food away. Marla's sipping tea. Gavin watches their mouths, waiting for them to include him.

"… course he thinks … good idea," Dani says, indicating Gavin with a nod of her head. She looks like she's going to say more when she realizes he's watching.

Still talking about Liam. BE HAPPY FOR M.

Marla gives Gavin a shy grin like he just told her the glass slipper fits.

Dani snorts. "He only asked because you got this thing going on." Dani rounds her stomach out so that it brushes the table, exaggerating. She laughs, patting it, but Marla ignores her. "Whatever. As long as you're still taking me to see Kamon later."

Gavin isn't sure who that is, but he wants to tell Dani that at least Liam is trying, even if he doesn't always get it right the first time. He'll be good for Marla. YOU NEVER GIVE L. CREDIT.

"Nope. When's the big day?" Dani asks.

Marla shrugs. "… haven't picked …"

"When are you going to move in?"

"I don't …" Marla says. She jiggles her foot under the table.

"What about parenting? Who's going to look after Liam Jr.?"

"… one thing … okay?" Marla turns deliberately to Gavin. "Thank you for breakfast."

"Point made." Dani takes a drink of ginger tea. She points at her cup. "This is fucking amazing."

Gavin nods, pleased. He clears the dishes, and when he returns they are talking about something else.

"Gavin's the one … model," Marla says, wiggling her eyebrows.

"Nude model," Dani corrects.

Gavin is so not going to be a nude model. He concentrates harder.

"For fat money," Marla says. She glances at Gavin and giggles. "At … gallery … art class."

Gavin grins. TODAY?

Dani laughs. "You're into that? Maybe I should take this smooth vessel over there." She runs her hands over her breasts.

Gavin is sure he's blushing, but Dani and Marla are honking

so hard they're practically falling off their seats. Marla doesn't know. He laughs with them, and Dani claps him on the back like he's one of the girls.

Eventually, all the snow melts, even the heaps along the edge of the street, leaving only pebbles and the months' worth of garbage that had been lingering below. Rainy slush takes over, but it is still too cold for the grass to grow green.

Marla takes her time at work, paying attention because each tip she gets goes in the spaghetti sauce jar to save for the baby. She's gotten her hours increased at the diner, and Bettina seems okay with the pregnancy thing. Apparently, she has a kid too.

Every day, Marla pours coffee for Mr. Markady, not too full, and makes sure he has enough creamers. He likes a lot of cream. "How are you today, Mr. Markady?"

He eyes her belly. "Slowing down." It's what he always says. "What will I do when you're not here?"

"Naomi can look after you," Marla says, watching his fingers shake as he opens another creamer. His hands are riddled with liver spots.

Mr. Markady glances at Naomi carrying a tray of pop. Some of it sloshes because she walks like a rig pig. "I don't know, Marla."

"You'll be fine. I'm not going anywhere yet." A couple of his old boys arrive, one in a motorized wheelchair, and she turns over coffee cups for them. "Good morning, Mr. Williams. Mr. Miller."

They let her go by first, all of them too wide to get through the narrow space between tables with another person in the way. This is the best part of being pregnant, that in her obvious vulnerability, people (old men especially), don't judge her. Marla wants to be pregnant forever.

After the lunch rush the restaurant dies. Marla is wiping down seats when Amber and Joelle come in. "Picking up your pay cheque?" Marla asks.

"Yep." Amber grins at her, and they head for the kitchen.

Bobby Love comes in too. "Hey, Marla," he says, startled. "Fuck!"

"What is it?"

"Nothing." He hurries to the back, where Marla can overhear Naomi telling him he was supposed to come in the back door and him bragging that he's a real back door man. Marla glances at Gladys, the only other person out front. Gladys shrugs her doughy shoulders, but is kind of grinning.

Naomi is loudly calling everyone idiots when Marla bursts through the swinging doors to the kitchen. "Surprise!" they call.

Everyone's there, even prissy Bettina—the guys wearing adult diapers over their jeans, and the girls with soothers and baby bonnets. Naomi ties a bonnet on Marla's head and pops a candy soother in her mouth. "Happy baby shower, Marla."

There's a stack of baby gifts—big pastel bags with tissue paper and ribbons, and Teddy bears with bows. Someone has made a banner: "Have One for Marla, Because She Can't Right Now." Bobby Love pops the top off a bottle of cheap champagne and everyone but Marla gets a plastic cup.

She hugs everybody, feeling their warm bodies and hearing their heartbeats. "You guys are the best. Thank you so much."

Would you and Liam come over for dinner this weekend?
is it a trap?
Please. We're long overdue.

Liam comes in quickly that afternoon, stomping his sloppy boots on the mat. "Where's Marla?"

Gavin sets aside his game of Solitaire. STILL WORK.

Liam paces. "two ... how can ...?"

PLS SPEAK SLOWER?

He stops moving and exhales, really looking at him. "Sorry, Gavin. It's just that I stopped at her work but she left early and she's not answering her phone. It's like she's avoiding me. Do you think she's cheating?" Liam hasn't even taken off his wool coat.

NOT HER STYLE.

Liam sniffs around. "Dani here?"

Shake head. Dani's out scoring weed, an indulgence Gavin allows because it's to do with her, but he can't tell Liam that.

"Something's going on between those two."

Gavin is smiling, but trying to stop, because Liam is mostly serious. DANI NOT GAY. MARLA EITHER, he adds.

"Really," Liam says, thinking, taking his time. There is something new in the way Liam's looking at Gavin. Something very adult. "You've been with her."

NO. Don't betray anything.

Liam is grinning, shrugging out of his coat. "What's she like?"

This is the exact second Gavin knows he must end it. CAN'T SAY.

"I won't tell Marla. Don't worry." Liam motions Gavin into the kitchen, leaning in close at the table. "I always imagined her being a bit rough about it."

SERIOUS?

Liam smiles the way guys do on TV. "And I'm right. There are bite marks on your neck."

So there are. Gavin is surprised to find himself more proud than embarrassed. He's sleeping with a woman, not just any woman, but an older woman who Liam (a righteous sort of guy) considers attractive. Gavin sits up straighter, feeling terribly manly.

Liam stirs the pot of veggie chilli on the stove, puts on some coffee. "I thought so. I'm glad you're enjoying yourself. Listen, has she told you how she met Marla?"

NO. WHY?

"No reason. Just seems odd, her being older."

Gavin doesn't even know how old Dani is.

"You should ask her. Let me know."

Gavin nods, feeling an immense sense of male camaraderie. GLAD YOU, M. BE MARRIED.

Liam glances at his phone on the table, then smiles. "Yeah. I think it's the right thing. I want her to move in."

YOU GOOD DAD.

Liam pours two cups of coffee. "It will be interesting. I mean, I know you two didn't have the greatest role models either, but I think Marla will be okay."

Gavin doesn't want Liam to pity her. She's not a refugee. NEEDS HELP, BUT M. STRONG. He wonders what Marla has told him.

"Yes. Did you find your mom?"

Gavin sighs. He's stopped imagining going home to his lonely apartment, and he's allowed the landlord to box up his personal items to rent it out. Despite not yet summoning the courage to visit his mom in rehab, Gavin feels in his bones that he belongs in this city. ALMOST. WAIT HER RETURN.

Liam's lips smooth into a long line. Tight. "My mother wouldn't go."

HOW?

"Alcoholic."

Gavin wants to ask more, but Dani comes in with the weed, all lit up. "If it isn't the knight in shining armour in my kitchen."

Liam doesn't bother to conceal his grin, which makes Gavin nervous. "Dani, how lovely to hear your voice."

She perches on the edge of the table in front of Liam. "Why are you smiling at me, fiancé?"

"No reason." Liam brushes against her as he rises, his forearm on hers. Gavin realizes he forgot to ask Liam about the cut on Marla's head all that time ago. He watches Liam rinse and wipe his coffee mug, his long fingers. He's not that kind of guy, Gavin thinks.

Dani takes Liam's seat and slips Gavin a joint, which he pockets in a panic, hoping he didn't crush it. "Hi Gavin," she says. She leans in, mouthing the words: *Why is this douchebag here?*

BE NICE. WAIT MARLA.

"Where is she?"

Dani stares at the two of them. "She's never this late."

Liam dries his hands. "I assumed she was with you, doing whatever it is you do."

"I'm serious, Liam. She's pregnant, there's sleet, and it's supper. She wouldn't miss a meal. Aren't you worried?"

Gavin is. SHD LOOK?

"Yeah, idiots." She's already putting her coat on.

NOT THINK BAD.

"Oh, it's nothing. Dani just wants to look like a hero."

She shoots Liam a look. "I'm calling her manager."

Liam looks at his watch. "I've got students tonight. When you see her, tell her to answer her phone. And get your buzz back on."

Dani sneers at Liam. "I'll tell her you stopped by."

"Do. I've got good news for her." Liam nods to Gavin and fingers a spot on his neck just under his jawline, where Dani's marks are on Gavin. "So long, brother."

All Marla's experience driving her shit heap has taught her a lot about judgment—most importantly, how to gauge following distance. Under normal driving conditions, a car with spongy brakes can stop for red lights, left turns and pedestrian crosswalks, so long as an appropriate following distance is maintained. Of course, Marla's shit heap is less than ideal under other performance conditions.

When the geriatric farmer in front of her loses a barbeque out of his pickup, Marla curses him for not having a tailgate, and for not thinking to tie down a huge hunk of metal. Knowing she can't stop, she swerves right to avoid the biggest chunk. She hits and then drags what she later discovers to be the grill, which causes her car to become an unsteerable projectile.

She slams into a parked car going sixty kilometers per hour. The impact throws Marla into the wheel and then the door as everything around her crunches and gets smaller. The passenger airbag deploys, bobbing stupidly in front of the hole where the seat should be. Her baby presents are jumbled around her. The pickup is long gone.

Someone on the street takes Marla out of the car and calls an ambulance. When the police arrive, they tell her several things she doesn't care to listen to, like her license is expired and she should have gotten the guy's plate number. She curses at them, and they ask her if she's drunk, make her blow into the machine, and order her to walk a straight line before she tells them under her winter jacket she's pregnant. They write her a ticket. Her arm throbs, and she holds it to her chest until ambulance attendants take her to the hospital.

Nurses fuss about her baby, asking her all kinds of questions, then X-ray her arm and tell her that she's going to have to learn to write left-handed for a while. She gets a cast and a sling, then waits in a plastic chair with her bags of baby gifts.

"Do you have anyone you can call?" a nurse asks her.

Right. Marla finds her phone—it's fine. She dials Liam to tell him she crashed the car like he said she would.

"Hi. I'm at the hospital."

"Hang on a second." Liam talks to someone else, one of his students, probably. "Why?"

"I broke my arm in a car accident. The baby's okay."

"You hit somebody?"

"A parked car." Marla's voice is small and tired.

"That's not good. Your fault, I imagine?"

"Yep."

"Listen, I'm sorry, but it's not a good time to talk right now—I'm teaching. Can I come see you tomorrow?"

"Yeah." Marla didn't think he could get out of work.

She calls Dani, who gives it to her for not calling sooner, then verbally unleashes on Liam for not picking her up. "We'll get a cab," Dani tells her. Marla leans her head against the wall.

When they arrive, Gavin hugs her without touching the cast, his arms soft. LIAM CAME FOR YOU. HAS GOOD NEWS.

That's hopeful. His audition must be over, so he's done practising. She forgets and tries to lift her broken arm to move the hair out of her face and then clutches it back to her chest and moans.

Dani scowls a young nurse into leaving the room. "This sucks. What a shit day."

It hits her that Dani's the first person to offer sympathy. Marla feels warm and cozy for three seconds before she realizes she doesn't deserve to. "Dani, I had to tell the police about the brakes, and they said it's my fault. I got a ticket. I'm lucky I didn't kill someone."

"Whatever. We're taking you home. Is there anything I should do, painkillers you have to take?" Dani says.

Marla shakes her head. "I have a prescription, but I don't get paid until Friday." Gavin's writing something, but Marla's too tired to wait. Or look.

"I'll find something." Dani collects the nurse she scowled at. Marla closes her eyes and waits on the hospital bed, her head heavy but her mind full, while Dani gets pills and fills out paperwork. Finally, Gavin drapes his jacket around her shoulders, and they ride home in silence, baby presents wedged between knees and stacked in their arms. Gavin pays.

Later, Dani tucks Marla into bed while Gavin stands in the doorway. She smooths Marla's hair. "Call me if it gets rough." As she leaves the room she says something to Gavin that Marla doesn't hear. He shakes his head and stays in the doorway as Dani brushes past him.

GOODNIGHT.

"Goodnight Gavin."

She lays in bed, unable to sleep. The doctor had said it would happen soon, and now it has: inside her belly is a tiny fluttering fish bumping into the side of its bowl. Her baby, steady and strong and reaching out to her. She smiles in the dark, her broken arm not bothering her at all anymore.

9. ICED CAPP.

THE NEXT MORNING, Marla takes the other two painkillers the nurse gave her and makes phone calls. The insurance company claims Marla owes five thousand dollars for damages to the parked car, plus some sort of deductible to write off her own wreck. And then the ticket. Marla is used to being a total idiot, but not on this scale.

Gavin sits heavily on a chair. Probably all deaf people are that noisy, but it's still annoying. CERTIFY INSURANCE CANCELLED.

He's ever helpful. "Yep. I sure did."

CALL WORK YET?

"That's next, okay?" Marla doesn't want him to know how flustered she feels. She waves him away and bundles all the insurance papers together, but drops some on the floor. She's surprised when he doesn't leave. He's waiting like a dog expecting a bone.

CAN GIVE YOU MONEY.

She bangs into the table with her bad arm while she bends to get the papers and scrunches her face in pain. "Gavin, leave me alone!"

Marla sinks to the floor. "Because I feel mean." All these years Marla prided herself on being a good sister, but she's not.

HAPPENS. STILL LOVE YOU.

"I brought you away from your job and your life, not to look after me, but so you could be a part of this. I wanted you to see it being good."

He gathers her papers and hands them to her. YOU ARE GOOD. CAN GO IF NEED SPACE.

She pulls him into her. "No, stay. I'm sorry I yelled."

Gavin sits back to back with her on the linoleum while she makes her calls, first to work to tell them she'll be late, and then Liam to beg for a ride.

"So, I was right about your car," Liam says.

Marla closes her eyes, squeezes Gavin's fingers. "Yeah. I have to figure out how to get to work at the clinic without it, pay for the insurance, and what to tell Dave and Elise."

"It's not their car."

"No, but they gave me some money to replace it, and I spent that on Gavin's bus ticket."

"You make some bad decisions. That's not going to go over well."

"I know, okay? Can you give me a ride?" Marla crosses her fingers.

"Okay, but I'll have to take you early—I'm doing a split shift at the restaurant." He pauses. "I hope they don't fire you."

"Yeah. They totally can't do that, right?"

"I'm glad your car is toast."

Marla says goodbye. Why didn't Liam say he was glad she's okay? She hates him and his job and his working car. His perfect clean house.

She releases Gavin's hand and they face each other. His patience unnerves her, and her words feel flat. "Thanks for your help."

FOUND MOM. WANT US VISIT.

Their mom. She doesn't want that for Gavin. Maybe he can't remember. She grabs his notepad and crosses out the last sentence. "Don't bring all that up."

SHE IN REHAB. I GO.

"So you can hit her back?"

Gavin shakes his head and Marla feels overwhelmed, like adding one more thing would make her head crack open.

PRACTISE FORGIVENESS. HARD BE A MOM.

Marla says the first thing that comes to mind. "Yeah, just look at Dani."

WHAT YOU MEAN?

"She has a kid, Gavin. She's trying to save money to get a place so she can have him back. She didn't tell you?" Gavin looks like he wants to write a paragraph, but she brushes past him into the bathroom. "Listen, I have to get ready. Liam's driving me to work." She squeezes foundation out of a tube.

LIAM GOOD MAN, DAD.

Marla draws eyeliner on, noticing the bags under her eyes. The baby. "Yeah, until our kid breaks his arm when Liam's working. It's not like he'll have more time if I have the baby."

Gavin crosses his arms. IF? TOO LATE FOR ABORTION.

"I'm just thinking, okay? You're the one that wants me to do everything right and make lists and be responsible. I don't even have a car, Gavin!"

MOM DIDN'T WANT ME EITHER.

Marla has never seen him talk like this. "That's not true, she just couldn't handle kids, even if we were perfect. You know her problems—don't make this all about you."

NOT. CAN'T QUIT YOUR KID.

Marla scoops her makeup off the counter into the drawer and slams it. "You would have been happier if you were adopted. Just saying."

THAT'S WHY YOU WON'T SEE MOM.

"What?"

YOU ARE JUST LIKE HER.

It's dead in the diner when Marla arrives. She waves with her good hand to Gladys, the day hostess, and heads to the back.

She's shrugging out of her coat when Bettina finds her, pointing to the cast. "Marla, what's that about?"

Marla pins her name badge over the stain on her ironed white shirt. She couldn't find her other one this morning, the nice one. It takes three tries to get the pin closed, and the badge is crooked, but she's not trashy, no matter what Gavin thinks. "I got in an accident, but don't worry. Everything's fine."

Bettina finger-combs her super straight blonde hair and makes tsk tsk sounds. "That's not good. You won't be able to serve during the rush and we can't put you back on dish pit. Or cooking or bussing."

Her mom worked at a biker bar, not a diner. It's totally different. Marla refills the ketchup bottles, which she can do no problem one-handed. "I'll hostess then."

Bettina taps her impractically-clad foot. "Yeah, but I've got five hostesses right now and they all want more time."

Marla finishes with the ketchup and looks around for something else to do. She usually folds cutlery in napkins next, but that's almost impossible with one hand.

Bettina does it for her, slipping paper circles over each set. "Well, for now I'll put you on morning coffee runs." Bettina's hair falls in her face and she blows it out of the way. Fine, wispy strands like spider's silk.

"That's it? I mean, I was hoping to keep my hours up."

"When the cast is off we can talk about thirty hours a week." Bettina twists her skinny hank of hair into a totally perfect bun. She carries a bin of silverware napkin packages from table to table as her phone starts singing. She digs it out of her back pocket to answer a text. "I'm off. Should I put you on the schedule or not?"

Marla counts trashy indicators in this diner: the grabby hook game no one wins at, signs on the bathroom doors (Customers Only), and cigarette burns in the carpet. The place is a total hole.

Marla takes one of the silverware packages Bettina just set and bangs it on the table. It clanks and Bettina looks up, surprised. Marla feels good, really good. "Don't bother. I quit."

Once Marla's left for work, Gavin walks to the bank, feeling the warm sun. It's the sort of spring day that makes a certain type of person sharpen their lawn mower blades for next month. There are new birds in the trees these days, robins even, in the sunshine. Crocuses.

Gavin doesn't look at his account balance, knowing it's lower than he'd like, hating that he's using money to solve a problem. When he gets home, he hides the cash under Marla's pillow and heads downstairs to talk to Dani. He's feeling all kinds of clarity this morning for not having slept with her last night, and he figures he'll be able to get everything straight if he just asks her.

Dani sleeps in the centre of her saggy double bed without sheets, bundled up in a comforter, Zigzag at her feet. She has a tab of pills on the floor beside her and is wearing a man's t-shirt, an old freebie from a case of beer. Gavin whistles until she notices his words on the notepad: MARLA SAYS YOU HAVE A CHILD.

"Shut up, Gavin. I'm sleeping."

Angry Dani was not what he was expecting, but then, Gavin doesn't know Dani very well. It occurs to him that she's not gotten high yet, and he's alarmed to realize how dependent she is.

WHY DIDN'T TELL ME?

"None of your business. Goodbye." She rolls over.

Gavin rolls her back. In his righteousness, he keeps his hands on her for a second too long, so Dani eyes him and reaches for his belt. He scoots back, feeling out of his element.

"What, can't get it up?"

JUST WANT TALK.

Dani laughs with her mouth wide open, suddenly awake. Gavin feels stupid, realizing he's part of a game he doesn't know the rules to.

WHAT ELSE SECRET?

"What ... blow you ... my resumé?" Her laughter makes her chest heave. Hard to understand her.

BECAUSE OF DRUGS?

"Yeah, genius." Dani hefts a glass ashtray from her bed and

hurls it at him. It bashes Gavin in the knee, making Zigzag piss on the carpet before he scrambles out the door. "You're one to talk, smoking pot here instead of going to school."

Gavin drops his notepad, holding his knee on the floor.

She's so close her spit sprays his face. "Listen—I don't need a soul mate and I don't want your help. I think you're a good lay, but don't talk about my son."

Marla's foster parents live outside Calgary in a sprawling bedroom community with three-car garages, tennis courts, and an irrigation reservoir made a hundred years ago by damming a slough. In early spring, Chestermere's high school kids park their parents' cars on the weak ice and are surprised when they fall through. Marla used to know those kids.

Elise answers the door in a showy apron with zero cooking stains and takes Liam's coat. "So pleased you could come. Marla's never brought a boy home."

Liam raises an eyebrow at Marla as Dave bursts up to shake Liam's hand.

"Welcome, and congratulations." Dave gives Marla a perfunctory hug, trying not to touch her belly with his body. He pats her back, and notices her arm. "What's this?"

"Nothing."

Elise serves bruschetta in the living room, where there are grad photos of Dave and Elise's much older real children on the wall, but not one of Marla, because she didn't graduate. Instead, there are pictures of Marla swinging in the backyard and doing the things kids do before they run away from home. Elise strokes Marla's shoulder. "Tell me what happened."

Marla swallows so she doesn't have to talk with her mouth full. "I crashed my car because it had no brakes."

Liam wipes his mouth with a napkin. "It was unavoidable."

Elise's colour is rising. "That's terrible! We would have helped you find a new car. Where is the money we gave you?"

"My rent went up."

"Is that the whole story?"

"Pretty much."

"Right, then." Elise sweeps crumbs from the coffee table and Dave excuses himself to check the roast. Marla knows she'll hear more later.

At dinner, Marla watches without surprise as Liam puts on his restaurant persona, pulling out Elise's chair for her and jumping up to turn off the oven timer. Marla catches Elise with a goony grin, wringing a pot holder in her hands. Marla's proud to be with a real man and not a punk or a dick: she's a desirable grown-up woman, not just some pity case with brain damage.

Liam places her napkin in her lap because she forgot and simultaneously brushes his arm against her breast, smiling at her, complicit.

"What kind of restaurant do you work at, Liam?" Dave asks, genuinely interested.

"A Thai place – it's called Kinaree."

"Oh, that's quite fancy," Elise says, star-struck. "I've eaten there myself."

"I'm also waiting to hear about a position at the University Music Department," he says, passing the potatoes.

"That must pay a lot."

Marla glares at Elise for caring only about money, but Liam doesn't notice. They talk about hockey, the price of oil and how it's affecting Dave's company, and why it's still supposed to snow even though it's April. After dinner, Dave persuades Liam to play Crokinole (which Marla knows is a very good sign), while Marla and Elise do the dishes.

"Liam is so together," Elise says.

Here it goes. "What does that mean?"

"I'm just glad he's not more, well, you know."

"You mean, like a pimp?" Marla dries dishes and stacks them neatly on the counter.

"Marla, I've asked you never to talk about that. I find it very upsetting. You don't want Liam to know about your past, do you? And the child? What kind of life would that be?"

"I don't live that kind of life. I'm getting married." The baby moves, and Marla wants to tell Elise, but her lips are all pressed together like she wouldn't listen anyway.

'Well, we still need to work on making good choices. You couldn't even buy yourself a safe car."

"It's hard, okay? I make minimum wage at the restaurant."

"We got you that job at the clinic—you should be making enough money there. And what about that woman—doesn't she pay anything to live with you?"

Marla stabs the knives into the knife block, saying nothing.

"Let's make a plan to finish your high school equivalency. Even Gavin has graduated." Elise leans in close. "I found a program that helps birth moms get funding for college. Remember? You were talking about massage school." For a second, Marla imagines herself hanging out with Naomi and her crew, having money to buy a bus pass. She could go out on Thursdays for $7 jug night like everyone else and make Elise proud. It's kind of tempting until Elise makes a very unsubtle gesture at Marla's belly, at which point Marla remembers she was never very good at school.

"I'm sorry I got pregnant. It happens." Marla hangs her tea towel on the oven door with a nice fold in the middle and shoves dishes into cupboards.

"You need a plan. Does he want the baby?"

"I think so."

"Very few women make good single mothers."

Marla edges behind her to put a dish in the cupboard. "That's not true. And I've got help. We're moving in together."

"Listen: I booked you in to see someone about adoption. I think it's a—"

Marla slams a drawer closed and hears the tinkle of broken glass. "Shit."

Dave and Liam come running. Marla opens the drawer to

find a casserole dish cracked into several pieces, which isn't what she intended at all. Those were scary words, and now Marla has gone and broken them so everyone can see.

Elise has her angry-disappointed face on. "I expect that to be replaced."

"Yeah. I'll work on that."

Elise puts her hands on Marla's shoulders. "Slow down and think things through. Your actions are costly."

Marla hates to admit it, but she knows it's true.

After some teeth gritting from Elise, calculated ignoring from Dave and too much nicey-nice from Liam, Marla puts her coat on and asks Liam to take her home. "That was less than ideal," she tells him in the car. She puts her feet up and cranks the radio.

He turns it off and Marla braces herself for a lecture, but he looks at her like he just found out horses aren't growing any more tails for bow hair. "At least you have a family."

"Some family."

Liam pulls over so fast that another driver's horn wails into the night as the car passes. His hands are shaking on the wheel. "Don't ever say that. Those people love you."

Marla doesn't want to tell Liam she envies him for having only a dead mother for family. "Okay, but she booked me an adoption."

"Because she loves you. I don't think you get it, Marla. Maybe you can't, I don't know."

"Well, then enlighten me, Liam."

He leans on the headrest, not looking at her. "It's simple gratitude. They took you in. Imagine you were me and had to stay with your real mom, looking after her."

"That would have been awesome. I wouldn't have had a curfew."

He turns so suddenly Marla reaches for the door handle on instinct. "Marla, that's immature. And harsh. My mom was a monster, cursing and raging and waking me in the middle of the night to practise." He shudders. "It was a nightmare."

Marla slouches like a teenager and they drive in silence. He's right. Everyone else is always right. She pictures Liam carrying his mom to bed when she passed out, cooking food for her before he went to school. He turned out all right. Amazing, even. To Liam, Marla's a girl who had the sweet life—rich foster parents and summer camp—and threw it all away.

"Dave told me about your condition."

That seems about right. "Yeah. I'm the damaged child of an alcoholic. *Ta-da.*"

Liam reaches for her knee. "Me too," he says softly.

When they pull up to her house, she says, "Wait here." He leaves the car running and she walks tall and deliberate because she has a crazy good idea.

It seems smart until Marla hears water running, splashing even. Dani's left the kitchen faucet on and water's all over the floor. The landlord is going to fucking lose it. Marla sops most of it up, dumping the towel in the sink.

Downstairs, water drips through the light fixture in the hallway, making a puddle the puppy paws at. Marla shuts the switch off in a hurry. That's it.

Dani's in the bathroom. Marla can hear her grinding up pills and clanking a spoon. She pushes the door open. "Why do you do it in here? It's not like I don't know."

Dani draws the solution up into an oral syringe from a shot glass and drops her pants. She reaches behind herself and grins at Marla as she plugs it. "Want some?"

Marla turns her head. She could very easily barf in this bathroom again. "That is so fucking gross."

Dani tugs her pants up. "Just bioavailability. Gotta keep it interesting."

"Yeah. Two things—one, you really ruined this light out here, because it's full of water."

Dani leans out the door, staring at it. "Yep. That's a fire hazard."

"Two, I'm moving in with Liam because he doesn't spend his time wrecking the place and stuffing drugs up his ass."

Dani sweeps the counter, her syringe and the spoon she was using pinging against the lino. "Don't think you're going to get what you want there." Spit flies out of Dani's mouth.

Marla backs up. "Yeah, I will. He's not like you."

"That is low. What about notice? What about Gavin?"

Marla hadn't really thought about it. "Gavin's coming too. He's here to visit me."

"And me?"

"The rent's paid. You can stay until the end of the month." Marla suddenly realizes this is what she wanted all along, just any reason to escape the constant spiraling clusterfuck that is Dani. An affirmation that it doesn't have to be this way.

Dani follows Marla upstairs. She pulls the curtain and sees the car running outside. "It's a drive-by pickup?" Dani laughs. Her face is red. "You haven't thought this through at all. Does he even know?" She tries to push past Marla to open the front door.

"Don't you dare go out there."

Dani stops and grabs Marla by the hair, pulling her in like a fish. She whispers through her teeth. "You fucking owe me." She kisses Marla, hard, pushing her tongue around.

Marla pulls back, bracing her hands against Dani's shoulders, but she's not strong enough to get away. "I don't belong to you."

"Oh, but you do." Dani twists Marla's nipples. "No one else would want you."

Marla runs out holding her breasts. Liam has locked the car doors, sitting there with his arms crossed. She pounds until he unrolls the window.

"What the fuck did I see in there?" The word sounds thick coming from Liam, she thinks. Heavy. The windshield wipers swish back and forth, spraying slushy snow.

"Dani's a crazy drug addict bitch."

Liam's breathing is fast, almost sexual. "You two have a thing going, don't you?"

Marla lets go of the door handle. "What? No. You think I want her?" The thought is bewildering.

"You just kissed her."

Marla shakes her head and reaches inside the open window to manually unlock the door. "She's high. I don't fuck her. I love you." She sits inside. "Take me home. I'm moving in."

Liam stares at her. "You two are done? You're not serious."

"I'll get my stuff tomorrow. Let's go."

Gavin takes the bus to the University of Calgary and runs through its carfree centre, edging by wide groups of young adults all talking at once. There are some beautiful low post-war buildings, but they are dwarfed by later towers that lurk without any orientation to grid. He sees himself overshadowed by their mess and creates a mental route to Marla's, running along 24th Avenue past concrete slab apartments and residences, then cutting through the playing fields to follow the near deserted 32nd Avenue in the dark.

He doesn't shower when he walks in, but lays in bed masturbating angrily. Dani has no right to hurt him. Gavin comes on his stomach and wipes himself off with the sheet. He's going downstairs.

The light's on in the bathroom. Gavin shifts his weight from foot to foot, like a boxer psyching himself up, but finds that he's limping, having run too long on the injury. He pushes the door open without knocking.

Dani lies in the tub with a wet towel over her eyes, her breasts floating in the soapy water. She doesn't look up, so he bangs on the side of the tub with his fist.

Dani startles, splashing him as she rips the towel off.

Gavin holds his notepad up. YOU HURT ME.

He can see her stomach muscles relax. "Let's see." She doesn't sit up, just rolls her head towards him.

Gavin pulls his pant leg up to show her the bruise on his knee. Seeing its purple colour, Dani grows a lazy smile.

"Looks painful," she says.

Gavin refuses to be emotionally manipulated. He will not be afraid. DON'T LIKE THAT YOU.

"I've had a shitty time." She looks at him, snide. "Marla moved out."

That's her fucking with him. He chooses to ignore it. She reaches down, fingers herself with a lost, big-eyed look. Gavin backs up but she keeps at it, her mouth open. She's playing.

Gavin points to the spoon and the lighter on the floor. NOT HOW A MOM ACTS.

Dani stops abruptly and rises partway out of the water, her hands braced behind her against the base of the tub. "I told you, my son is none of your business."

Gavin's pant leg hangs awkwardly, his hairy calf showing below the bruise on his knee. DID YOU HIT HIM?

Dani sinks back into the water and lathers her leg. "You and Marla. Neither of you understand a thing about love."

WHY HE NOT HERE? I DON'T TRUST YOU."

"I don't trust anyone, Gavin. That's the way it is." Dani runs her razor from ankle to knee, watching Gavin's face.

TOO LATE, THEN?

"It's been too late since I can remember." Dani laughs, her face contorting like a funhouse mirror person. She goes on with it too long, mocking him or lost in herself, he can't tell. She waves the razor in the air, her mouth wide open.

He writes, DON'T EVER ATTACK ME AGAIN, rips the sheet off and presses it to her stomach in the tub. She lurches up like she's afraid and for a moment, he congratulates himself.

10. TRIPLE SCOOP ICE CREAM CONE

Moving in with Liam. picking you up tomorrow
what? why?
be ready

EARLY THE NEXT DAY Marla returns to pack. She grabs garbage bags, shopping bags, and the plastic bin they put the bottles in from under the sink. Everything is immaculate: dishes neatly done, her spice jars labelled. She looks for Gavin in his room, but he's not there.

He's cleaning out the hall closet, part of what she sees as his relentless makeover of her and her stuff. Pretty soon everything will be categorized and organized and sanitized and empty. Gavin's looking through a suitcase of their mother's clothes that Marla has been telling herself she would throw out for three years, ever since Candace forgot to come back for it. Like Marla really believed her mother could get her shit together.

"Why are you limping?"

Gavin holds a sequined top and shakes it at her. WHAT'S THIS?

She sees something wrong in her relationship with Gavin, something ominous, but can't put a finger on it. She refuses to think about it. "Why are you going through my stuff?"

Gavin gives her a look, as if to say she was his mother too. Like it's Marla's fault. DIDN'T KNOW YOU HAD THESE.

"Take them." She edges past Gavin into her bedroom with her bags and starts filling them with her own clothes.

Gavin folds in the hallway, watching her. Vest with a fringe. Acid washed jeans, size 2. He makes everything neat. As if it was symbolic of something, as if it really mattered. This is what I come from, Marla thinks. A lost woman with slutty clothes.

WHEN YOU LAST SEE HER?

"Years ago, when she was going to recovery again. She'll never change."

BUT YOU KEEP THIS.

"Didn't you get my text? Why aren't you packed?"

He waves her question away. YOU SHD FORGIVE.

Marla shoves her belts and purses into a garbage bag. "Aren't you angry at her?" How can he not remember? Marla pushes down the thorny business in her child welfare file that threatens to overwhelm her, but it's too much. Gavin holds her hands and gazes into her eyes with such calm that she feels release.

REMEMBER HER DOG, POO-POO?

Marla does, and watching movies together, leaning against her mom's chest, and the birthday cake her mom got her from Dairy Queen when that was the only thing she wanted. But it hurts Marla to think about her mom loving her and Gavin because it seems like every other emotion she feels must balance on that.

SHE BROKEN TOO.

Marla gets up. That doesn't excuse anything. "Yeah. And I can't fix her."

Gavin helps her fold her clothes into bags. DANI SAME. TELL ME WHAT HAPPENED WITH HER SON.

"Why?"

WHERE IS HE?

"Away from her." Marla ties up a garbage bag and throws it towards the door. She starts packing her poetry binders into a shopping bag. She hefts it, then double bags it.

HOW OLD?

"Five. Why don't you ask Dani these questions?" She takes clothes from the closet and packs them in the bin, hangers on.

I DID.

"If she doesn't want to tell you, I'm not going to."

SHE DEPRESSED. THINK USING HEROIN.

Marla raises her eyebrows. "You can't save her, Gavin. Can you get your stuff? I want to get this done before she wakes up."

I STAY, HELP HER.

Marla turns away so Gavin won't see her mouth hanging open. Staying? It's an ugly kind of relief, knowing someone more fresh and giving than her is going to be dutiful. Someone with less at stake. She pushes the lid on the plastic tub and clicks it closed. "Whatever you want," she mutters.

OKAY, RIGHT? He chews his pencil.

"Yeah. Great." It's not like he doesn't know what kind of person Dani is. Gavin will be safe. Just in case, Marla gives him what she considers the need to know: "The baby was taken away when he was two and a half because she was using crystal meth." Marla doesn't tell Gavin about Kamon waiting in the car while Dani turned tricks.

Gavin does a deaf-guy whistle that makes him sound like he's blowing up a balloon. WHY NOT QUIT?

"She did, but she had no place to live—she and Kamon were staying in shelters or with friends, people who weren't baby material. She only had a certain amount of time to get everything together, and it just didn't happen. Her mom stepped in." Marla remembers them living in Dani's car, Dani tucking Kamon into bed on the backseat. Then she didn't even have a car. Poor Dani. "It wasn't all her fault."

WHERE THE FATHER?

Marla hesitates. "She doesn't know who the father is."

Gavin gets her to repeat that sentence. He sits, thinking. CAN HELP. SHDN'T BE ALONE.

He's so earnest, her brother. She hugs him. "Maybe you're right. Just be careful. She's pissed at me." Marla pulls at the tote bin with her good arm but can't lift it.

Gavin takes it from her with one hand. I'M NOT AFRAID OF

HER. Gavin's biceps flex as he heaves her stuff out the door, out of this place forever, which makes Marla forget how strange it was for him to say that.

Gavin leaves Dani alone all the next day, thinking about her son and how he must be the child of a rape and that's why she's dug herself into such a hole. At night, he creeps downstairs with the untouched money from under Marla's pillow, following the blue glow of the TV. He feels bigger this time, ready to help.

As he rounds the corner at the bottom of the stairs, some guy strides past him, not saying anything, brushing Gavin's shoulder. Gavin is so startled he flattens himself against the wall. A robber? He's not sure whether to chase the guy or make sure Dani's okay. He looks: she's folded into a pink blanket on her chair, flicking through channels like nothing's wrong, Zigzag sleeping at her feet. He runs over.

She jumps up, startling the puppy. "Fuck, Gavin. I could have killed you!"

He's panting, adrenaline roaring through him as he scrambles to write. YOU OKAY? WHO THAT?

She laughs like he's ridiculous, but doesn't answer his question.

HE TAKE ANYTHING?

Dani's leaning over the edge of the recliner without getting up, so he's not sure if she's read what he wrote. She slides a wooden baseball bat from under her chair, raising her eyebrows.

Gavin backs up instinctively, having lost his swagger in an instant.

"No, come here. It's for just in case. You know."

Gavin does not know. Is it for the guy who was just here, or are there other people peering in windows or sneaking in? Gavin wonders if she's hiding here, like the rapist father was a stalker who knew her every move and now she can't live in her old place. But that would have been a long time ago.

BROUGHT YOU THIS. He hands her the cash he withdrew for Marla. HELP YOU.

Dani hands it back to him. "No."

OR YOUR SON.

"You want to pity me?"

WHAT?

"We can do that. I see him once a month. His birthday is February 17. He had a soft blue car that he drove around. I got him potty-trained the week they took him away. It was right before Hallowe'en."

Gavin strokes her hair. I'M SORRY.

She pats the arm of her chair, and he sits. She exhales, and he can feel her breath on his arm. "No, I'm sorry I'm such a cunt about it. Kamon lives with my mom, and I'm trying to get him back."

Kamon. SO YOU MUST BE GOOD.

"I should be better." She fishes in her chair for some pills in a small Ziploc bag and holds them in her hand, fingering them. She hands him the bag.

I DON'T—

"No, I know. Flush these for me."

He does, excited that she's going to get well. She won't be angry and fucked up anymore. He makes a mental list for her: open the curtains, cook together, spend time outside walking, learn more about her son. He walks back down the dark hallway to Dani.

She reaches for him with her eyes. "How come you're not all moved out with look-at-me Marla?"

He keeps his eyes on hers, his jaw loose. An almost imperceptible shrug.

She caresses her breasts. "A guy like you can't leave all this behind, can he?"

He shakes his head, holds her hand in his, putting it on his chest, then pointing to her: *I love you*. Dani doesn't care that he's deaf, doesn't treat him like he's delicate. He would never leave her behind. He sets the money on the table and takes her in his arms, softly at first, as if Dani was not quite real. She opens her mouth to meet his and lets him hold the back of her neck, arching into him this time like she's small and desperate and needs him more than he needs her.

Don't forget our appointment this afternoon.
yep. got it.

Not even twenty minutes after making love, Marla and Liam get up. It's not like her house, with leisurely coffees and Dani's music blasting. They dress and get right to work unpacking her scented oils, binders of loose leaf poetry, and rock concert T-shirts. She stuffs things into the hall closet and the cupboard on top of the fridge. She puts away her garbage bag full of shoes and Liam does her clothes. This is the kind of house where anyone could feel purposeful and together—just look at how they're working as a team!

"Elise wants to take me to the adoption agency today."

Liam is hanging skirts by colour. "I wish I could come, but I have to work."

Marla knows she's not dumb enough to be tricked into adoption, especially now that she has a fiancé who actually wants a baby. Sort of. "But we don't need that. I mean, we're not going to, you know."

He shrugs. "Just go see, that's all. Make her happy."

So, later Marla is waiting for Elise on Liam's couch in her fancy clothes when a different older woman wearing expensive jogging gear enters with twin boys. She's surprised to see Marla and puts a hand out to stop the boys from taking their shoes off. "Sorry, I didn't realize Liam was with another student." She eyes Marla's broken arm. "I guess we're a bit early."

Marla can hear Liam tuning his strings down the hall. She puts on her grown-up voice, which is like the one she uses to waitress, except less slutty. "I'm not a student, I'm his fiancée."

The woman does a double take. "Oh my." She stares at Marla's pregnant girl-body. "Are you expecting?"

"Yes, in July." Marla aims her belly out, smoothing her shirt over it. The woman looks kind of impressed.

Liam emerges from the bedroom, wiping his hands on his pants. "Mrs. Jackson," he says, surprised. He glances at his watch. "I must have lost track of time."

"Don't worry about it. I think we're early." Mrs. Jackson gestures to Marla. "I was just chatting with—I'm sorry, I don't know your name—"

"Marla," Liam and Marla say together, their eyes on each other. She knows it's his way of telling her to be normal for a woman who pays him every week. She sits up straighter and gives a fake smile to prove herself.

When the little boys have dropped their backpacks on the mat and followed Liam down the hall with their mini cellos, Mrs. Jackson sits on the couch and takes wool from her bag.

Marla puts down the magazine she was reading and props her chin in her hands. This is a primo research opportunity. "So. Twins. Do you ever just wish for one?"

Mrs. Jackson looks up, a bit startled. "Not anymore. I felt pretty overwhelmed at the beginning, though."

This gal is in the real woman club. She has her stretch marks and knows how to put on a diaper and when to call the doctor. "What's it like?"

Mrs. Jackson crosses her legs and laughs nervously. "Parenting? It's good. It's hard."

"Did you always want kids?"

"It was a whole thing, going through IVF and being on adoption wait lists. Really stressful."

"IVF?" Imagine having a price tag on your kid. "How long were you on an adoption wait list?" Mrs. Jackson looks up from her knitting. "I mean, I don't know much about it."

"The approval process alone takes months, and then it can take years to be chosen."

Chosen. Marla didn't know that. She thought the agency assigned every unwanted baby a mom and dad. "But those are your actual kids, right?"

"Yes, our biological sons. We're very fortunate to have Lincoln and Grady."

Marla runs her hands under the coffee table, feeling for gum she can squeeze, but of course there isn't any. Mrs. Jackson sets her knitting needles down and leans forward. "Can I say something?"

"Sure."

"I don't want this to sound rude, but there are lots of really good families waiting for a baby. I mean, if you're not sure."

Marla jumps up and puts on false cheer. "Oh, no. We're very happy. Liam's always wanted kids." Mrs. Jackson smiles politely, and Marla sees Dave and Elise pulling up outside. She grabs a jacket and takes off out the front door without a word like a twelve-year-old. Marla wishes Dani were here to tell her Mrs. Johnson's clothes are obviously so tight as to have cut off the circulation to her brain. Dani wouldn't listen to a know-it-all music mom for five seconds.

The office door reads "Choices" in splashy letters, as if the font alone might make a woman whimsical and carefree. Through the glass Marla can see another pregnant woman in the waiting room. As Dave opens the door, Marla hears her talking on her phone, tapping her nails on the glass coffee table. "Yeah, I said I'll do it. Don't give me that shit."

There are posters of babies on the walls of the adoption agency, which makes loads of sense to Marla: the real customers come here to get a child. The babies are round like babies should be, smiling mostly, sitting in pudgy piles with each other, wearing only diapers. The message is clear: this is a baby store. Marla thinks about all the babies in the world and hopes they will all be as happy as her and Liam's baby is going to be. She smiles at the other mom on the phone, feeling glad that a place like this exists for women like her.

Elise leads her to the counter. The receptionist is warm and squishy like cooked spaghetti. "So glad to have you here, Marla," she says, as if adoption is the only logical decision and this gal decided so while Marla was on her way. "Please have a seat."

Marla sits between her foster parents, noting with some satisfaction that this baby-grabbing facility at least has the decency not to fill the racks with magazines about parenting.

"Marla and family: follow me, please."

The adoption counsellor's accent is pure poise—New Zealand maybe. She shakes Marla's hand while holding a big blue teacup. In her office, the counsellor gestures for everyone to sit on the couch, a long smooth number that feels too red. Her office has a view of the mountains and joggers on the river pathway. There are paintings of opening flowers, making this place as soft and cozy as someone's living room, not where you would go to give away your own child. "I'm Cynthia. Pleased to meet you."

Marla nods a greeting as the door clicks closed. There is no street noise, no music, no sound, just the slippery noise of clothes on leather as she and her foster parents sit.

"Hi. I'm Marla, and this is Dave and Elise."

Cynthia nods to them, and Marla can tell she and Elise have met before, or at least talked on the phone. "Tell me, how can I help?"

Marla knows this is where she's supposed to start gushing about wanting the best for her baby and the many totally competent couples who can't make kids of their own, but that's not her. "I don't want to give my baby up. That's my mother's idea." Marla was going to say foster mom, but it sounded too trashy.

"You're here now," Cynthia says. "Please, tell me your story."

Marla juts her chin out. "I would be a good mom."

Cynthia leans forward and uses a conspiratorial tone. "And?"

Marla sighs. "I quit one of my jobs. And—like they probably told you—the baby was unplanned."

"What about the father? How is your relationship with him?"

"We're great. We just moved in together."

Elise interjects. "They haven't been dating very long. And he's very busy."

Cynthia pulls a pamphlet from one of many file folders in her desk drawer. "You might want to look at this." The pamphlet is titled, "Co-Parenting Questionnaire."

Marla scans the items: Are you and your partner committed to co-parenting for eighteen years and beyond? Have the two of you planned for who will be responsible for day-to-day parenting tasks such as feeding, bathing, and putting your child to sleep? Have you and your partner discussed parenting decisions such as religious education for your child, what kind of school your child will attend, and how you will deal with discipline? How will you and your partner maintain and continue to build your own relationship with the added stress of raising a child? A whole page of that. "There's a lot of stuff on this list."

Cynthia pours her voice on Marla as if it were hot tea with honey. "All parents need to address these issues, both before their child is born and as their child matures and changes. Have you and your partner talked about these things?"

"I live in the moment. I don't really nail everything down."

Dave nods, crossing his arms. "Marla needs help making decisions and planning for the future. She has FAS."

Cynthia smiles at him. "That doesn't mean Marla can't be a good parent," she says, and Marla does a silent cheer. "What you need to think about is how you are going to be the best parent you can be. Do you have a plan?"

It looked good for a second, but now this woman sounds like Elise. "Well, I just have to stay away from my drug addict ex-roommate, get my fiancé to pay for everything now that I have a ridiculously low income, and ask my deaf brother to watch the baby so I can get another job. It's not like it's impossible."

Elise holds Marla's hands. "A baby is forever." For a moment, she looks like the Elise who used to wrap Marla's knee when she sprained it playing volleyball or hold her when a boy dumped her. Marla tries to picture herself in her forties, her baby grown up, and can't even get past the birth. She faces Elise.

"Here's the stuff I think I would be good at: reading to him, snuggling and watching movies, playing outside, making fun food, teaching him to dance. Helping him be patient and kind."

"What about the parts you'll need help with?" Elise knows how to phrase it.

"It'll be hard to keep up with his appointments, like for vaccines and doctors. And I don't think his room would be spotless. I go on gut for everything, so anything logical will be hard. Math homework, but Liam could probably help with that."

Dave says, "What about setting boundaries? Helping him navigate his relationships with others and make good decisions for himself?"

"Yeah. That's hard. And knowing what's a big mistake and what is just a normal one, keeping enough money in the bank to feed him, finding good people to be around him when I'm at work, teaching him to wait for the things he needs and how to control his feelings. All that stuff." Marla turns to Cynthia. "What if I am interested, just a bit?"

Cynthia holds Marla's gaze for a moment before she stands to embrace her, the baby between them. She pats Marla's back, whispering, "You are a very courageous woman. Strong."

Marla sits down, shaky. "You say it like other girls can't do it."

Cynthia holds her hands across the coffee table. "If you choose adoption, it will be the hardest thing you ever do. I can tell you that from my heart. I've been there myself."

Marla tries to picture a shivering Cynthia handing over a baby in the hospital, her fingers clutching at the baby's blanket. If she looks past the couch and the accent, Marla can see it. There is something milky in Cynthia's eyes that tells Marla the truth.

"Do you see your kid?"

Dave clears his throat, but Marla needs the answer, leans forward to hear it.

Cynthia looks out the window. "Everywhere I go, I think I see him." She turns back to Marla, inhaling, composing herself. "Open adoption wasn't common then."

Marla looks at the school pictures of other kids on Cynthia's desk. "What do you do?"

"I wait." Cynthia's voice breaks. "On Mother's Day, you know."

Marla passes the tissue box, taking one for herself and handing another to Elise. "I'm sorry. I just like to know who's legit."

"Don't be sorry. Sharing our stories is what makes us stronger. My son's adoptive parents gave me this." Cynthia shows Marla a ring she wears on her first finger. It has a blue stone, the colour of an old dog's eyes. "Aquamarine," Cynthia tells her. "My son's birthstone. He has the same ring. He would be old enough to wear it now."

"Okay," Marla says, not to agree, but because she wants to stop herself from bawling. How many guys has she met that might be this woman's son? He has no idea, and wouldn't even have her accent. "I think I want to go."

Cynthia nods. "Come again and we can talk some more."

Marla nods, barely, leaving the three of them thanking each other, and heads for the waiting room where she accidentally meets the eye of the beaming receptionist. Nope. She'd rather be outside. Her baby begins to hiccup as she gets on the elevator. Alone with the mirror, Marla realizes she's crying.

Gavin signs the visitor sheet at the reception area as a frowsy counsellor stands over him, talking as he writes. He signals for her to wait and hands her a card.

She looks him up and down, then shouts like a moron. "Visiting hours are almost over!"

Of course they are. CAN I STILL GO?

She shrugs and leads him through the kitchen area to

the common room where several young adults and some rough-looking middle-aged people watch TV. The counsellor points to Gavin's mother, who's playing ping-pong against an acne-ridden teenager. Candace swings wildly, spinning around in her slippers. Her black hair shakes. Gavin thinks she looks the same, but he doesn't have any pictures of her. The image he has of her is a teenager.

Gavin waves, then scribbles hurriedly. HI, MOM.

He was too slow. Candace Parker walks right past Gavin, takes a mittful of juice boxes from the fridge, and sucks one back before she sits heavily at a table. He follows her, sitting across from her. Candace looks at Gavin with the slow shock of recognition. Puts her juice down.

"Long time, trucker." She bats her eyelashes, tucking her hair behind her ears, sitting up straight.

IT'S ME, GAVIN.

Candace takes another look and yelps. She stands up so quickly she rocks the table with her knees as she comes to hug him. "My baby." She sits again and looks up at him. "Thought ... your dad ..."

Gavin can't remember his dad, or even seeing a picture. His dad is a different man than Marla's father, an oil patch worker who never came back. YOU THINK I LOOK LIKE HIM?

"Exactly ... but such ... retard."

Gavin feels something hard in his gut. SOMETHING WRONG WITH HIM?

"... nice guy ... neighbour ... using his disability payments ... pay rent ..."

Gavin has been trying to remember a man in the house, not a neighbour. There were so many of those—the old guy at the Dutch store, the truckers who stopped at the diner, Randy with his scratchy beard who used to play trucks with Gavin, using scrap lumber for ramps.

YOU MEAN RANDY?

"Yeah, Randy. Your dad."

A crippled giggler of a man is his father. A guy Gavin's never lived with. And now he knows his name. WANT TO FIND HIM. Gavin sees himself sitting on a step with a guy who chewed tobacco and slept with his mom and wonders what they'd do together.

"Why ... change anything."

But Gavin knows it might change everything. If he only knew exactly what kind of retard his father was, how people talk to him, whether he wears stained jeans or is missing some teeth. Those are the important things Gavin can't remember. And why his father couldn't look after Gavin when Candace tanked. WHERE IS HE NOW?

"Fucked off to ... where."

He swallows and writes, WANTED TO SEE YOU. CAME FROM ONTARIO.

"... haven't taught ... talk, eh? Fucking deaf school."

Gavin doesn't want to tell her he can talk. She used to make fun of him for how he sounded, kicking him when he made noises with his toys. He played under the table after that, but she would haul him out.

FINISHED HIGH SCHOOL. HONOURS.

Candace nods, purses her lips to whistle. "Okay. Now what?"

HAVE SCHOLARSHIP TO U. OF T. He doesn't tell her it was for the winter session that began in January. WANT TO BE AN ARCHITECT.

Her eyes are darting around like she's not really following. He makes a fist under the table, squeezing hard, and waits.

Candace finishes another juice and nods at him, starting a new conversation as if they weren't already in the middle of one. Talking about herself. He can tell by how many words she's using. "... doing the work ... life back together ... program." She gestures at the other clients and the counsellor at the desk. "I should tell you I'm sorry." She makes a heart out of her two hands and presses it from her chest to his, which somehow makes Gavin feel even emptier.

MARLA'S PREGNANT.

"Yeah?" Candace picks at a gouge in the plastic tabletop.

SHE LIVES HERE.

"I know … not stupid …" She's mumbling, turning away.

YOU SHD VISIT.

"She came to me once. I told her to go home." Candace looks him in the eye, daring him to say it: *You're a bad mother.*

WHY DIDN'T YOU WRITE ME? Even as he says it, he knows it's ridiculous.

"Write? Like letters?" She starts laughing, so Gavin hands her his phone so she can type her number in.

I'LL TEXT YOU.

Candace shakes her head. "… don't … one of those. Hey, you smoke?"

Gavin shakes his head.

"… couple bucks?"

Gavin takes two twenties out of his wallet, surprised there aren't more. She stuffs them in her bra.

They sit in silence until she pokes him, points to the ceiling. "… announced it … gotta go now."

Gavin nods. He can't bring himself to write "I love you," so he writes down Marla's address. He wishes he'd brought Dani. She would have known what to say.

The doctor at the clinic where Marla works asks to talk to her, and Marla grits her teeth. Katelynn stares as she walks by, still typing. It's serious, then, if Katelynn knows. Marla's all set to tell the doctor she hasn't been reading the files because she is super keen about patient confidentiality, but that's not what he wants to talk about at all.

He sits her down with a paper cup of water and looks apologetically at her stomach. "It's just that Alex is studying nursing and we only have the budget for one practicum student. I'm sorry, Marla." Dr. Leal gives Marla her last cheque and ushers her out of the office, past Katelynn who waves and Alex's vest hanging on the coat rack. Marla shrugs like it's no big deal and walks out into freezing rain. She lets the weather sting her face, ready to feel something concrete.

How is she supposed to save anything for the baby? She won't be able to get another job now that she can't hide her bump. She has basically no money, like two hundred bucks, but she doesn't want Liam to know. She takes care of herself, pays her own way, which is why she would never take Gavin's money. Marla waits for the bus, staring at the warm mall across the street. She checks the schedule: twenty minutes, if the bus is on time. She eyeballs a wad of frozen phlegm on the glass of the bus shelter and picks up her bag. She heads for the baby store.

It's snuggly and pastel and just about perfect inside. People really have thought of everything, like little leggings, banana-shaped pillows to nurse with, and very techy strollers or hiking backpacks that convey the message a baby is an add-on you just need the right gear for. She checks the prices: hundreds of dollars for everything except the strap-on booster chair, and even that is fifty bucks.

Marla walks through the cribs, beautiful fake bedrooms without babies. Matching walnut dressers, bassinets, and changing tables. What kind of diapers will she use? There are potties that sing and baby butt wipe warming contraptions.

Marla looks at the clothes, hoping for something she can afford even though she has no job. The newborn onesies are impossibly small. A little suit with a monkey on the front hangs by itself. The size is ten pounds. Jasper, Beckett, Gavin. Marla clutches it and feels like she might cry.

A very pregnant woman and her partner are trying to get by in the narrow aisle. "I said, excuse me," the woman says pointedly, gesturing to her watermelon shape. She is thirty-five plus, carrying a dainty leather purse. Her partner wears a suit and tie and carts a swack of baby stuff under both arms. One of those big exersaucers.

Marla sticks her own stomach out, pulling her shirt taut over her little front. "Sorry. Didn't see you there."

The woman doesn't roll her eyes or push close for a bump-off like Marla wants. She gives her partner a look of pity. "Aren't you a bit young, dear?"

Her partner pulls her along. "What a shame," he says, looking at Marla with disdain.

That shit really pisses Marla off. They are so ruining her moment here. She grabs the little monkey suit and follows them to the till. "Hey, I think you should apologize."

They ignore her, making their backs a wall. The man has his arm around the woman, who fidgets. The cashier rings their stuff in.

"You think I can't buy this kind of shit?" Marla flicks their blue plastic bathtub with gizmos hanging over it. Her good arm brushes the woman's jacket, making a plastic-sounding rustle. The woman steps away in alarm, clutching her womb.

The man has had enough. "Get your hands off her," he says to Marla. He waves his hand in the cashier's face. "This teenager is harassing us. Can't you do something?"

The cashier is post-menopausal and afflicted with severe eczema. She gives Marla a warning look, then lifts the intercom phone beside her till.

Marla glances at the monkey suit crumpled in her hand. She drops it on the floor and stomps out the door.

Outside, she can see her bus pulling away. Marla sprints for it across the parking lot, holding her belly. Any other day she would have made it.

After he returns from visiting his mom, Gavin stays with Dani, leaving only to get cigarettes for her. He brings her upstairs, helps her into the tub, and tucks her in his bed. She sweats and throws up and he rubs her back, brings her ginger ale and face cloths, candy. She gets bad headaches and the shakes, but she doesn't take her withdrawal out on him. She tells him about her son, about her plans, and he thinks Marla was wrong about her. Dani has it inside herself to change. He can tell.

Marla tells Liam the whole story while he practises endless scales and patterns.

"Then what happened?" he asks. His bow saws at precise angles.

"I ran away like a baby."

"At least you didn't steal anything. Or start something."

Marla sits on the floor beside the cello, her hand resting on the back of the instrument to feel the vibrations. "They started it."

"You have to know when to walk away." He plays teensy weensy scales high on the neck. Liam's back is so straight Marla thinks he would fall over if she blew hard enough, like a balanced pin.

"Are you mad because I lost my job and now I have no money? Because I'll pay my own way."

Liam hangs his bowing hand down by his side and holds the cello at arm's length. "Never—I'm happy to give you whatever you need. But you should look at the image you present to the world. You're young, and you walk around in a cheap coat and stretch pants picking fights. What are people supposed to think?"

Marla stands up in her stretch pants and her too tight shirt. "So, I'm impulsive." She sees the face of the woman from the store on Liam. Same sniffing disdain. She rips the clip from her hair and shakes it. "You're on their side."

"No offense, but you're the one who looks bad."

Marla wants this fight. No one will tell her the truth, which is that, yes, she is different. It doesn't matter that she's almost always friendly and generous and makes her hair pretty. Whenever it's her against someone else, the other person always looks better, just because. "Why won't you talk about it? You think I don't know people look down on me? They'd look down on you too, if they knew."

"I don't let anything that happened define me. Not my mother, not my cheating ex-wife. I make my own reality." He turns the page in his technical studies book and starts another one. Minor this time.

She closes the book too hard and it flaps to the floor. "Why doesn't that work for me?"

"What do you want me to say? That you're going to be the one who breaks the mould? You'll be some sort of wonder mom that everyone else will be jealous of at parent-teacher night who never gets angry and whose kid asks for more vegetables? Get real."

"Yes. That's exactly what I want. Someone who believes in me."

Liam looks her up and down. He shrugs. "I'm just not seeing it. You are different: you have to work way harder than most people." He edges her out of the way to make the slightest adjustment to one of his fine tuners.

Marla wishes they were still fighting about her scene at the baby store. "Look, I'm sorry I'm not perfect, but it wasn't fair."

She's waiting for him to tell her that of course he loves her and she's a good person, if a little flakey. But he looks at his watch. "I'm sorry you had a crappy day, but I have to practise." He opens his book again with his bow and gets in ready position to attack the strings.

"Why is that? Your audition's over."

Liam bangs his heel on the floor. "Because I want to, okay? I don't want my head full of someone else's drama."

Marla wants to kick his stand over, but she doesn't. She proves to herself that she can walk to the bedroom without freaking out.

He calls after her. "How about this—you don't have to keep the baby. You don't have to prove it to anyone."

Marla screams into the pillow, the sound of Liam's exercises filling the house.

11. EGGPLANT

GAVIN FEELS THE WARMTH of spring and senses the change in the angle of the sun as it enters Dani's basement window. Her body is healing and the trees are budding and Gavin feels like everything is right in the world.

They walk daily—to the grocery store, Bowness Park, and the library. Now they sit on the steps and wait for a cab because she's going to visit her son.

They're supposed to be out of Marla's basement at the end of the month, but Gavin's not sure if Marla really followed through with the details. He doesn't know where to live, and he's out of money, so he's tentative. WHAT JOB YOU WANT? WHEN AT YOUR OWN PLACE?

Dani looks at him like he's a little boy. "Oh, honey. I'm not hurting for money."

That doesn't make sense, because she must have pissed away a lot on drugs even if she did get a big settlement from that car accident. And she doesn't really have a lot of nice stuff, but then some people aren't into that. HOW?

She waves him off. "I'm fine. What about you? Will you go back home, go to school?"

Gavin shakes his head and is pleased to see relief on her face. MIGHT APPLY HERE INSTEAD. GET A JOB CLOSER TO MARLA. AND YOU.

"I know some people. Maybe I can set you up with a job until September."

Gavin picks a hair off her sweater. CAN WE STILL LIVE TOGETHER?

"You ready to tell Marla? I've been waiting to talk to that girl."

He nods, feeling good. Everything's falling into place.

Marla is lonely in Liam's house, finding him no more available than he was when she didn't live here. Sure, he apologized for yelling at her, but she can't shake the feeling that he doesn't know what to do with her, like she's the same sort of disappointing person as his mom. Except at night, when their sex is angry and mostly amazing.

One gorgeous spring afternoon, Marla opens the door and Dani rips into Liam's house trailing Gavin. They've brought fast food takeout in big greasy bags.

"Happy housewarming, you fuckers!" Dani's voice bounces around the house like a basketball. Marla can hear a distinct pause in the screeching bow from Liam's studio down the hall.

"Shhh," Marla says. "Liam's teaching in the back."

"We're celebrating your new big-shot life. Don't you want to see us?" Dani drops the bag on the couch and picks Marla up to twirl her around. Dani's body is so much softer than Liam's. So much sturdier. Marla gives her a peck on the neck and lets go. "Yeah. I missed you."

Dani dumps a pile of music books from the coffee table to the floor. She sets up four meals, dividing burgers, fries, and chicken nuggets onto napkins, then stuffs a handful of fries in her mouth, talking through them. "*Voil*à."

Marla hugs Gavin. "How are you?"

Gavin smiles. BUSY. SORRY DIDN'T COME SOONER. He doesn't touch his meal.

Dani turns on the TV, skipping through channels until she finds a trashy talk show and laughs raucously.

There are ten minutes left in the lesson before the kid's mom comes through the front door. Marla has to get Dani out of here. "Listen, I have something for you. A makeup present." Marla takes a vase from the bookshelf and upends it into her palm. She hands Dani a bag of weed. "Here."

"He smokes pot?" Dani laughs so hard she slaps her leg. She flounces around the room with the bag, peering in the f-holes of Liam's double bass and tipping paintings away from the wall. "Where else does he keep it?"

Marla swipes the bag from Dani and pushes her towards the kitchen "Shhh! We're going outside." Dani giggles and does The Mexican, her r's rolling everywhere.

When the lesson is over, Liam stands in the patio doorway frowning, first at Dani in general, then at the joint she's holding. She licks the edge of the rolling paper like it's a chocolate-covered strawberry.

Liam slides the door open. "Thanks for leaving your garbage everywhere. Makes me look really classy."

Dani holds up Liam's bag of weed. "No, this is what's classy."

"That's for emergency use only." He walks onto the deck in his socks and takes the joint from Dani. She raises her eyebrows as he lights it. He smokes it like he does everything else—no hesitation. He looks at Marla. "I hope you're not having any."

She shakes her head, incredulous. She knew he was keeping it around, but she's never seen him use it. "Don't you have more students tonight?"

"Nope. The sisters cancelled." He flexes his fingers and gives a sudden cringe. Marla takes his hand in hers and massages it.

Dani's nodding. "So that's what you've got. My grandma had that. Couldn't knit anymore."

Liam takes another hit and passes the joint to Dani. "It's a lot better than it was." Dani offers the joint to Gavin. When he inhales, Gavin holds his breath for a long time, like he's done this before. He doesn't cough.

Marla's impressed. "Look at you, all grown up."

Gavin exhales, and smoke gets in her face. For a second she

worries about what he and Dani have in common and what they've been filling their days with. TV?

"I got a little phone call today," Liam announces.

Marla knows what he's talking about immediately, just from his eyes and how they get soft and sparkly just for her. "You got the job?"

"Did I ever." Liam beckons them in close. "Tell me if this is wrong: there's this one kid who comes on Wednesdays. She has so much ear wax I almost can't concentrate—I just want to use a cotton swab. I don't know how she hears anything." He puffs on the joint. "I don't have to worry about her ears anymore."

Dani slaps Liam on the back. "I never knew you could be disgusting. I like it." She starts snapping, humming a jazzy little riff, singing about Liam's waxy kid. To Marla's surprise, Liam joins her, harmonizing and tapping a syncopated rhythm on the railing.

Liam wraps his arms around Marla and Dani. "Let's go eat. I'm ravenous." They all shuffle through the patio door like people playing choo-choo train.

Inside, Gavin drinks pop, finishing half the giant cup in one slurp. Marla raises her eyebrows. "I could be wrong, but I'm thinking sugar's involved there."

He drinks and writes at the same time. SO GOOD. SO SOO GOOD. OOOOOO. He starts giggling in his weird deaf-guy way and drops the pen. It rolls across the old, sloping hardwood, and he limps over to get it.

Liam sits beside Marla, his arm around her. "What's wrong with your leg?" he asks Gavin.

Gavin shrugs and points to Dani. She sits up primly and looks down at them over her nose like a teacher would.

Marla doesn't understand why Liam is laughing. "What?"

Dani gives a theatrical eye roll. "I threw an ashtray at your brother, but he's fine. He's just faking it now."

"That's not very nice," Marla says. She wonders what it

would take to get that angry at Gavin, but it's ridiculous. More likely it's Dani being crazy; she should get Gavin out of there. She motions him over and rolls up his pant leg to check the bruise. It's ugly and green. Marla gapes at Dani. "Why'd you do that?"

"The guy wouldn't leave me alone!"

At this, Liam laughs even harder, trying to hold it in this time. Dani licks her lips at him. Marla glances at Gavin, who looks like he's almost enjoying this. Everyone's laughing except her. "What's going on?" Marla asks.

"I've been making love to him," Dani says, deadpan.

Gavin and Dani are exchanging a look Marla doesn't like. "You mean ..."

Everyone looks at Gavin, who nods and gives two thumbs up. He's proud of himself, the little fucker.

Marla throws a french fry at Dani. "You messed with him? What's that going to do to him?"

"We're grownups. He's my sugar-daddy." Dani winks at Gavin, who's clutching his notepad like he wants to write but can't miss anything.

"You're paying her?" Marla asks Gavin.

Before he can answer, Dani pulls a wad of twenties out of her bra. "I'm getting my own place, and you can't come there," she sings.

"Slut," Marla hisses, and before she can think she's smushing Gavin's untouched burger into Dani's face. "Once a whore, always a whore."

Dani stands up, taller than everyone in the room except Gavin. She wipes at a patch of melted cheese on her face, eats it. "I'm a whore, you're a whore. Who hasn't fucked for money?" She smirks at Marla. "I don't see your hand up."

Marla feels all the air get sucked out of the room. She's suddenly back on a dirty mattress kissing Dani. Checking car doors to make sure the locks hadn't been disabled.

Dani leans into Marla, her breasts soft, her hands on Marla's neck and trailing down. "I was always gentle with you when we were fucking. You remember, right?"

Marla was stupid to think she could keep everything hidden with her past living in her basement, everything ugly she's pushed down. She shoves her friend away. "You didn't just do that, Dani."

"Stop." Liam's face is white, and Marla feels the room go frozen like it's been abandoned for years. "Tell me she's lying," he says.

Marla has to get that look off his face. "It was in high school. I ran away from home."

Gavin's hand shakes as he writes. WHAT YOU SAY?

Dani dumps a tomato from her shirt onto the table. She grabs Gavin's face and mouths the words at him, cups her breast. *We hustled.*

Liam backs away from Marla. "You're a prostitute. And the two of you—"

Dani waves her hand. "Well, not this week. Think of it as temporary work. Seasonal. Debt dependent."

Gavin waves his hand in frustration, holding up his notepad. CAN'T HEAR.

Liam nods. He says, slowly, through clenched teeth, "That's how they know each other."

WHY?

"Doesn't matter. I'm not like that anymore," Marla says.

Gavin throws his pad, and it flutters to the floor. "Oh, I'm sorry. Isn't that what you just said? Once a whore, always a whore?"

It's been so long since she heard his voice that it takes her a second to understand, like listening to someone speak underwater. He sounds like a man. He's shifting his weight, his breath hitching.

Marla reaches for him, confused by how many feelings are happening, thinking that if she could hug him it would be okay, but Gavin pushes her away, hard enough that she falls backwards. "Filthy," he says, his voice dragging on the floor. "Don't touch me."

Marla sprawls on the ground, shaking with the same rage she used to feel at her mother. Gavin takes no notice, glaring at Dani.

"Whoa, buddy. She's pregnant." Dani is watching Gavin the way Marla's seen her watch men before. Checking. Making sure.

Marla slaps the floor in frustration. "Listen—" Even as she speaks, Gavin's walking out the door. He doesn't want her apology, and somehow, that's worse than any of it.

Gavin's heart races. He kicks through black dirt in a flowerbed just to watch it scatter on the sidewalk, and punches a cinderblock wall hard enough to leave blood. Filthy, that's how he feels. He shouldn't have drunk all that pop. And no more weed. He laughs to himself, a snide laugh. That will be easy without Dani. He walks down Edmonton Trail past the bus stop and the snarl of small businesses crammed where the road divides, and onto the bridge towards downtown. There are still some hundred-year-old brick buildings from when this was an Italian working-class neighbourhood, but the scale has been altered by condos. Everything in this city is ballsy but haphazard, like a dream that happened in fragments. Gavin appreciated it at first, but now the city's renegade character stings and makes him long for home.

Tap on the shoulder. He turns around and there she is, her smart mouth. "Get back here, you idiot."

"Fuck off." A man wearing a suit and an ID badge turns around, but Gavin doesn't care who hears his retard voice.

"The bus is back there," Dani says.

"Think I'm going with you?" He must be yelling, because some kids on the bike path approaching the bridge are laughing at him. He knows they think he's drunk. There's no room for error when you're a retard, because a retard always looks worse than a regular person, even with immaculate grooming and excellent posture. A red-eyed guy fighting on the street with a woman wearing pleather, too much eye makeup, and scuffed pumps is as bad as it gets. Of course she doesn't know who the father of her son is. How could he not see? Gavin stumbles and remembers he's high. Dani laughs, and he wants to hit her.

She hands him his notepad and points to the bus stop. Gavin grabs it away roughly, ripping the cover. People are watching. She shrugs and walks away, and Gavin holds the railing of the bridge, leaning forward to let cyclists, students, and office workers pass. It's the end of rush hour, and everyone's going home. Not Gavin. He looks over the water. The river runs cold, a current Gavin can almost feel, as if ice-covered horsemen were rushing under the bridge to a war just around the bend. Gavin wishes it had been Marla who walked out so he could commiserate with Liam. Why would Marla sell her body when she had a family? Cause she liked it? He finds Dani in the crowd, watches her step right in a puddle, splashing grey water on the back of her legs, then stomps after her so he can keep being angry.

Gavin grabs her by the shoulder and turns her around. YOU USED ME.

She pulls a file from her purse and buffs her nails. "Okay, yeah. But only for today."

AND YOU LIED.

"I did."

YOU RUINED MARLA.

Dani shakes her head adamantly. "Nope. I met her on the job, and when I realized what she was about, I helped her get out. Where are you going?" She puts the nail file back in her purse.

DON'T CARE. Dani has lured him and turned everything inside out with her breasts and her hand jobs. Without her, he wouldn't be smoking weed and sleeping till noon. He would be a regular guy with friends and school. Normal. Except that now he's out of money and he has no way to get back to Ontario. He pictures himself hitchhiking, people knowing right away that he's deaf and how he'd spend the whole time looking over his shoulder.

"Don't be stupid." Gavin hates the way she looks at him like she knows he's got nowhere better to go. He feels naked and afraid, like a kid who got his pants pulled down. A kid who would rather go home with Dani than worry about getting messed with walking downtown.

Gavin can see the bus coming around the bend in Memorial Drive. YOU'RE BAD FOR ME.

The bus driver lowers the ramp for Dani and waves them on, impatient.

Dani straightens his jacket and dabs with a tissue at the blood on his knuckles. She's so gentle. "I'm here for you. Think about it."

Marla blots grease stains out of the carpet, using a special spray until Liam takes it away from her. "Don't use that. You're pregnant." She can't read his tone, whether it's weary or angry or disappointed. Probably all of the above.

He gets on his hands and knees to use both hands on the rag, doing a much better job than she did. He's practically sweating, and she just stands there, useless and guilty again. She suddenly has more compassion for Elise—cleaning broken casserole dishes and calling all around to find Marla when she ran away, filing reports, reminding everyone that a young girl was unaccounted for. It feels enormous, the endlessness of how she is.

"It was only for one summer."

Liam looks at her, the muscles in his forearms standing out as he scrubs back and forth. He doesn't say anything.

Isn't it enough that she feels horrible? "I'm not a whore, you know."

Liam throws the rag in the bucket and the dirty water sloshes. "I know. You're a child." He shakes his head, then leans down to sniff the carpet. It's still bad.

Marla hates this useless anger he has. The room is dripping with tension. "I'm a woman, actually."

Liam uses more spray, disgusted. The stain isn't coming out. He lifts the bucket with one hand underneath in case the handle breaks, holding it away from his body as if it's toxic sludge. "You put on a big show of being this beautiful woman, and you seem like you have it all together, but you don't." Liam takes the bucket into the bathroom to dump it. She can hear him muttering over the sound of the dirty water splashing into the toilet. "I think this is over."

She follows and installs herself in the doorframe so he's forced to look at her. "You don't want to marry me because of some teenage mistake? I've definitely made some bad decisions, but so does everyone."

Liam throws his arms out to the side in exasperation, still holding the bucket. Water slops on the tile floor. "Marla, I can't trust you now, about anything!"

This is so, so bad. "I don't have other secrets. There's nothing else I'm ashamed about."

He empties the rest of the water, sets the bucket beside the toilet, and flushes it, then stands up stiffly, like an old man. "You're not understanding me. I want a family, not just a baby. I want a wife who doesn't lie to me, a mother for my child who's not coming off life as a sex worker."

That's not fair. Marla wants to throw down a foolproof comeback about all the hooker moms she knows, but the list is pretty dismal. Dani. Her mom.

Liam edges past her with the bucket. She can hear him in the living room stuffing the fast food containers in a garbage bag, swearing at the carpet. The baby kicks, and Marla can't even bring herself to pat it because she feels so futile about all the yelling she's done tonight. The poor thing is probably clutching its umbilical cord in fear. The whole house seems to sag, like all the fancy books and weird wire sculptures are sliding to the floor in a horrible heap with Liam in the middle.

She kneels to help him clean. When he puts his hands on her shoulders Marla feels hope rising inside. Her belly brushes against him, and she wills the baby to kick again.

"Marla, I'll say this in the gentlest way possible. This—" Liam indicates the garbage bag full of floor food and the dirty rag in the pail behind her "—is not for me."

Marla doesn't believe he's serious, except that he's stopped cleaning. He's standing totally still. "But I have the ultrasound tomorrow, and my stuff is here. Are you asking me to move out?"

"I don't mind if you stay for a few days. But after that, I don't know."

No. This is not happening. Marla feels like a piece of hamburger picked off the floor and held between two fingers. Dropped in a garbage bag.

Liam takes the bag and the pail to the back door. She doesn't wait. Marla puts her shoes on without doing them up and grabs her jacket off the banister so she can be gone before he even gets back to the room.

Dani's body is warm and soft in the twilight. Her room smells like yesterday's pizza and unwashed feet, and Gavin is crying. He shakes his head like he could throw the tears off. He should have kept it simple, stayed in Belleville where there was nothing to care about. He clenches his fists, hating himself.

Dani holds his head on her lap and finger combs his hair. He thinks about how she's done this before, soothed men, tamed them. Been used by them. How Marla has too. He feels ashamed that he is a man like that who uses women like this. He knows it's all fake, that he's not actually interesting or good-looking enough to warrant this kind of attention. She does it because it's what she does. He shrugs away from her touch, rolling onto his side to stare at the smudges on the wall.

Dani pulls him back so he can see her face. "Here." She hands him the money back, each bill still crisp and new.

He waves it away, turns on the light to write. He does not deserve that money. GIFT TO YOUR SON.

"You really mean that?"

He nods. BUY HIM SUMMER CAMP OR SWINGSET. Gavin stabs his stubby pencil into the page, feeling like an idiot. He can't even talk in front of a woman he's slept with.

Dani tosses his notepad on the floor, and Zigzag tears away with it, shaking it to kill it. She leans over Gavin. "Stop hiding behind your deafness and just talk to me."

Gavin doesn't know which is worse—that she was pretending to care about him, or that a woman so full of baggage wants him. He's half hard and snotty from crying, lying wrapped in Dani's down quilt that smells of sleep and flesh and being a man. "Do you have STDs?"

"Nope." She strokes his arm, staring at him like it's any other day and they're going to fuck before he falls asleep in the smell of her hair.

STILL HAPPENING? He looks at her carefully, trying to see in her eyes if she feels bad, guilty.

"Not often. Say it—you think I'm disgusting."

The easy way out would be to tell her she is a worthless person who he hates, which would make her rain ashtrays down on him, but he's too afraid. She would hurt him because it's easy, then she would laugh at him. Gavin would have to sit alone upstairs watching the door to see if she's coming in, looking out the window for her light on. She's not afraid of him.

And there is no easy way out of love. "Was it bad for you and Marla?"

"Yeah. But we looked after each other."

"You hurt her tonight."

"She's pretending, and that never works. I didn't think you'd shove her. You can't do that."

Gavin looks at his hands. He's got to get out of this town. "I hate this about you and her."

Dani lifts his chin. "I don't love it either."

"I feel like an asshole, like I'll never be able to hold everything in."

She lays propped on an elbow. "You're my asshole."

"You don't know me."

"Yeah, I do. And you know me." She smiles at him, her face open and unconcerned. Loyal.

Gavin is overcome with regret and hatred. Somehow even a prostitute is a better person than he is. One last time. Then he'll go home, hitchhike if he must.

She kisses him, gentle at first. Tentative, and it's nice. Neither of them hear Marla come home. Then Dani straddles him, and he leans into her in wretched defeat.

you suck, Dani
je regrette, ma chérie
everything's out in the open
as it should be

The next morning Marla wakes up in her stale old bed with her clothes still on. Dirty light spills in around two tacked-up towels. One of her diner shirts is balled up behind the door, un-ironed. That's where it was. Her cell phone alarm is ringing. Reminder: ultrasound.

She rolls herself out of bed, her hands on her belly. She tries being happy, thinking about a chubby baby from a diaper commercial giving her gooey grins from the floor, but it's totally disgusting. Her room is cluttered and gross, full of half-finished diet pop bottles and shoes. One of Dani's ashtrays overflows on the dresser. Marla tells herself that the baby could have its own bedroom if she kicked Dani out. Or she could clean up and put a crib in here and a rocking chair, but how do you nurse in one of those? Will she nurse?

Marla hangs her bathrobe on the repaired bathroom door and brushes her teeth, pinching her face in the mirror. She's gained weight for sure. She looks rounder. Bags under her eyes from crying. Thick, long black hair that seems really shiny. She drinks three glasses of water. She takes her T-shirt and panties off and doesn't turn the shower on, just stands there looking in the mirror.

There are six scars, all faded white except the thickest, on her thigh, which is ropey and red. Dani put her back together that night with medical tape and cheap pink wine. Now with her broken arm curled into her body, her belly looks heavy and safe. An anchor right in her centre. Something that belongs.

The bathroom door bangs open, and Gavin stares at her, his face white. He slams the door before she can say anything.

She wraps herself in a towel and opens the door. He's sitting against the opposite wall with his elbows on his knees, his head in his hands. He holds up SORRY without looking at her.

She kneels, wiggling her fingers in his face. "I'm sorry too. And I should have locked the door."

He gives her a quizzical look: palms up, expectant.

"I live here again, of course."

LEFT LIAM?

"No, he kicked me out." While Gavin takes forever and a day to think out what he wants to write, Marla interrupts him to think out loud. "I have to get to my ultrasound appointment."

YOU SAD?

Marla was mad at Dani and afraid Gavin wouldn't speak to her, which would be the worst. She feels a sense of relief at not having to lie or worry what people think. These people like her anyway. Well, except Liam. "Yeah, but I can get over a man. You?"

SORRY ABOUT LAST NIGHT, FOR SHOVING YOU.

"You were upset."

STILL. THINK I LOVE DANI.

Dani, who Marla now thinks may have orchestrated last night to break her and Liam up, not out of hatred, but concern. She'd better be done hustling if she's got Gavin in love with her. She wonders what Dani's told him. "It's okay. She could use it." Marla hugs him, towel-clad, hard enough that she feels him catch his breath. The towel is scratchy on her skin, and the baby bumps into Gavin's upper thigh. After a second, he wraps his arms around her too.

Gavin thinks Marla's body looks small on the table. The examination room is dark, with just the glow from the screen flickering against the white-tiled floor and the off-white walls. This is definitely the wrong place to tell her he's going to hitchhike back to Belleville. Gavin shivers and wraps his arms tighter around himself.

The bearded technician says something to make Marla scooch closer. He tugs at her pants, and she slides them down a couple inches to expose her pubic hair. Gavin tastes something sour in the back of his throat.

He gets up to leave, but Marla grabs his hand. "Stay," she says, her eyes big and soft. Afraid. Sad. He doesn't know. Gavin sits down, and Marla resumes staring at the ceiling.

If he cranes his neck, Gavin can see his nephew on the screen. He's amazed at how much it really looks like a baby. It must be magnified. The view changes, and the baby looks like a skull, then a pulsing flutter that can only be his heart.

The technician doesn't speak to Marla. Gavin worries that Marla can't see the screen and motions for the technician to turn it. "Sorry ... can't... position ... pictures ... end."

He writes for Marla. YOU SEE?

"Not really."

Gavin takes a deep breath. "Your baby—" The technician is staring at him. Not frowning, just staring. This guy probably thinks Gavin is the father, some drunken puncher who caused Marla's broken arm. Gavin sits up straighter. This is his sister who talked for him when he could not. Marla, who has always defended him. He tries again. "The baby's eyes are wide-set. He's sucking his thumb, no it just came out. He's kicking."

Marla touches her abdomen, but the silent technician's wand is there with its conductive goo. She holds Gavin's hand instead, turning to face him. "Thank you," she says, her eyes welling up.

The technician interrupts to say something with a frowny face, and Marla heaves herself around to more properly face the wand.

Gavin knows she would want him to keep going, so he tells her about how perfect the baby's feet are, taps the heartbeat on Marla's arm, says that the baby is strong and big.

After the ultrasound, a young, smiley doctor with gelled hair comes in. He scans through the ultrasound results on screen with the technician. His face goes serious as he says two or three sentences to Marla, who looks stunned. But the heart was beating—Gavin saw it. The doctor turns to him. "... the father?"

Gavin glances at Marla, miserable Marla. She doesn't say anything, and Gavin nods to save her further pain. Sure. He'll say he's the father, because he's not going anywhere. Gavin Parker doesn't do abandonment, at least.

"... soft ... syndrome ..."

Gavin is lost. He hands the doctor a card. WHAT DOES THAT MEAN?

The doctor is honest. "We don't know yet."

12. COCONUT

AT THE BUS STOP, Marla thinks, sorting the words. Soft markers for chromosomal abnormalities. Recommended genetic counselling and amniocentesis. Only two blood vessels in the umbilical cord. Echogenic intracardiac focus: bright spots on the baby's heart.

Marla hadn't considered there could be anything but a healthy baby growing inside her. Even Dani had a normal kid. "They want me to have an abortion," she tells Gavin. "They just can't say so."

Gavin looks broken. He's licking his lips. DEFORMITY?

"Not an obvious one, but he said I'm more likely to miscarry or have a special needs baby."

They get on the bus, and Gavin reaches into his backpack to pull out his handbook. He draws a round smiling face with tufts of black hair and wide-set eyes. A smile with no teeth. BABY IS A BABY, he writes.

Marla shakes her head. "What if he needs special appointments? What if he can never go to the bathroom by himself or can't walk and doesn't talk?"

"I don't talk, Marla."

People on the bus stare, and Marla sucks in a terrible breath. "That's not what I meant. You know that."

"Your body is making a baby who needs faith and love. I know, okay, because I didn't have that."

"I can be scared, Gavin."

"Don't quit."

Marla shakes her head, more at herself than Gavin. "I won't do that. I never have."

She's not sure if that's true once she factors in the lying and the prostitution and the drug use, but she doesn't want to think about how often she's chosen something that made sense on the surface only to realize she couldn't stop what went wrong.

Gavin pulls the cord to get off. "Where are you going?" she asks.

He takes off his shoes and socks, arranging them in his backpack. "Running. See you at home."

baby might be messed up
What do you mean?
chromosome stuff
What did they say exactly?
get an amnio. big needle thingy.
We're so sorry, Marla. Have you called Liam?

When Marla hears Liam pull up, she is waiting for Gavin on the tiny back deck. She decides that she can pull this off without getting emotional. She could co-parent with an ex. Lots of kids live like that.

"I got your text." Liam looks concerned, not in a boyfriend way, but an afraid way, like she might talk too long and make him late. He's probably on his lunch break.

She goes business-like. "I want you to know I'll do whatever it takes: special classes, doctor's appointments, leg braces—anything."

He nods, distracted. "We need to make a decision. As I see it, you have two options." He says it like he's been rehearsing in the car.

"Me?"

"Yes." Liam lists options on his fingers. "Adoption or parenthood. I talked to Elise. She said you can get funding from some program?"

Great. Now Liam is her mom. There's a scraping sound from the basement as the window slides open wider. "Who told you to talk to Elise?" Dani hangs her head out like a garden gnome with a cigarette.

Liam ignores her. "Let's go somewhere else."

"I'll be ready in a jiff," Dani says, and Marla can hear her bounding up the stairs.

Dani slams the screen door and then sits on the bench beside Liam, no shoes on, blowing smoke rings. "Where were we? And what are you doing here, girlfriend?"

Marla rolls her eyes at Dani. "We broke up, dumbass."

Dani nods like a sage. Ash from her cigarette drops on Liam's shoes. "Mmm hmm. And?"

Gavin bangs through the back gate, his feet muddy and his jeans rolled up. He looks like a man who wrestled an alligator and then ate it. Dani grabs him around the waist and sits him down beside her. "Hey. We're just helping Marla decide about her baby."

Liam turns his body away from Dani and speaks quietly. "Marla, don't you think in light of last night, and your test results, we should consider what's best for everyone? This might not be an ordinary child."

"What's the matter?" Dani asks Gavin.

"Baby's not perfect." Gavin twirls his finger around his ear, then makes it into a gun. Bang.

"What the hell was that for?" Marla asks him. Gavin shrugs.

Dani waves it off. "They say that to everyone. Everything's going to be fine."

"Dani, I'm not fine," Marla says, wilting. In her centre she feels the enormity of her baby, the heaviness of him, and she thinks about all the things she's been doing wrong. The cigarettes she had before she knew, the hair dye she used, the car accident. The kale she bought and let get slimy in a bag in Liam's fridge because she didn't feel like eating it. All she's really done is doodle baby names.

Liam sidesteps Dani to put his arm around Marla. "Please, let's go together to the agency this time." Gavin puts his hands up, confused.

"Whoa, what agency?" Dani bobs behind Liam. "Why would she give her baby away?"

Liam exhales in frustration. "Stop it, Dani! Don't talk for her."

She stands in front of him, arms crossed. "I look out for her, asshole. We look out for each other." For a second Marla sees the Dani that Liam must see: bags under her eyes, dry skin, out here on this deck eavesdropping because she has nowhere better to be. A woman who's irresponsible.

Marla thinks about what Dani said, that Marla needs looking after, and what it says that her caregiver is Dani. "Babe, leave it. You've done enough."

She pulls Liam to the side, but she can still hear Dani and Gavin cooking up plans. "Please," Liam says, and in the way he lowers his eyes then forces them back up to her she can see he needs looking after too. He's nervous, and he wouldn't be if he didn't care about this child.

"Yeah," she says, ignoring Gavin shouting about abandonment. "I'll go."

There's a guy smoking pot in Dani's basement. He has eyeliner on and red jeans he's walked the bottoms off of. The same guy who was here before.

He nods at Gavin. "I'm E." He gestures to the pizza box. "Have at 'er."

Gavin doesn't sit. WHO THIS he asks Dani.

"E." Dani says. The man is laughing, his mouth open and his head thrown back. "My old dealer."

A dealer. Of course. Dani doesn't go out, so the pills were coming to her. Gavin is so busy congratulating himself for figuring this out that he's handed a piece of pizza before he can refuse. It smells amazing. MARLA WTF, RIGHT?

"Yep. That girl thinks she suddenly doesn't need me. Or you." Dani chews a hole in her slice, catching a piece of pepperoni that was sliding off.

EASY TO TAKE EASY WAY. Gavin glances at Dani, then takes a big bite, allowing the cheese to string down and melt on his two-day beard. The pizza is greasy and thick, sitting heavy as a stone in his throat. Gavin eats angrily. He's been a health nut for so long, GF, SF, CF, only buying organic, saying no every time people celebrate. Why shouldn't he have what he wants?

"You're hungry," Dani says, her head jigging in approval. She stretches her bare legs out on the coffee table so Gavin can see her crotch. E. grins and stuffs his pipe with weed.

Gavin looks away and finishes the slice, then motions for the box. E. feeds some crusts to Zigzag and passes what's left to Gavin. He brings the box close to his face, admiring the salami islands submerged in grease, the cherry tomatoes and stuffed crust. He eats it without looking up, just in case Dani was going to ruin this for him with her magnificent body.

"Don't offer me any, hey?" Dani snorts good-naturedly and pours him a pop in a plastic cup. Gavin eats and drinks but it only makes him feel emptier. Pizza spills on his pants, and he wipes it off distractedly.

When he's finally had enough, Gavin sits on the couch beside E. and gestures for the pipe. E. nudges Dani. "… see … he needs a job."

Dani explains. "Told him you're looking."

Gavin rubs his thumb against his fingers in the universal sign for cash.

"… really … talk?"

Gavin does the "monkey no hear, monkey no speak" thing that everyone gets faster than they can read his cards.

"I've heard him talk," Dani says.

E. says something to her that Gavin can't see. She laughs.

E. twists around to look right at him. "… birth … never … women squeal?"

Gavin almost laughs. He mimes holding a woman, arches his back, opens his mouth in a not ugly come face. He catches Dani's eye.

E. punches his thighs in delight. "You're a fucked up guy," E. tells him.

Here it's okay to eat pizza and wear whatever you want, and no one thinks you're a retard. Gavin feels like maybe he got it wrong with trying so hard. He thought all grownups had it together and didn't get afraid, but that's not true. At least these people don't pretend.

Dani throws Gavin a beer from the fridge. "E. knows a guy."

"Yeah. Carpet layer … looking … someone clean."

Gavin laughs at the irony of anyone in this basement being considered clean and thinks about riding the bus and bringing home a pay cheque to buy beer and pizza with. Hanging with guys like E. who would give him a hit after work and sleeping in the truck on the way to fancy houses. Gavin cracks the beer and nods. He'll do it.

E. uses his phone to set everything up while Dani sucks pop out of her 7-11 mug, crossing and uncrossing her legs. "You're in. You start tomorrow."

Gavin starts to get hard, watching Dani's mouth. He likes the inertia of this, letting things happen. Letting go. He has more time to feel like a failure this way.

This time at Choices, Marla tells herself she is a chirpy bird. She's worn bangles so she jingles, and her favourite jeans with a long shirt of Dani's to cover the fact that her fly's not done up and anyone looking could totally see her ugly granny panties. She tells herself this is just market research—she doesn't have to commit to anything—but she's nervous. She reaches for Liam's hand, but he pulls it away, adjusting his perfectly straight glasses. Right. "This is just an idea, though, isn't it?

Because we haven't even talked about shared custody."

"That's an option. But it would be hard. Think about this baby, Marla," he says, and she does. He would have Liam's green eyes. In all her fantasies about the baby, Liam is there. But she has to admit to herself that it might not be like that. She'd be alone, but worse. She can see from his expression that they would fight about who would get him on his birthday and they'd have to sit at school performances and soccer games with this same awkwardness. The only time their son would see them together is in a mall parking lot every week when they shared him like a favourite sweater no one could cut down the middle.

In her office, Cynthia sips from her blue teacup. "Okay. Let's talk positives."

Marla pulls a list out of her pocket. She wrote it on the personalized post-it notes of a real estate agent that were left in her mailbox.

Go to concerts.
Do massage school.

Marla reads it over. She's not like Liam with a new job to love and all the glory of the world. "It's a pretty lame list."

Liam clears his throat. "Her mom and I have been trying to get Marla to make some real goals. There's this program—"

Cynthia nods, her hands folded. "Marla has lots of time to make life plans." She looks meaningfully at Marla. "We're so glad you've started."

Cynthia explains the process, and it seems casual, one step after another. The way she breaks it down, anyone could do it. The first step is just some paperwork. Marla looks at Liam and thinks about Elise and hating her own mom and decides she could easily write her name and birthdate down on some forms. Adoption's an option.

Cynthia gives Marla and Liam envelopes of forms to fill out.

Marla reads over them, fingering her bangles. The standard stuff—her age, ethnicity, does she smoke. There is a lot of health stuff about her and her family. But it gets personal fast. Do you or have you ever used intravenous drugs? Do you or have you ever received money in exchange for sexual favours?

"Do I have to answer all of these?" She glances at Liam's forms. He's already halfway through the first page.

Cynthia nods. "It's important to be honest."

Marla knows what that means: there are people who won't choose her child because of the things she's done, the person she is. She sets her form on the glass coffee table. "No one will want the possibly deformed baby of an ex-hooker with FAS."

Marla said it for shock value, but Cynthia isn't shocked. She sits beside Marla on the couch and hands her a tissue. "I can help you fill it out. You're in control here: you choose the right family for your child."

Marla reaches for her stomach as if her baby might have disappeared, but he's still there, moving and growing. He deserves her strength, so Marla wipes her eyes and writes her age on the form.

When the forms are complete, Cynthia asks them to talk about the ideal parents for their child.

Liam ticks items off on his fingers. "Financially secure, university educated, have other children."

Marla wasn't thinking about any of those things. She searches for a moment, then decides she doesn't care whether she gets the right answer. "Well, I'd want parents who weren't too old and don't just watch TV all night. A dad who remembers to change the smoke alarm batteries and can cook huge family breakfasts. And a mom who cheers loud at school assemblies, and for them to have a house with a garden. With sunflowers. And I want to be able to see him."

"I'd be more comfortable with closed adoption, if possible." Liam sits primly with his hands folded.

Cynthia sees the look on Marla's face. "Tell me more about that, Liam."

He pulls on his earlobe. "I'm not ready to be a parent, and I don't want to explain that to my child. He's going to hate me, just like I hated my mom."

So, Liam does have thoughts about all this. All Marla had to do was come to a fancy office. She admires Cynthia's sympathetic expression and sees an opportunity to look like she knows what she's talking about. "We could learn to be good parents to him if we're around and he has his own family too. It could be extra good, with lots of love coming at him from everywhere and ..." Marla searches for the right words, but realizes it's not what she actually believes. When has that been true for her? How did having lots of foster families make up for not having a real relationship with a parent? They would be putting a burden on their child either way.

"I'm glad you're talking about these things," Cynthia says. "Of course, your level of participation in this child's life is completely up to you as individuals. It's something you will have to work out with the adoptive parents if you choose adoption."

Liam's phone buzzes but he doesn't answer it. He's looking at the table with the Kleenex box, his shoulders slumped. "Being forgiving is easy for you, Marla, but lots of other people find it hard. Like me."

Marla wants to tell him she's making it all up, that she doesn't know the first thing about stability and commitment and that's why she's here, because she's afraid. That he's right to want to go through with this and choose other parents for their child because Marla just faked a bunch of happy she doesn't have, like she always does. His face looks so raw she gives his shoulder an awkward sideways pat.

Cynthia offers Liam the tissue box. "It's okay not to know," she says. "Take each feeling as it comes and be confident you can make the decision that is right for you and your child."

Cynthia is looking at Liam like she's saying this for the first time, not the hundredth, and in that moment, Marla loves her.

After midnight, Gavin gets Marla out of bed. MOM'S HERE.

Candace is outside swinging a tin can on a string, banging it into the screen door. She looks old, Marla thinks, the lines on her face deep under the glare of the porch light.

"I pissed in your bucket, you know." Candace indicates a five-gallon pail Marla was using to collect rainwater and starts giggling to herself, nervous. "I thought there was body parts in there, you know? Like the missing women? Voodoo shit that had to be stopped." Then she sees Gavin. "My baby—" she says, and paws him like a slobbering dog. Marla thinks it's supposed to be a hug.

He stuffs his pad in his pocket and wraps his arms around her reluctantly. He mouths over her head at Marla: *What's going on?*

"She's fucked up, Gavin. You told her where I live?"

Sorry. I didn't know—

Candace spills all the way inside and spits on the floor. "What the hell are you saying?"

Marla ignores her and rummages in the kitchen, piling up apples, leftover takeout, pop, beef jerky. She hollers down the stairs for Dani to bring some tampons. She can solve this problem in two seconds.

"I'm not here for a goody bag." Candace belches, then winces, and Gavin backs up a step. "I'm just here to see you, say hi." She looks Marla up and down, wobbling. "You're a house. When's your baby coming?

"Summer."

"Your arm—remember when you broke it before?"

Marla remembers. "Next question."

"Whatever. My own kids think they're better than me because he's got some scholarship, and you're living here with her. How'd the two of you get pregnant anyways? Always thought that was failsafe." She scrunches her face and laughs like a hyena.

"You have a scholarship?" Marla asks.

Gavin looks down. HAD. MISSED START DATE.

Dani comes up in her robe holding a box of tampons. "Hey, Mama."

Candace leans, misjudges the distance from her arm to the table, and falls. "Fuck." She blinks, then throws up—pathetic globs of upchuck puddling under her chin.

It's at this moment that a tousled E. appears at the top of the stairs wearing nothing but boxers. "Hey sexy. How you doin'?" Candace says, getting up, fixing her hair. He lights his bowl and stumbles into the kitchen, then lots of things happen fast.

Gavin's voice rumbles. Marla can't believe it, but he's actually growling. He pushes past Candace to hold E. by the throat. "You fuck her?" Gavin says.

"Yeah, man. Don't you?"

Gavin cocks his arm to punch E. in the face, which Marla knows would be so stupid, considering the kinds of people that E. knows, but Dani gets between them, wrapping her fingers around Gavin's fist. "Don't do it, tough guy. Not even a little bit."

Marla steps behind the table, watching them talk with their eyes, saying complicated stuff. Someone has to back down. It's another moment she doesn't know the mom response to.

E. cracks his neck and dusts himself off. "Fuck. Take it easy. You are seriously melodramatic, man." He takes a hit and then bumps down the stairs, smoke trailing behind him.

Gavin's voice is heavy with anger. "Why is he here?"

Dani chews her lip. "Don't worry about it. It's nothing." She waves to Candace. "Look after yourself, babe."

"Feels like something." Gavin blocks Dani's way downstairs, his arms on the doorframe, a monstrous look on his face.

"Gavin, stop it!" Marla says. She swats at him so he'll look at her. As if she needs this drama.

Dani speaks softly. "You want the truth? I'm paying a debt. All right? You happy?"

Gavin snarls and breathes wet through his teeth, staring Dani down. When she doesn't blink, he turns on his heel and bangs out the door.

Gavin stays out all night, running, then walking, then running again, knowing this city and feeling its air in his lungs. He runs past shabby mom-and-pop groceries in Bowness and Montgomery, concrete slab student apartments on the edge of University Heights, and through the winding tree-lined paths of Confederation Park. He cuts across the river at the pedestrian overpass and snarls at the miserable and foreboding grey wall of institutional buildings forming a phalanx around City Hall, two homeless kids fucking under a blanket by the river, and women waiting for tricks. They call to him, showing the curve of their hips. Well after they finish for the night, Gavin runs back along the river, from the zoo past the downtown that is both fortress and heart, past the skate park and leafy neighbourhoods where everyone is tucked in, past tall condos, and all the way to the forest angling up the ridge at Edworthy Park, panting, where he lies down on a giant rock to sleep.

When the sun rises, Gavin awakens by the river. It seems constant, but it started small, carrying water from the Rockies through an enormous watershed. He imagines the water growing as it joins the Oldman and North Saskatchewan rivers and travels the country to drain into Lake Winnipeg. Looking at the river, Gavin feels he can go back.

Candace is gone, but E.'s shoes are still at the back door. Marla must have cleaned the puke up.

Slut, he thinks. Dani's soft arms and her brown eyes. Lying. All those times the door was locked. There is so much to hate. He slams the cupboard doors in the kitchen, looking for one of Marla's sugary granola bars. Nothing.

Like all health nuts, Gavin goes to the grocery store to get high. He tells himself no one will see him, no one knows him. He can buy orange juice and chocolate bars and tuna and his own bag of those amazing crusty buns and eat it all on a park bench if he wants to.

The old Gavin is used to being in charge in the grocery store, knowing everything he can about what he buys and secretly lording his immaculate basket of food over the plebs who eat extruded dry cereal and long beans from China. But today he's not going to ask produce managers why they don't stock the Alberta asparagus that is in season. Today he's going to buy pepperoni sticks from the deli and a carton of chocolate milk. And chewing gum that is coated in flour and full of chemicals. He feels a giddy glee.

Gavin has a full basket of fun, normal food and he's just thinking about whether to get a can opener for the tuna when he feels it coming. He leaves the basket and runs for the double doors at the back, hoping there's a public washroom there. Guys wheeling dollies give him sideways looks, unable to get out of the way fast enough.

He pushes through to the bathroom. Full on liquid shit.

He's sweating, breathing fast. This is what it's like, he tells himself. This is who you are. He can't eat food like regular people. All of it makes him sick, makes him angry. He punches his thighs. There's a long future looming.

He stays there for a long time, so long the handle jiggles because someone wants him out of there, probably asking if he's okay. He's not. Gavin can't stop thinking about his basket full of pleasure. He sees himself carrying it right out the door and across the street, down the block to the park. He sees himself by the duck pond biting into a hunk of cheese and gulping pop. He flushes the toilet, then looks at himself in the streaked mirror. He's going to buy all that food, even if it makes him sick. Maybe because it makes him sick. He grins at himself, a tight little smile that feels nasty and exciting. Gavin knows that if he allows a transgression, he might not be able to stop.

After a slushy start, May brings a warmth that Marla needs. She spends her time in the backyard digging up grass to make a garden, planting potatoes, pulling dandelions—anything to keep out of the house. Marla is so sick of Dani and Gavin avoiding each other and not talking to her about it that it's almost a relief to be back at the agency.

Today, Cynthia has eight or ten books arranged artfully on the coffee table in her office. Some are fancy, with glitter-glue spelling and upholstered covers. Others are more like things Marla made for school: binders with sticky labels.

"Are you ready to look at these?" Cynthia says it like you can't go back after, and Marla hesitates.

"I mean, isn't that what we're doing here?"

"Yes," Liam says. He's making her nervous. It takes Marla a second to think about what's different: he's not hurrying or looking at his phone. His attention is unsettling.

"I'll leave you to it, then." Cynthia takes her teacup and closes the door with a click.

Marla shifts the binders around the table, feeling each one. She worries the people in these books won't understand her, will judge her and shame her to her own child—which scares Marla, and, to forget about the fear, she thinks about how satisfying it would be to mock them. That's exactly what she intends to do when she picks up a satiny binder with ribbons glued onto it. It's stuffed like a quilt, and in the centre is a circular picture of a tidy couple with landscaped haircuts that probably get trimmed every three weeks. They're wearing matching his and hers windbreakers. Marla opens to the first page, the letter.

"As if a letter could convince me to give my baby to a stranger," she tells Liam.

He shrugs, reading.

It's predictable: full of statistics and status. A husband who is an engineer. A master's degree in nursing. A list of charities supported and countries travelled to. Marla is annoyed at how much time this couple seems to have, how quickly they can earn unfathomable amounts of money and the things they do to unload it.

"They seem nice," Liam says.

"No, perfect. In a bad way."

"Let's look at another one." Liam offers her a binder with sparkly writing.

Marla shakes her head. She chooses a sketchbook with pictures glued inside and little stories underneath: the child who was adopted two years ago, eager for someone to play in the sandbox with. He has made a card for his future sibling, painstakingly glued pieces of tissue paper and tinfoil in the shape of a heart. Plans for a playhouse the father is building for his son. The open adoption they have, with visits to the birth mother every month, who is called Mimo by the child. There is another letter from the adoptive mother's parents, who live on a farm. Pictures of all their grandchildren riding ponies. Marla sees her child there and stops breathing for a second. It is overwhelming how right it feels, and she slams the book shut.

Marla sobs, her tears spilling onto the cover of the sketchbook, afraid she will make this choice.

"Hey, you're really thinking about this, aren't you?" Liam hands her a tissue from the box on the table.

She wraps her arms around him, probably getting snot all over his jacket. "It's easy to keep your baby," she says. Easy to be selfish.

"None of it's easy."

She thinks about the baby being here right now, in this room. Not a baby, a little boy, gluing pieces of tissue paper in a heart shape. He is hunched over it, knees on the floor, black hair in his face. He raises his head to look at her, a soft smile on his lips. But he's not looking at her. Marla's not there.

Marla sets the sketchbook on the coffee table gently, trying to breathe calmly, but it's impossible not to make sounds she doesn't want to hear. Liam places Marla's hands on her lap and walks to the door. "I'll be right back," he says. She can hear him calling for Cynthia in the hall.

Her baby is a rock inside her, sleeping. Oblivious. Will another mother play with his hair? Sing Liam's cello songs to him? Marla had thought about pulling her son in a red wagon to the little lake on Nose Hill and bringing a bag of bread so they could feed the ducks. And Gavin. How could her child not know Gavin? But she can't stop thinking about those kids at the farm and how happy they must be.

She pushes her bump from side to side, wanting to feel something. There: a kick. Marla doubles over, her fingertips searching for little elbows and feet. It's the worst feeling, because the baby doesn't know yet, but also the best. She's doing this for them both. "I'm sorry," she whispers to him. "I don't think I'm going to be your mom."

13. HONEYDEW

GAVIN BELCHES as he shuts the door before he sees Dani and Marla at the table, smoking. He rips the cigarette out of Marla's hand and stubs it out. "Don't be an idiot. That suffocates your baby."

Marla's eyes are red like she's been crying. "I know."

Dani rubs her back and leans over to put her own cigarette in Marla's mouth. She looks Gavin up and down. "You look like crap."

Gavin feels like crap—bloated, angry crap. All he wants to do is crawl into bed for the rest of the day. Alone. He ignores her. "What's the matter?"

"... decided ... adoption," Marla says.

Gavin doesn't move. "Because you're a quitter."

Marla stares blankly for a second. Gavin tallies it up: the drugs, the whoring, the shitty place. Marla is like Candace, maybe exactly like her.

Marla wipes her hands on her jeans. "Actually, I feel proud of myself. Something I wish for you too."

There is no way that Marla is going to make him feel bad, so he digs into her. "At least I'm not a coward."

"That's the kind of thing people say when they're afraid." Marla keeps her fingers on her belly, brushing at her skin so soft, and he wants to take it all back, tell her that she's right, he is afraid and now that someone else knows he might not have to feel that way anymore. But Dani's glaring at him.

"Stop being a dick, Gavin." She helps Marla up and adjusts her hair, using the reflection on the microwave. They put their shoes on.

"Where are you going?" Gavin asks.

Dani shrugs. She leans down and puts her hands on his jaw so he'll look at her. "Getting some pills."

"Failed again?"

She grins at him, and he feels her fingernails sharp on his skin. He shakes her off and doesn't look up until he's sure they're gone. Liam was right. She and Marla can have each other. Gavin pulls a chocolate bar out of his pocket and eats it.

Peter's Drive-In is a mess on Friday night with line-ups ten deep in front and cars idling down the block waiting to order at the two drive-thru windows. Marla worries she won't be able to get a picnic table, but then she sees Liam waving to her, there already, wearing the vest like he said he would. Finally, after looking through endless books, they're meeting their first couple.

"I haven't seen them yet." Liam pats the tabletop. "Sit up here. You're easy to spot."

"Listen, I wanted to apologize for before, for being dishonest. I'm going to make that up to you."

Liam helps her up. "Thanks, Marla. It's not easy to say that." He smiles at her. "I'm sorry I haven't been there for you. I was selfish." They hug, then he glides to the window like a dancer, leaning back to let kids pass, then resuming his incredible posture. She thinks about him naked, his back arched in pleasure, his perfect alignment interrupted.

She texts Gavin: *meeting a couple. nervous.*

"Hi. I mean, excuse me. You're Marla, right?" A black-haired sprite of a woman has materialized holding a big purse. No fingernail polish. Practical shoes. Hair done with a curling iron, but like it's her first time.

Marla nods. "Hi." She's not sure whether to get off the table, but before she can attempt it, Cassie is hugging her, her purse bumping on Marla's back. Marla looks around for a man.

"This is Hank." He's even better in person, blond with shaggy hair and wide-set eyes. He looks like he just walked off a beach volleyball court with his beefcake arms and his muscle shirt, like he never gets cold. Marla checks for sand on his knees.

"Um, hi. I'm Marla."

Hank grins and shakes Marla's hand up and down and all around. "Nice to meet you."

Marla can't believe her luck. She thinks about telling Naomi at work about the major hunk who's going to raise her son—she's so lucky!—but then Marla remembers she doesn't work at the diner anymore. For the first time Marla considers what will happen after she gives birth. She could get her cast off and have her old job back. Or she could get into that program and go to massage school.

Liam returns balancing a milkshake tray waiter-style and carrying a white bag. He sets it all on the table and shakes hands, smiling.

They sit, and Marla squeezes herself onto the bench. Cassie doesn't eat. "I'm sorry, I'm just really, really nervous." She sucks noisily on her straw and picks fuzz off her skirt.

"Don't be." Liam sets a burger in front of her.

Hank eats half his burger at once. "Cassie just wants this so bad." Cassie gives Hank a crestfallen look. "I mean, we both really want this for each other and our relationship," he says.

There's an awkward silence. Eventually everyone looks at Marla, at the baby she will bestow on whoever wins her private lottery. Marla pictures the adoption ceremony, the baby wrapped in a fuzzy blanket and Cassie tripping over an IV stand and apologizing. And Hank carrying a jock bag of sports equipment and asking everyone to play some soccer or do lunges in the hallway. Except Cassie would be picking fuzz off the baby blanket.

Towards the end of supper, Cassie asks a lot of questions about the pregnancy. "You're feeling nauseous, right? I mean, that's supposed to be a good sign. Not like barfing all day though, right? I mean, do you still have to? I'm sorry—that would be really hard."

Marla smiles and smiles, but she can't shake the idea that she doesn't feel anything at all about this couple. Sure, it would be nice to give a baby to two people who really wanted one. But not these two people.

When the mosquitoes come out, they all rise and shake hands. Cassie gives Marla a tentative hug, and Hank grins.

As soon as they're gone, Liam shakes his head. "I can't see it."

Liam gets her. She knew it all along. "I know, right? I mean, Cassie looks like she would drop a baby and then stand over it on the floor not knowing what to do."

"What about Hank?"

"He seemed alright. But Liam, I want someone tough who can make everything okay."

"I know." He gazes at her in the twilight while cars inch forward in the drive-thru line-ups and teenagers smoke and posture. "Are you going to get the amnio?"

"I read they can cause miscarriages. I'm going to see what my next ultrasound says. I'm getting them all the time now."

"That makes sense."

Marla picks at the remains of the fries. "So, we'll look at more books next week?"

Liam sits almost close enough that people might think they're a couple. "Yeah." His arm brushes against hers, and then he reaches for her hand. "I'm glad we decided to do this. I feel really good about it."

"Me too. As long as it's some other couple."

"You got it. How's Gavin?"

"Okay, I guess. He's working with someone Dani knows." She thinks about how he was this morning, and his angry thing with Dani's dealer. About being honest. "Actually, he's been an ass. He and Dani are fighting."

"About what?"

"Relationship stuff." She feels a raindrop. The sky looks ominous. "I should go."

Liam stands up. "I can drive you."

"It's fine. The bus is right over there." Marla doesn't want to tell him she's practising being alone. She scoops all the garbage into one of the fry trays and throws it in the bin.

"Wait," he says, and she closes her eyes because she wants it so bad.

"Yeah?"

"Maybe we could get coffee somewhere."

Even if it's not really a date it will feel good just to be with the one other person who knows exactly how she feels. Marla leans into his chest, and he holds onto her. "Yes," she says. "I'd love that."

Gavin has all these plans for what he wants to say to Marla, how he can convince her she's just not thinking straight. He waits in the kitchen for what feels like hours, watching the flicker of light from Dani's TV on the lawn. She's probably laughing down there, eating pills, nothing wrong. He tries to meditate, but all he can conjure up is E. tucking his stringy hair behind his ears, fucking Dani. The look on her face when he comes in her. When Gavin opens his eyes, the sky is dark.

He knows Dani's down there, not going anywhere. He stomps down the stairs to give her lots of warning.

She's microwaving pills with the bass pumping. Fucking junkie. "Happy now?" he asks her.

She grins and shakes the bottle, but Gavin doesn't smile. She tilts her head and pouts. "Are you here because you're done being mad?" Her mouth is red like candy. Like a circus clown. She slides a bottle of beer along the table towards him, and he steps out of the way to watch it hit the floor and break.

She lets her hand fall from the microwave door handle, and suddenly her body is tighter, her eyes more alert. "That was fun, but now I'd like you to leave."

He shakes his head. "I want to know, what were you getting from me? Was it just money?"

"Asshole. You can have it. I have enough."

"Yeah, I know how you get your money. I'm just a pity trip, fucking a deaf guy?"

"Yeah, that's what it was." She holds a pretend pencil to write on a pretend notepad, licking her lips and biting them, making slow mouth shapes. "I'm deaf, but I can read lips. All I've ever wanted."

Gavin feels it, that white-hot blast of rage. It's ugly, filthy, like this room, and Dani in it with her bathrobe and her lips and her pills. He reacts, not even trying to push it down, just moving. Forcing it out.

He sweeps the table with his forearm, sending an ashtray into the corner where it smashes, spilling cigarette butts and powdery ash. Dani doesn't back up, she comes right at him, scratching and punching.

Gavin grabs her by the shoulders and throws her down. He feels good doing it, strong. It's easy, and he thinks he should have done it before. No more cowering, no more fear. Just action. The puppy barks.

Dani springs up with the bat from under her chair. She wields it, waiting to swing, waiting until he gets closer. "Don't fuck with me, Gavin."

He hesitates for only a second, but that's just fear eating at him, the fear that he can't do anything, the same fear that he is over having. Gavin darts forward, full in, and rips the bat out of her hands. He throws it into the wall, making a sizeable hole. He holds her arms by her sides. "You think I'm funny?"

"Let go of me." Her face is shiny, and in her eyes is a new look, like she's taking him seriously for the first time. He feels her breasts against his chest, her breath coming fast, and knows exactly what would make him feel better.

"It's just business," he whispers in her ear.

She whips her head around, trying to brain him. She goes

to bite him, but that can't happen. He uppercuts her jaw shut so her teeth clack together.

"You motherfuck—"

He kicks her legs so they buckle, and together they fall to the ground. It feels hard under his hands. Gavin's heart is banging in his chest, so loud he can almost hear it, but it doesn't seem important.

This is hunger and momentum, that's all. Inevitability. He's got her bathrobe up around her belly, and she's reaching for the pizza boxes beside the TV. Probably has something in there. He leans over her and scatters them, crumbs and bits of dried up meat flying all over. Gavin feels her holler, but no one can hear her.

It's better than sex is, just the right kind of dirty without any vulnerability, in this room with its fluorescent lights and its makeshift furniture. It's cheese smell. She's crying.

"Don't you cry," he tells her. He's being yanked out of the moment; it's a trick she has, a trick to make him give up. Her nostrils flare. She can feel it.

It can't be like this, he thinks. He's in charge. He thrusts harder, and Dani laughs at him, her mouth curled up and her breath hot on his skin. She bangs her head into his nose, and the room wavers. She scrambles out from under him, and he kneels where he was, waving his hands until he can see her. The air in the room has changed again, everything brighter and smaller and completely over.

She spits blood on the floor, then wipes her face. "I got those pills from a doctor, asshole, because I loved you. I finished with E. the night Candace came." She's holding the bat above her head, her arms steady. No emotion.

Love. Her eyes tell him she'll do it—she'll bash her best friend's brother to death in this basement. Her lover. But that's not what he is anymore. "Dani," he whispers. His tongue feels thick, his mouth shape all wrong. She will never understand because there are no words.

"Get out," she says.

He stays down. "Do it," he says, arms behind his back.

"My pleasure," she says, and swings.

It turns into a date when Marla veers down the street with Liam's umbrella and the hot chocolate he bought her to take him to the flea market. She feels strong, full of love for him instead of just need.

Marla sorts through rip-off brands, jostled by deal-hungry regulars, tourists, and children, until Liam puts his hand on her waist and keeps it there. She pays a dollar for a jazz record for Dani, then they eat Ukrainian sausages and drink imported pop in the six-table cafeteria that smells like every morsel of street food in the world, sharing their table with a family of four. It's too noisy to talk, but not so crowded that Marla can't feel the way Liam's body is relaxed or see the crinkle in the skin beside his eyes when he laughs.

When Gavin comes to, the only movement in the room is a record going around and around the turntable. There's a twenty-dollar bill stuck to his face, and many more on the floor. Dani is gone.

His head is throbbing, but from the size of the lump, he knows she could have hit him much harder. He hates her pity. Inside he is drowning and sick and wrong, a fucking coward. Gavin sees his own face above hers, the way she's crying, how Dani looks when she's afraid and how it felt good to make her that way, finally seeing himself for what he believed himself to be all along: an animal.

Gavin buttons his jeans and scoops up all the broken glass with his fingers, wiping the beer with his shirt, the blood. The hole in the wall gapes at him. He can feel the bass from the stereo and it beats like his heart, going too fast. He should get out of this basement. Gavin takes the money and breaks a lot of stuff in his room because he's afraid that if he doesn't smash something, he will have nothing to hurt but himself. He shreds the handbook and hurls the pages against the wall but they float down in an infuriating way. A sheet of paper drapes over a baby crib he was building with fancy wood. He kicks it apart board by dowel then collapses onto the shreds on the floor. So many little pieces.

Gavin wanders Bowness Park in the rain, looking by the dock and the boat sheds, but Dani is not there. Just graffiti and ugly florescent lights.

He rides the bus downtown, shaking. No one will sit with him, and he prefers it that way. He gets off at Centre Street and walks by the river where the hobo camps are. He calls her name. Kids whip past him on bicycles in the wet dark, and he stumbles.

She's not here. He won't find her. He rubs dirt between his fingers, looking over the river. It carries all the rain and snow from the mountains, impossible faraway places. The high water gives him a plan that's garbled and ugly.

In the cold wet, Gavin conjures Marla and casts about for a safe place to put himself, for her sake. She's probably riding the train or walking with Liam. He'll look after her.

Maybe Liam is at the restaurant. Gavin scrambles up and runs. He doesn't look when he crosses the street. His shoe comes untied and he kicks it off, not stopping.

The Thai place is busy, with people still waiting for tables. Gavin edges in the door and around groups sipping tall drinks. He brushes hair off his sweaty face.

The hostess is saying something. "... many, Sir?"

"I'm looking for Liam." As soon as he says it he wishes he brought his notepad.

The hostess widens her eyes like Gavin he might eat her. He glances at his wet, muddy jeans, his missing shoe. She's still talking. "... going to have to speak up."

"Liam," he says, slow and clear. Pointing.

The hostess is now in conference with a male server, who looks

Gavin up and down. He says it again, standing up straight, trying not to pant. "I'm looking for Liam."

She's shaking her head. Maybe the music is loud, but that doesn't occur to Gavin. The concerned look on the hostess's face is one Gavin can't stand.

He kicks over a decorative planter, feeling the vibration of it hitting the floor. "Liam!" he bellows. The waiting patrons have backed away and are staring. Gavin shakes his hair and snarls.

The male server puts his body in front of Gavin's. "Sir, I'm going to have to ask you to leave."

Gavin turns in half-circle, feeling cornered. People have stopped eating. The kitchen door swings open and shut, open and shut. None of the curious wait staff are Liam, because Liam would have come running. There is nothing in the room but disdain.

He runs, his one shoe hitting the pavement hard. Gavin knows only one thing: he is the worst version of himself that he could be.

14. MICROWAVE POPCORN

A HORN'S HONKING outside at six-thirty in the morning. Marla rolls over, trying to ignore the noise, but it's incessant: Gavin's ride to work.

She hauls herself up, barging into his room. He's not there. It looks like hell, with pieces of wood all broken on the floor: the crib he was building. Marla feels sorry for a second, then just annoyed at more of Gavin's useless anger. He's here, makes a huge mess, then takes off without leaving a note?

She leans out the front door, still in her pyjamas, and hollers to the guys in the truck. "Gavin's not here!"

They mutter to themselves, then a skinny guy in a backwards hat yells back. "He's done then." They roar off.

It's like having a kid, but worse, because he's old enough to know better.

Marla's cell phone alarm rings with a reminder about Dani's meeting with Kamon. She twists the doorknob to go downstairs, but it's locked. She picks the lock with a hairpin she keeps in the drawer for that purpose, but the door still won't budge. "Dani!" she yells. Must be something against the door. Like having two kids. She walks out the front door barefoot, around the side of the house where the bucket is. She sniffs at it, curious. Yep. There's piss in there. She leans it over carefully so the pee runs into the flowerbed.

Marla bangs on Dani's window, then slides it open to peer inside. Dani is wrapped in a quilt on the floor holding her bat, her head back against the wall. Passed out.

Marla backs herself into the window, something she's done many times, but not at her present girth. She can feel Dani's dresser with her feet, but her bump's not budging. She kicks around, banging her feet into the wall. "Dani—get up and help me."

"Why?"

Marla stops wiggling. "What do you mean, why?" She sucks it in, and yes, she can feel herself sliding through the window frame. She crouches awkwardly on Dani's dresser.

Dani's rolling her bat on the floor. "You look like Pooh Bear." She licks her lips. Her cheeks are really red.

"You're fucked up."

"Yeah. You want some?"

"You're supposed to see Kamon today."

Dani slams her head against the wall. She punches herself in the jaw. "Fuck, fuck, fuck."

Marla grabs Dani's hand to stop her from hitting herself. Close up Marla can see a bruise on her chin and Dani's split lip. "Listen, I'll call and reschedule, okay? I'll tell her you're sick." Dani slumps down, clenching her fists. "Dani—"

Marla's phone's ringing. "Yeah?" She pats Dani's arm, squishing her phone against her chest. "I'll get rid of them."

The voice on the phone is authoritative. "Can I speak to Marla Parker?"

"Yeah. I mean, speaking."

"Are you aware that you are the emergency contact for Gavin Parker?"

Marla's hand falls away from Dani. "Gavin?" Her voice feels small, like it's coming from far away. "Um. Yes."

"I'm calling from the Foothills Hospital to inform you Mr. Parker has been admitted and you should probably come in."

Gavin. Marla drops the phone and presses her hands to her eyes. She's let him down, and now something is wrong. "Dani, we gotta go."

meet me at foothills
baby?
no. gavin.
what happened?
don't know. please come.

When Gavin opens his eyes, Liam is there, pacing the room in a suit. Gavin sits up, blinking. Liam puts a hand on Gavin's shoulder. "Hey, you broke your ankle and bashed your head. Marla's on her way."

Gavin feels down his body, hating that it all still seems to be there. He should be underwater. He hops to the bathroom, staying longer than he needs, sweating with the pain. He deserves it.

When Gavin gets back to bed, Liam hands him a clipboard with old dot matrix paper clamped into it. Institutional paper. "What happened?"

JUMPED OFF CENTRE ST BRIDGE.

Liam is frowning so hard he tears up. "Why?"

Gavin remembers her shaking beneath him. DID BAD THING.

"The nurses say you were belligerent."

THEY THINK I WAS DRUNK BUT I WASN'T.

Liam holds a glass of water to Gavin's lips. "I'm going to get you something from downstairs. A salad? Fruit?"

Gavin closes his eyes and nods. Stupid. Tired. Don't want to care and can't help it. And all the cold water rushing up around his bones and heart.

He feels the room change and snaps his eyes open. Dani. Through Marla's weepy babble and officious patting, he watches Dani in the doorway, staring him down. She's wearing Marla's jacket over sweatpants. She taps her foot, her face red, her neck long and her arms braced on the frame.

"What'd you do, fucker?" She drums her fingers on the wall.

Gavin wishes he could pull something beautiful out of his pocket, like a stalactite or a tiny teapot, but he has nothing.

He can see his marks on her face. "Jumped into the river." His voice feels wobbly but he stops it. He doesn't deserve sympathy.

"That wouldn't kill anyone."

"No. Guess not."

Marla flaps in his line of sight. "Gavin, that's horrible." She's crying. "You need help."

Gavin doesn't agree or disagree. He holds his eyes on Dani.

Liam returns with a bag of food that he presents with two hands. "Eat," he says. He embraces Marla, saying something or other. Dani sits in a chair by the window. She hasn't taken her eyes off Gavin.

He stands, hopping on one foot and pushing his IV pole out of the way, but it catches on a leg of the bed and tips over. He rips the IV out of his arm. "Dani, I'm sorry." He gets down on one knee in front of her, sticking his broken ankle out to the side. "So sorry."

She raises a hand to examine her nails. "They all are, you know." She looks beyond him. Marla must be saying something, but Gavin doesn't turn around.

"I want you to press charges." He should be in jail, pissing in a stainless-steel toilet, sleeping on a plank. Now he craves her anger, thirsts for it. He juts his chin out at her in an invitation to flare off. Dani bites off a fingernail and spits it on the floor. She doesn't move. The expression on her face doesn't change, and the love Gavin feels for her, his admiration, eats him alive.

Liam is beside Dani now. "... he talking about?"

Dani looks at Gavin. "He got a little carried away." Marla opens her mouth and closes it like she has a lot more to say. She holds his hand with the hospital admissions bracelet on it, squeezing him. He stays kneeling in front of Dani.

"You never have to see me again," Gavin says to Dani.

"Perfect." Dani bites her lip at him, suggestive, angry, and before he can say anything else, she leaves.

Marla tries to pull Gavin back to his bed, but his body feels heavy, like dead weight. He yanks his hand to go on his own, and Marla feels she will never understand.

"Did you hit her?" she asks, tentative. It's the only thing that's coming to mind, yet it feels ridiculous when she says it. "Did Dani hit you?"

Gavin curls into a ball with his arm over his eyes. "It's my fault. I did this, all of this."

"Right, but—" Marla trails off when she notices Gavin isn't looking at her. She picks his arm up off his face. "Look at me, Gavin. You owe me that much."

"I'm seeing you."

"I'm sorry I didn't notice the signs or whatever, but now I'm freaking out. You jumped off a bridge? You and Dani won't tell me what's going on—something's really wrong with you." Marla knows as soon as she says it that it's bigger than just Gavin. It's all of them, something to do with pretending and perfection and not really knowing anything at all about what to really do. "With all of us."

"I don't believe in me anymore."

"But you can. I'm learning too."

Liam has his mouth open, but he's almost frowning too, like Marla read his mind. "Marla," he says, but then Gavin's crying, turned away. The emotion is gone now, floating in the room unclaimed.

Liam opens the bag of food Gavin left lying on the bed. "Maybe you should eat something, Gavin. I brought you a chicken Caesar—no dressing, no croutons."

Gavin picks at the cheese on his salad and looks like he's going to burp or throw up or both. He pushes it away and folds his arms over his chest.

What if he won't eat the whole time he's here? Marla tries to squish down the panic inside her into little boxes—the adoption, Dani's chaos, the sort-of relationship she has with Liam, and now her easygoing, perfect brother crossing his arms in a backless gown because he's in the hospital for throwing himself into the river—and she can't do it. There's a tingling sensation in her breasts, a heavy feeling she doesn't understand, and she squeezes her arms around herself to make it stop.

Liam touches her back, leading her to a chair, as if this was a perfectly normal thing to do, sit and watch Gavin cry and stare at his sheets. She sits, reluctantly. The room is stifling with the sun blasting through the windows. "Aren't any of you hot?" She fans herself with her hand, flapping it faster and faster. "I can't do this."

Gavin looks away. "Marla, you're good. You're going to be fine." He closes his eyes and rolls over.

Marla lays beside him on the bed and whispers to his back. "I'm not fine, Gavin. Nothing about this is fine. I'm having a baby in a month and you're in here, and I lost my jobs. You lost yours, too." He can't hear any of it. She squeezes her arms around him, and he allows her to, which feels good until she realizes the bed's shaking because she's crying, not him. He's just lying there like a rock.

She shakes Gavin's shoulder until he looks at her. "Why'd you do this?"

Gavin shrugs, his face empty.

"You apologized to Dani twelve times and you're not going to talk to me?" She holds his face in her hands like she used to when he was little. "I need you, Gavin. I love you."

He brings his arms up, and she thinks he's going to hug her, but he uses them to nudge her off the bed.

"Maybe it's not a good time," Liam says.

Marla feels awkward here, too big and mostly useless. She backs up into the doorway, but Gavin doesn't notice. "I'll go, then," she says, but he doesn't turn to look.

Dani's sitting in the hallway, mouth breathing. "Can we leave now?"

"Yeah. I can't fucking believe this. Should I leave him? Did you know about this?"

Dani looks at Marla like she's an eight-year-old. "He's a big boy now. He can manage." Marla helps Dani up, noticing the sweat stains under her arms.

The nurse at the desk calls to them. "Are you the family?"

Dani snorts. "I'll be downstairs."

Marla nods. "I'm his sister. He's staying with me."

"What about other family?"

Marla thinks about Candace, Gavin's dad who doesn't have a last name. "We don't have other family."

"Very well. You should know he will likely be evaluated. We strongly recommend he voluntarily transfer to the Psychiatric Unit."

Liam emerges to shake the nurse's hand and nod like a dad. "We'll talk to him. Thank you very much," he tells her.

"My brother's not crazy!" she yells after the nurse. "Being sad doesn't mean you're crazy—he gets mugged because he's deaf and his mom's a junkie and he's lived on his own forever. He's building me a baby crib!" The nurse doesn't turn around. "He was." Liam wraps his arm around her to shush her, but Marla pushes past him to pull Gavin's file out of the plastic holder outside the door and read it. It's a record of vital signs and medications administered for the pain in his ankle. "It doesn't say crazy in here!" she shouts, but people here must be used to that kind of thing. It says attempted suicide.

Marla is flipping the page when Liam takes the file out of her hands and replaces it in the plastic holder. He pats her on the back. "Shhh."

Marla edges against the wall to let a stretcher wheel past, then a boxy meal cart. A nurse gives her one of those grandma grins when she sees Marla's big belly. The next time Marla comes here will be to have her baby. And give him away. She rolls her head back on the tile wall, listening to the nurse's shoes swish and squeak on the floor. "What should we do?"

"I'm going to ask Gavin if he'll come home with me," Liam says.

"What? Why?" Despite herself, Marla feels a ton of relief.

"There's something really wrong with him and Dani. I think she might have gotten him involved with drugs."

"Oh shit." Dani was a good doctor for Marla too, drawing up syringes and making everything okay. "He's supposed to be in school."

"I know. I'll talk to the admissions office. Just worry about you. Go to your prenatal class."

Marla nods, pushing it down. This is what she hates, this acquaintance talk. Liam re-enters Gavin's room, and Marla takes the elevator alone to collect Dani, who'd better tell her what the hell is going on.

When Gavin next opens his eyes, the sun's gone down and he can see the streetlights shining in the window. Liam's typing on his phone.

YOU SHOULDN'T BE HERE. Gavin's head feels like it's full of mice.

"Why not?"

SHOULD BE PRACTISING. WORKING. Gavin looks around at the shit hooked up to him and kicks his foot around in the bed until the sheets come untucked. He hates that he's here, that he's anywhere at all.

"I want you to stay with me."

That means Marla's kicking him out. Dani told her, and Liam probably, out in the hall. The nurses probably know too. Gavin feels that crawling sense of panic in his throat, and he bites his tongue hard to feel something else.

"Gavin, are you okay? Do you want me to get a nurse?"

Gavin's mouth fills with blood, and he swallows it. Shakes his head. He deserves for everyone to know what he is, what he does. He's not fit to live in Liam's house with its arched doorways and crown moulding.

Liam holds up a finger before answering his phone. "Hello?" He talks fast, nodding. Explaining something. Probably Marla.

The thing is, Gavin would love to live at Liam's place: chatting on the couch, drinking expensive wine. Watching movies and cooking together, but that's all fantasy.

SO YOU KNOW ABOUT THE RAPE.

Liam glances over, still on the phone. He reads it. Reads it again. "I'm going to have to let you go." He slips his phone into his breast pocket and sits on the bed. Concerned.

DIDN'T WANT SAY TO MARLA.

Liam nods, his eyes full of pity. "Tell me anything."

No. This is going all wrong. Gavin speaks so loudly he can feel the words vibrating in his chest. "I raped Dani."

Liam leans close, glancing at the open door. He taps Gavin's clipboard. "What do you mean?"

Gavin speaks slowly, deliberately. "I mean, I held her down and raped her." The words were angry in his head, but he feels his voice break and has to look away.

Liam shakes his head. Confused. Looks at the bed sideways like he's thinking hard. "But you guys have been—"

"I know the difference."

"I think you must be exaggerating."

An orderly comes in with a plastic tray and sets it on Gavin's lap. She opens the lid, and a hospital food smell flops out. Jell-O and microwaved chicken.

Gavin lies and stares at the ceiling, tears spilling down his cheeks. "She was screaming. I felt it." The orderly raises her eyebrows at Liam. Gavin sees it.

When she leaves, Liam paces the room. He takes his phone out of his pocket, then puts it back. "So, it was happening, then it got nasty, right? You had a fight?"

I STARTED IT. PUSHED HER DOWN.

"I don't think you know what you're saying."

I KNOW EXACTLY WHAT I'M SAYING. Gavin shudders and wraps his arms around himself. The food smells like he will eat it.

"Don't do this to yourself. You're probably still in shock."

Gavin backhands the tray to the floor. "This isn't about me!" Red Jell-O cubes splat into red Jell-O blobs.

Liam takes hold of him. "Gavin, listen to me. The doctors want to do a psych evaluation on you. Once they fill out those forms, that's it—you're committed and you can't leave. Is that what you want?"

Gavin remembers Candace in rehab with the ping-pong table and the juice fridge. He shrugs, angry. It would be a kind of jail.

A nurse comes running, and Liam lets go of Gavin. "He was trying to sit up and knocked the tray off." Liam gives Gavin a deliberate look. "It was an accident."

"I'll have them bring a new one," the nurse says, her face unreadable. Businesslike. She leans over Gavin so her breasts are right in his face, then wraps her arms around him to lift his upper body while she pushes a button on the bed to move it into a sitting position. She arranges pillows behind his shoulders and closes his hospital gown behind him where it came open at his neck, then reaches down, tucking in his sheets. "Better?"

Gavin's chest feels hollow and heavy, like he could rip his own arm off and still not feel anything. "Yes. Much better."

She pauses in mid-bend to stare at him. "You're deaf?" she asks, signing at the same time. "My son is deaf, but he doesn't lip read. Where did you learn that?"

A deaf son? Gavin fingerspells O-N-T-A-R-I-O. He signs, *I went to deaf school.*

The nurse nods, interested. "I wish my son could have something like that. He's the only kid in his school who's deaf, and he has a translator who sits with him. It's hard."

Gavin's hands remember signing, how much faster and cleaner even Signed English is than all the lip reading and writing. How beautiful. *He will be a strong person at the end. Deaf people are always strong people.*

The nurse puts her hand on her chest, touched. "You know, I wouldn't normally say this, but could I bring my son to meet you? There are so few people in his life he can sign with, and he could really use a role model."

Gavin looks at the splattered food on the floor, then at Liam nodding. A role model. It would be nice to really talk to someone, even if he is a kid. Maybe especially if he's a kid. *Yes. I would love to meet your son.*

The earnestness on her face makes Gavin want to weep. "I can bring him after school. His name is Justin. He's fifteen." She nods her head towards the mess. "Someone will be right in to clean that up." She squeezes Gavin's hand before she goes.

Liam steps over the spilled tray. "See? You don't need the psych ward. You just need to get out of Marla's basement."

Gavin glances at his pad. What he wrote about Dani is still open on the bedside table. "You don't believe me."

"I believe there's a problem. Stay with me."

Gavin wants to do the right thing, but there is so much inertia. The wallowing is what he wants, what he's feeding off of. It pulls at him, tempting him. He could lie in the psych ward on a scratchy couch watching daytime TV and eating hospital toast, signing to a psychiatrist all day. But there are other ways to punish himself. He nods. "Okay. I'll come."

Marla decides to let Dani sleep it off before asking her what the fuck is going on. She tucks her into bed, removes all the pills from her room and sets the microwave timer for six hours. It counts down the seconds as the clouds bunch up. It's going to rain again.

Thanks to Gavin, Marla's house is now perfectly organized and sorted except for her room and his. It feels fake, like no one real lives here, but also full of spaces that are calm and clean. Something he couldn't keep up.

Marla is suddenly certain that if she can finish what he started, he will be all right. She rips the clothes out of her closet and stuffs half of them at random into garbage bags to donate. She bins up books she's not going to read, an old computer that barely works, her old phone, unused photo albums Elise gave her: donate. She throws out loads of paper—old bills, grocery lists, movie ticket stubs from her first dates with Liam.

Removes dirty plates and plastic bottles. She keeps her high school poetry binders and the drawing of a werewolf Liam gave her as a gift. She stores them high in the closet.

This puts her eye level with the baby stuff she's accumulated: presents from work, a box of newborn diapers, little hats, the stuff Marla's neighbour saved from when her daughter was a baby, Gavin's wooden blocks, bibs, and a baby bathtub. It's so much stuff it doesn't fit on one shelf anymore. She removes the box of diapers to donate, but feels wrong about it. Why shouldn't her baby wear these? Would it be wrong to give someone a baby and baby presents? Marla remembers Cynthia saying Marla would be like an aunt. An auntie might bring presents, right? Maybe.

Marla takes all the items out one by one on the pretext of packing them into a box to give away. However, she doesn't have a box, nor does she get one. Marla finds herself playing with them, stroking them, laying little outfits in rows on the bed and smoothing down wrinkles. Tying the bow on a lacy bonnet. She assembles a plastic push toy and pushes it around the room on her knees, flipping the flaps and pressing the buttons, surprising herself with how satisfying it is. She opens the diaper box, takes out a newborn diaper, and opens it up. It smells like a baby, or what she imagines a baby smells like. Baby-powdery. Soft. She holds the diaper to her cheek and brushes it alongside, closing her eyes. That feeling happens again, and a bloom appears on the front of her shirt.

Marla abruptly stuffs the diaper back in the box, but it won't sit the way it was before, factory-packed in shrink-wrap. This isn't something she talked about with Cynthia. The diaper bunches out of the hole Marla ripped in the plastic, looking crumpled and used.

She told herself once she chose adoption the hardest part was over but no one thought about this closet full of guilt. Marla grabs garbage bags and starts stuffing. It takes three bags, one just of teddies and blankets people made by hand. She puts the bags in the donation pile, but they look so lumpy and sad Marla changes her mind. She piles them on the floor of her closet and shuts the door.

She can't stop now. Marla reaches under the bed with the broom, and when that doesn't prove satisfactory, she heaves the bedframe around the room to clean the rest of the floor. She pushes hard, feeling good to be so physical, so strong and clean.

After everything is immaculate, Marla can see dust scattered in the air. She lies on her bed watching the drizzle on the windowpane, deliberately not thinking about Gavin or adoption or anything, and falls asleep.

When the timer dings, Marla rustles Dani awake and hands her four pills. "Crush these. You're going to baby class with me."

Dani salutes and snorts the pills. "I thought you'd never ask."

"Bring a pillow."

Dani licks her fingers. "Awesome. Do I get to massage you?"

Marla holds the door open for Dani. "You better."

Dani kicks a stone on the way to the bus stop, making a few good ones before stumbling, her eyes half open. Marla takes it the rest of the way, winding up and aiming it right at the bench. It bounces off and scrabbles into the long grass.

She can't wait any longer. "What was with the bat?"

Dani waves this off like it's nonsense. Like she wasn't a shivering mess this morning. "Don't worry about it." She picks at her nails, watching now and then for the bus to come.

"You were extra fucked up."

Dani stands up as the bus rounds the corner, steadying herself against the back of the bench. She gives Marla a look like Marla's boring her. "Call it a bad night. It's over."

Marla knows she can press Dani more than other people can, but, looking at the bruise on Dani's jaw, she's not sure if she wants to. On the bus, Marla sits on her pillow and drums her feet against the wheel well. "Did you get Gavin high?"

Dani stares out the window and doesn't look at Marla. "Only pot."

"You guys got physical?"

Dani shrugs, still not looking at Marla. "You could say that."

"So, Gavin did something? I really wouldn't have thought—"

Dani faces Marla, grabbing her wrists. "Look, everything's peachy. I'm completely back in action now, ready to be your labour breathing support person extraordinaire."

"Um, okay." They stand up to get off. "So, you're good, Gavin's good?"

"I'm not speaking for him." Dani has the tiniest hint of a frown, just for a second. "I'm fine," she says firmly.

In class, the instructor lists pain medications for labour. Dani raises her hand repeatedly, talking too loud. "You don't need that shit, ladies. If I can push out a baby, so can you." The other moms-to-be are listening. They're all first-timers, most of them oldish with husbands. One young woman with her gay friend.

The baby class lady forges on, talking about medical emergencies and showing how big ten centimeters really is with a piece of PVC pipe.

"Those are just scare tactics. Labour isn't going to kill you." Dani looks at Marla. "It's the rest of life that does that."

The instructor hates Dani, and tells her so at the break. "Please keep your opinions to yourself."

Dani's not fazed. "Or what? You'll kick me out?" Marla was proud of Dani in the class, but now, in her oversized hoody and her hair spray, Dani looks cheap, like someone you know will waste a lot of time.

Marla pulls her aside. "Just be quiet, okay?"

Dani rolls her eyes, but she stops interrupting. The instructor talks about bathing babies and breastfeeding. How to burp. Each woman is given her own doll to practise diapering. The doll is weighted and lifelike with a head that flops horribly on the table. The doll's lips are puckered like it might smile.

Marla tries to get the diaper on, but it's upside down, so Dani puts her hands on Marla's, helping her lift the baby and slide the diaper out to flip it around. "Like this, Marla," she says, softly.

Marla strokes the doll's onesie, runs a finger along its head. Feels like real hair.

The instructor honks out a laugh. "If you leave your baby lying like that, you might get the golden shower!"

Dani gets right up in the instructor's face and whispers in a harsh, low voice. "Be nice to her. She's planning an adoption." Marla hears the word bounce around the room. It feels like everyone in the class is staring.

She puts her hand over the baby's face and turns away. "I can't do this."

The instructor is quick to butt in. "No, of course, I mean, I had no idea—"

"No." Dani's voice is firm and her arms are strong as she steers Marla to face the infant. "Pick her up. See what she feels like in your arms."

Marla knows this will start a wobble in the fine balance she's achieved of not thinking too much about anything, but she slides her forearm under the baby's head anyway and wraps her other arm around the tiny body. She's surprised by how heavy she is, and her forearm quivers. She holds the baby tighter to her chest. There's a part of her that wants this, the weight of a child. She cradles the baby's head, staring into its glass eyes.

Dani squeezes the baby's foot. She whispers to Marla, "See. You know what to do. Don't let them tell you that you don't."

Marla drops the doll on the table. It makes a thunking sound, then rests with its legs splayed. "Don't do this to me, Dani."

"What? Believe in you?"

"Mess this up. I have to get through this." The rest of the moms only pretend to diaper their babies. The young mom has her mouth open like a whale ready to swallow everyone.

Marla puts her warm hands on her belly. She tries to use a big voice, but it only comes as a whisper. "I'm making a brave choice."

Dani nods, slowly. "Oh, shit, Marla," she says, and puts her hands over Marla's. Dani drops her head, tears in her eyes, which Marla hasn't seen in years.

"What is it?" Marla uses her body to shield Dani from the instructor, who is hovering like she wants to make it all better.

"It's just—I'm sorry, you know?" Dani faces the rest of the class and points to Marla. "I look up to this woman." She holds onto Marla, and her breath hitches in Marla's ear. The last part comes out kind of choked up. "You're so much braver than I was."

The young mom nearest Dani pats Marla's shoulder. Her friend wraps his arms around both of them, and Marla feels everything slow down.

Women leave their plastic babies on tables and bump into Marla and Dani, soft and quiet and strong, until Marla is in a cave of love, encircled.

15. CHICKEN

JUSTIN IS TALL in an awkward way, with expensive clothes and a straight-brimmed hat like the little thugs in Belleville. Gavin can tell by the way he stands away from the bed, looking at the chair, that he is nervous.

He uses Signed English haltingly. "My mom ... spoke ... you deaf."

Gavin shakes his hand. *Pleasure to meet you, Justin.* He fingerspells his name. *I'm* G A V I N.

Justin gestures to the bandages on Gavin's head. "What ... wrong ... with ... you?"

Broke my ankle. No sense burdening a kid.

"On purpose?"

And there's no sense being dishonest. *Yeah. Attempted suicide.*

Justin comes closer, sits in the chair, taking off his hat. "I tried ... too."

Justin's mom leans on the doorframe, watching. Gavin likes her for not interrupting, and finding exactly what her son needed.

He's a nice kid, into drawing and rock climbing. Girls don't like him yet, and he has no deaf friends. Watching him, Gavin feels ordinary, but in an older way, like he's seen this part of the show already. He wonders if Justin will find love and then obliterate it. He wonders what kinds of mistakes a person can learn to live with.

Later, Justin leaves for his job at the library shelving books and his mom steps in, thanking Gavin. They make some plans to get together again, and then she says, "Sounds like you'll be discharged tomorrow. Take care of yourself."

When Marla and Dani get home, Dave and Elise are waiting outside in their SUV. They clamber out awkwardly, weighed down by shopping bags.

"Oh shit," Dani says. "I'm out of here." She scuttles through the gate and in the back door.

Elise rushes up, waving her arms like she's doing jumping jacks. "Marla, we're so sorry about Gavin."

Marla shrugs it off like her only biological family member who's not regularly in rehab trying to commit suicide is as important as what she ate for breakfast. Otherwise she might start crying again. "He's fine."

"We brought some things."

Right. They want her to let them in. "Why are you bringing stuff here? He's at the hospital."

"For you."

Inside, Marla opens the bags—a bunch of notebooks and pencils. A new laptop.

Dave claps his hand on her shoulder. "In case you want to go to school, after all this is over with."

The delivery wasn't perfect, but Marla's impressed by the sentiment. "Wow. Thank you, that's—"

Dani crashes up the stairs. "Where are they, Marla?"

The pills. "Plastic bag in the toilet tank."

Elise looks worried, like she might flutter. "Are you getting drugs for her?"

Marla speaks in a hushed voice. "It's a prescription. There's this thing with her son." And then she remembers Dani's meeting with Kamon. Fuck.

Elise shakes her head. "What a shame. There are so many people out there who really want children."

Elise obviously did not see Dani meticulously get dressed and put together presents on the last Friday of every month to visit her son. Except for the one day Marla and her dysfunctional brother screwed it up. There's a flicker in the hallway that Marla knows is Dani, listening to make sure Marla's not getting reamed out on her account. Marla sits up straight. She can handle this. "Listen, Dani looks out for me. She even came to baby class."

Dave nods, impressed. "That's positive."

Elise chews the inside of her lip like a dog with no bone. "What about the adoption? Have you found any nice families?"

"A few. We're meeting another couple tomorrow."

"I worry this might be too much for you. Are you on track with your timeline?"

Marla takes Elise's hands. "Yes. I made a list, okay, of things that I can ask for help with— like looking for a job, learning how to cook new recipes—and I can add applying for school. I would love your help, but not with this."

"We just want what's best for you."

"I'm all over it."

Dani nods in the hallway. *Better fucking believe it,* she mouths. Marla smiles in acknowledgment, feeling pretty grown up.

Gavin being discharged tomorrow.
Will he see me?
Don't know.

This time Cynthia is there with her smart heels and her shoulder bag. She's wearing social worker incognito, which looks a lot like what Liam calls business casual: a solid colour power skirt that goes to the knee, blouse, and a scarf tied really pretty with tufts that Marla admires.

Cynthia allows Liam to pull her chair out for her and push her in, and she smiles at Marla as she opens her napkin and lays it on her lap.

Marla, who had been seated by Liam five minutes ago, promptly opens her own napkin, dumping the cutlery on the table with a loud clank before spreading the napkin carefully under her baby. She can't get as close to the table as she would like, even by turning her chair slightly sideways.

"They just texted that they're parking the car," Cynthia says. "Hannah didn't want you to think she would be late."

Marla feels immediate sympathy for Hannah, who she pictures looking in the flip-down mirror to check her hair and makeup, smoothing her dress, anxiety rising in her throat, asking her husband if she looks okay, because this could be it, we really want to be on our best here and I can't believe the traffic! She's probably got a real hustle on, running carefully so as not to appear out of breath or windswept. Josh is probably holding her purse for her and clicking the car locks without looking back to see if he rolled up the windows.

"These people are amazing on paper," Liam is saying. "They were my first choice."

They have good jobs and lots of education, but Marla likes them because they seem really normal. They ride bikes along the river and try a new restaurant every month. "They love each other," she says. Who wouldn't want that?

Marla knows it's them in the doorway as soon as she sees them. Hannah is breathing with her hand on her chest, her lips pursed like the baby lady told Marla to do when she's in labour. Blowing it out. She looks just like her picture, which Marla's been holding in her head: Hannah with her head softly tilted, gazing up at the camera from the beach. This Hannah is just like that, Marla tells herself. Please be just like that.

Josh is grinning and looking around, and when he sees Marla parked right up to the side of the table he loses all the tension in his shoulders and clasps his hands. Something is wrong with the way he is looking at her—she can't read his eyes, and then she realizes it's because they're watering. All gratitude.

Cynthia notices Hannah and Josh and waves them over, but Marla has already gotten up. She bumps between tables, sideways-ing it, her arms open until they meet in the middle of the restaurant. Hannah enfolds her in a hug. Josh has his arm around them both.

"Hello, Marla," Hannah whispers.

Marla wants this moment to last forever, the way she's crying and being held and holding someone else and the baby is between them, a person with so much love. She meets Liam's eye across the restaurant. He's on his way, nodding and biting his lip to keep from spilling over too.

We found them.
found who, honey?
a mom and dad. so perfect.
will they let us visit?

Nephew measurements:

Weeks	Waist
15	29 inches
18	30.5 inches
19	30.75 inches
22	31.5 inches
25	33 inches
26	33.5 inches
28	35 inches
30	36 inches
33	38 inches
36	39 inches
38	39.5 inches

Marla sleeps in Gavin's room because he's not answering her texts. Except she can't sleep because the broken crib makes her cry. She picks through the pieces, looking for what is salvageable. She takes the sandpaper from the shelf and smooths the rough edges, thinking about what she should do.

She texts Liam. *need to see Gavin.*

The pages of his handbook are scattered around, and she

sets down the wood to collect them. Every page is something different: poetry, drawings, origami in pockets. An eggplant recipe. Pieces of a patchwork quilt.

Her phone buzzes. *He's working out some stuff and said no distractions.*

It's killing her she doesn't know what happened. *What stuff?*

Not up to me to say. I think he's actually an angry person.

Angry? Marla uncoils the orange scarf she's wearing and examines it. It's just right: soft and vibrant. Marla shears it into long strips, then cuts the strips into angular shapes. Rectangle, square, rhombus, triangle. She glues them onto the thick cardboard of the diaper box, making bumps in the fabric on purpose. There's an art word for this that Elise would know, but Marla doesn't care. She's going on gut.

I'm coming tomorrow morning. She unravels a pink baby toque and glues bits of yarn here and there like cotton candy drizzle. This is how she would make her binder if she wanted to adopt a kid.

I'll let him know. If he wants to visit he can be there.

Liam and Gavin are kinda similar, now that she thinks of it. Rule-oriented. Careful about how they look. Don't like surprises. Didn't have fathers. While the front and back covers dry, Marla lays out the ripped-up pages and tapes them back together. She uses scotch tape and stickers and band-aids. She draws faces and trees. She traces the words Gavin wrote and cries.

She cuts out an ultrasound picture and tapes it down. She writes "Gavin's Nephew" below it. She binds all the pages together with clips she's lifted from the medical clinic, and elastic bands them between the covers. On the outside, she writes with permanent marker, "A Handbook for a Beautiful Person."

Marla brings the handbook for Gavin, and for Liam, one of the nude drawings she sat for. It's a picture she loves because of the geometry of her body: her triangle leg and her half circle arm, her watermelon baby and her dark round nipples. She's going to ask Gavin to move back in with her.

Gavin is watching it storm from a lounge chair on the deck, his crutches by his side. He's shaved his head, which makes him look smaller. Younger. Lightning snakes against the sky, and he taps the chair, counting the seconds like she taught him to years ago, his other hand flat on the glass so he can feel the thunder. She puts her hand on his. "Come inside," she tells him. "I miss you."

His smile seems hopeful, like he was afraid she wouldn't come. "How are you feeling?" he asks. He signs at the same time, and Marla's taken aback.

"I'm good. How about you?"

Gavin ladles something off the stove into a mug, something meaty with bones in it, which makes Marla think of hot dog water. "Working on getting better. I met with another deaf guy today, a mentorship kind of thing. It's part of my list." He unfurls it to show her.

It's a huge list, with bullet points and cross-references. She skims, getting the gist of things. Meet more deaf people, find his dad, a bunch of dietary and training stuff. Go back to school. "This is a lot to do."

"I know." Gavin takes a sip of the steaming meat water and looks down. Marla doesn't like to see him stooped over.

"But you're signing again. That's good."

He nods at Liam. "He's into it."

Marla feels instantly better. This is the Gavin she knew, the guy who just needed some encouragement. "Sure. I mean, we could sign too." She points for "we."

"Look, I have something to say to you, Marla."

Liam shakes his head almost imperceptibly. Just the way he looks at Gavin makes Marla think she doesn't want to know.

She dodges. "Sure, but first, I brought this." Marla pulls the handbook out of her coat. "I thought it was such a shame it was all torn up—you should have it back now that you're getting better."

Gavin leaves the book closed, as if admiring the front cover. Marla's feeling all proud of herself for the excellent gluing she did and how the letters are all the same size when she notices Gavin's crying on it. He hands it back without opening it. "This isn't who I am." His signs are angry, jerking and big.

Liam holds Gavin by the shoulders. "This might be too much for you."

"No, I want to tell her." Gavin looks afraid and yet defiant, like how Marla imagines he looked before he jumped. His voice is loud. "I raped Dani. That's why I tried to kill myself. Because I'm a rapist."

For a moment Marla finds herself back at the Banff Springs Hotel. The pudgy, spectacled man had paid extra for her because Jim told him that Marla was only thirteen. It was a lie, but a lie she was used to. She played it up, acted the part of a little girl because that was what she was good at. Pretending. Something about the straightness of her hair, her long stomach with the hipbones pointing out, the smell of cigarettes. It's hot, and for a second Marla forgets what summer she's in. What afternoon. A fuzzy feeling, like the sound of shattered glass.

"I don't feel right," she says, but her voice seems far away. Liam hardly turns towards her before she collapses.

It's Gavin who understands what's happening, who drops his crutches and hops with his arms outstretched. She feels herself slipping down into his arms. Slow and soft and black.

"We have to call your doctor, Marla." Liam is leaning over her with wide eyes.

The lights are brighter than before. The handbook is on the floor beside her, some of its pages loose. "Where's Gavin?"

Liam helps her sit up, and she has a sick, embarrassed feeling in her stomach like everything is wrong. Liam pulls at his earlobe. "He's not here."

Her suicidal brother is out in a thunderstorm. Her brother who is deaf and imperfect and full of self-hatred because he raped Dani. "We have to find him."

"You're not leaving, Marla. You're nine months pregnant, and you just fainted."

Marla shakes him off. "It's the humidity. I'm just hot." She feels the baby, but there's no kicking right now. "Did I fall on the baby?"

"No. But I think you should get checked out."

"Okay. As soon as I find him."

Liam hands her a glass of water. "He has an umbrella and a bus pass. He said he'd be back after lunch."

Oh. Marla tries to shake it off. It's just another thing that's going to be in the back of her head every time Gavin is late or testy or looking at her funny. Yet another thing. "Did he really do that? I mean, with Dani?"

"You should talk to her, Marla. Make sure she's okay."

Marla swallows. She wants to think Gavin wouldn't do that, couldn't do that, but she's forced to admit she doesn't know. Marla feels fiercely protective of Dani and wants to get home and wrap her arms around her friend and spend the night punching pillows until they both feel better. There were other times like this.

Marla grabs her coat. She leaves Gavin's handbook on the floor. "Let's go to the hospital, then."

"What about Gavin?"

"What about him?"

Marla doesn't sit in emergency long before they bring her to the maternity ward and put her on a bed. She tells them about the fainting: no, it hasn't happened before; no, she hasn't had any contractions or bleeding. Thirty-eight weeks. She keeps her knees up, feet together. Liam stands beside her, holding her purse.

"Have you had the fetal monitor before?" the nurse asks.

Marla shakes her head.

"We're going to listen to Baby for ten minutes, make sure everything's okay." The nurse bustles around the room setting it up.

Marla pretends she's not there. "I think Gavin's right. Dani should press charges."

The nurse smiles at Marla like she didn't hear. "Your first baby?"

Marla nods, barely glancing up at her.

"That's wonderful. Boy or girl?"

Marla shakes her head. Something happened within the last month. Everyone who judged her when her bump was a cantaloupe is now bamboozled by the baby. Marla doesn't factor in at all anymore. "We don't know," she says, tight. She slides her legs down on the bed, scraping her shoes against the paper sheet.

Liam clears his throat, embarrassed. "It will be a surprise," he says.

The nurse lifts Marla's shirt to wrap a belt thingy around her belly. "So long as Baby's healthy, right? That's what I always say." She runs a finger along the scar that used to be under Marla's breast and has now travelled onto her ballooning shape. The nurse's eyes go hard. "What's this about, dearie?"

Dearie? "I don't want to talk about it."

The nurse cocks her head like she knows everything. "Why not?" She leans down close. "You a cutter?"

Marla looks her square in the eye. "It's from a rape, okay? A guy cut me up while he was raping me."

The nurse's face immediately falls apart, and Marla feels sorry. "Oh," the nurse says, dropping something on the floor. "I'm sorry." She glances at Liam as she retrieves it, a clicker-type thing attached to the monitor. "This button, press it every time Baby kicks," she says, and scurries out.

Liam puts both hands on the scar, his fingers on the crest of it as if he could push it back together. "Why didn't you tell me?"

Marla shrugs. Click. "I don't talk about it."

He runs his thumb down its length, looking into Marla's eyes. "Maybe you should. I mean, with Dani too."

Marla sucks in a breath through her teeth. This feels like a conversation she had with Dave and Elise once, hundreds of years ago when she was the only person that mattered. "I feel so shitty for her." Click.

"She needs you."

Click. "It's my fault. I mean, it's my own brother." Marla knows that men undressed can be different than men in their clothes. Some are scary—sweat dripping from their faces. Some are cold and hold their jaws firm, and some just laugh.

"It's okay to be angry."

"No, it's more like total shock. Gavin? I looked after him, cared for him." *Click. Clickity-click.*

"Let me worry about him."

Liam and Gavin. Marla and Dani. Marla hesitates. "We make a good team, you know? Getting through crazy stuff."

Liam gives Marla the kind of smile a person gives to the homeless. An afraid, sad smile. Click.

The nurse returns and reads the printout from the fetal monitor. She's put on a chipper face. "Baby's busy, hey?" She pauses for Marla to respond, but when she doesn't, the nurse just smiles a big empty smile. "Five more minutes."

Marla waits until she leaves, then sits up, shifting the belt thingy so it doesn't scratch against her skin like a giant belly bra. "I want it to be just you and me." *Click.* "Not like a daytime talk show where the baby's born and we never see each other again."

"Is that what you think? Oh, Marla." Liam holds her hand. The fetal monitor beeps and blips.

"Look, I'm sorry I never told you everything. It's not pretty."

"Marla, I can handle not pretty. I just wish we could have started the hard stuff sooner." Liam turns away.

Marla stares at the ceiling to stop herself from crying as the nurse returns to unstrap her and take the printout. She glances at the wiggly lines and nods. "The doctor will have to look at this, but I think everything's fine. Baby is active, your vitals are normal. I don't think you need to worry." She wipes the ultrasound gel off Marla's abdomen and sees Marla's red eyes. She leans close. "I'm sorry about before. I didn't realize."

Marla reaches up and hugs her, pulling the nurse against her body. The nurse is surprised, but folds her arms around Marla like she's seen loads of people cry today and she made them all feel better. She smells like bar soap and laundry detergent. Flowers and spring.

"Everything's going to be okay, right?" Marla asks.

"Of course it is." The nurse rubs Marla's back and smiles at Liam. "Come over here, Dad." She takes Liam's hand and puts it on Marla where her own was. His hand feels cold and stiff. The nurse moves it around for him. "Just hormones, hey?" She squeezes Marla's knee. "I'm going to ask the doctor about that cast, too. It's probably time you had that off."

When she leaves, Liam mumbles something about the parking meter or the vending machine and Marla curls up and stares out the window. Cars are driving by on 16th Avenue, headlights racing down to Bowness.

Marla rubs her belly. Of course her rock star baby is fine. He's strong and right and totally undamaged. Something sticking out of her pocket scratches her arm, and Marla pulls it out—the nude drawing. Her faraway eyes are the second thing she sees. The baby takes up her whole middle, frozen inside her forever in the sketch.

This baby is all she has, and now he's almost gone too.

Once Marla gets her cast off, Liam tells her all the right things in the car: you're going to be okay. We can do this. I care about you. He just forgets the one she really wants to hear: I love you. He applies the brake gently so Marla and her bump can ride comfortably. He takes corners like an old person just for her. He listens to jazz. She bends her arm this way and that as if it's a totally new limb. She refuses to cry.

After Liam drops her off, Marla pretends to go in the front door, watching to be sure he is gone before reaching for the cigarettes hidden in the mailbox. She lights one and sits on the step, wishing it was dark so she could see the flickering lights of Dani's TV on the lawn and know everything is okay. Dani should have heard Marla come home—should be waiting for the car door slamming and Marla's footsteps on the stairs—but Marla can't face her yet.

The sky looks heavy again like more rain is coming. Marla needs the power of these storms to wash away the dust and make the trees grow, to give and renew because she feels so empty. The worst part is the way Dani's going to smile and brush this off like it's nothing at all, and then lie because that is something Dani can do like no one else. Lie for Marla, because she would always choose Marla over herself.

Marla smokes the cigarette with shallow puffs just in case that's better for her baby. She read somewhere that light cigarettes are just as bad so she bought regular. As soon as Dani comes, she's going to put it out. But Dani doesn't come. She holds the cigarette until the filter is burning, then stubs it out and hides the butt under the steps. She tiptoes inside past Zigzag sleeping on the couch, then down the stairs, not sure what she's afraid of, only that the silence is overwhelming. "Dani?" Her voice sounds an echo, and she wishes someone else were here. Anyone else.

When Marla rounds the corner, she can see the TV on mute. There's a bowl of fluorescent cheese puffs spilled on the table, and Dani's pop mug beside it. Fast food garbage is heaped beside the chair where Dani sits with her head back and her mouth open. Sprawling and grinning. "Marla, you're here already!" she slurs. She shakes her head hard, waking her eyes up.

Marla feels responsible. This is exactly how it wasn't supposed to be. "I'm sorry, Dani, about Gavin. He told me what happened." She leans close to put her arm on Dani's shoulder, like patting her would help.

"That was nothing. You think I'm put out by a little fucking?" She rocks back dangerously in her chair.

Marla struggles to find something to say, something that will mean anything. "It's shitty of him. I hate him."

Dani laughs, a sputtering sound. "I already forgot him." Dani pulls a baggie of meth from under the cushion. Marla thought she gave that up years ago for Kamon.

"Where's the pills we just got?"

Dani shrugs, waving her lighter around.

Marla backs up, tripping on a cardboard burger box. "Gavin won't bother you anymore."

Dani lights the bowl and inhales deeply. "Nothing bothers me anymore." She laughs so hard she starts coughing. "Fuck."

Marla wants another cigarette and hates herself for it. She should go.

"Just you and me, babe." Dani starts singing some old song in a perfect falsetto. It's silly at first, but Dani can't help getting serious. She's breathing with her diaphragm, signalling the beat with the fingers of her left hand. It sounds so beautiful that Marla starts crying. "Don't stop, Dani," Marla whispers.

Dani leaps from the chair and uses her dirty old spoon as a microphone. She wails it out, not even singing words, just scatting around the basement in her housecoat. Her breasts bounce and her hair flaps against her head as her moves get very disco. She John Travoltas it, puts in a spin, then moonwalks, her feet smooth and solid. Her sound is bright and sharp, and for a moment Marla forgets.

Dani gives one last vibrating yowl with her face pointed at the ceiling and ends with her fist in the air. "Boo ya, Marla. I haven't done that shit in so long."

She flops back into her chair, panting, but it's Marla's chest that heaves, like she's the one who's been dancing at a club with lots of noise in the near dark with too many people beside her. Marla's breathing too fast.

Dani takes an empty fast food bag from the floor and holds it over Marla's mouth. "Breathe in. You're gonna live." She strokes Marla's hair with her other hand. "Look how many people care about you." The bag fills and deflates.

That's what Gavin said: no one worries about her and she'll be fine. Marla smashes the full bag with a satisfying pop. "I'm sad, okay? I'm allowed to be sad."

"Sure. Be sad. I'm sad all the fucking time."

Marla holds the broken bag in her hand. "Shouldn't you do something about it? Shouldn't I?"

Dani takes a huge hit then offers the pipe to Marla. "Stop dwelling, girlfriend."

Marla takes the pipe and the fluorescent lights buzz. The pipe looks pretty in her hand with the designs in the blown glass, and nothing would be easier than to let Dani show her a new trick, but there is something about how the light is glinting off it. It takes Marla a moment to remember who else was mesmerized by holding Dani's pipe: Kamon. Marla dumps the bowl out on the floor and then throws the pipe at Dani. "I'm having a baby, dumbass."

Dani jumps out of her chair, suddenly much larger than before. "Do not do that, Marla. Now I gotta pick this shit out of the carpet."

Marla doesn't bend down to help. Crystal meth. Fuck. "Seriously."

"You're shitting me, right? Did I not just make everything all better?" Dani talks in a baby voice that Marla can't stand.

"No, you didn't. You mess everything up and then wait for the worst to happen." In Dani's dark basement with its fast food smell, Marla says the first thing that comes to mind. "I think you asked for it."

Bad move. Dani cups Marla's face in her hands so Marla can't back away. "Learn with me a minute, Marla."

Marla is sure Dani can hear her heart thumping. "What if I don't want to?"

"You do, or you wouldn't be here mouthing off like a little punkass. I know he's your brother. I respect that. But you owe me some dignity. I just—" She lets her hand fall from Marla's face and closes her eyes.

"What is it?"

"Nothing."

"Liar. Talk to me."

Dani pulls her in close, crying. "It's never been like this."

Marla holds Dani, stroking her hair, getting it, finally. "You loved him."

"That shitty fucker. Yeah. I did." Dani wipes her eyes with her forearm and sinks into her chair. "Serves me right."

"Don't say that. No one deserves that."

"You're damn right."

Marla lights a cigarette and holds it, lets it grow a long leg of ash while she watches the news with no sound, trying to think. A red ribbon's been running along the bottom of the screen. "It says there's a flood warning."

"We'll be fine. It didn't happen last time."

Marla flips to CBC. "They're evacuating people to rescue centres."

"Whatever."

Her phone rings. Liam. "Hello?"

"Did you hear?"

Marla doesn't recognize the river she sees on TV. The water is just a foot and a half below the lower deck of the Centre Street bridge. It's coming hard, brown and angry, full of trees and debris. The path alongside the river has been washed out in places. People are hanging over the edge of the upper deck, watching water run. "I'm just seeing it."

"I'm coming to pick you and Dani up. Is she there?"

Marla looks at Dani with her housecoat spilling open. "Yeah. I don't know if she'll come."

Dani raises her eyebrows. "Is that your boyfriend?"

"No," Marla says, softly. "It's Liam."

16. PUMPKIN

GAVIN DOES TRICEPS DIPS in the spare room at Liam's house. He is shirtless, sweating. When he's done one hundred he can check them off his list.

He stands up, and Dani is right in front of him. "Sorry," he says, startled.

Dani spreads out in the doorway, blocking it. She slurps from a pop can. "This would have been a better week to jump." Marla and Liam peer from the hall, looking unsure whether to intervene.

Gavin grabs his shirt. "I'm leaving. I won't bother you."

"Where are you ...?" Marla asks.

"To a hotel." Gavin glances at Liam. "I should have left already."

Dani snorts, and Gavin jumps. "Don't bother. You clearly can't be alone. I'm going to bed." She trails down the hall to the couch and crumples onto it.

She's here, and this is it. Gavin knows it. There's no time to be afraid. He kneels by her head to whisper even though he knows Marla and Liam can probably hear from the kitchen because he whispers like a deaf person. "I hate myself for what I did to you."

Dani nods, deadpan. "I hate you too."

She's trying to make light of it, make it easier for everyone. Gavin looks at the makeup line under her jaw where she hasn't blended it in, her red eyes. "Don't be funny now. Please."

"I'm not. Look, you're this sensitive, journaling fucking kid. You're not even old enough to know what you're doing."

"Not true." Gavin can't say it, how he wanted to punish her for never hiding anything. "I'm going to turn myself in."

"No one's going to put you in jail over me. You have major anger issues, but you don't need to quit." She pulls her pipe out and lights it. "Keep trying."

"Like this?" She allows him to take the pipe from her, and the lighter, her fingers against his. He puts the pipe in his mouth and flicks the lighter.

"No, you dipshit." She yanks the pipe away, then sits up abruptly and empties her pockets onto the table. Pills and rolling papers, a spoon. Needles. "This is what it looks like, how I keep myself from getting sick, okay? I can't even get high anymore." She kicks at the table, but carefully, so nothing falls off.

"I know."

Dani fits it all back into her pockets. "Doesn't matter. To you and everyone else I'm just a burnt-out hooker." She jiggles her breasts.

He shakes his head, and tears spill down his cheeks. "No. You're my friend. My best friend." Gavin reaches for her hands, tentative, because he sees a tremble in her lip that means something.

She slaps his hands away. "You can't touch me anymore, Gavin. You don't know what friendship is."

"You're right." She looks away like she's tired of talking to him, but he has to say it. "Before this, you helped me, you listened to me, and I am so grateful for that."

Dani leans in close, her nostrils flared. "You think it's your deafness that sets you apart, but it's not. It's the way you punch things up when you freak out. It's fucked up." She stares him down, and he turns away.

In the kitchen, Marla slams things around, not putting them away, just picking them up and banging them into new places.

Liam takes the teapot out of her hands, so she picks up the toaster instead. "You love her." She drops the toaster on the table in front of Gavin like a challenge.

He whispers, worried they'll wake Dani. "I'm sorry, Marla."

Marla's talking like she hasn't heard him. "How ... rape ..." Gavin sucks in a terrible little breath at that word.

Liam reaches for Marla, folding his arms around her middle until she leans into him. "Be angry, if you have too." He signals Gavin to get his bag.

She shakes her head, disentangles herself from Liam. "... not good enough ... me."

It's hard to look at her. "I'm going to make it up to you, to everyone. I've got this list and a counsellor—" Gavin's voice shakes, wobbling between his useless ears.

"You'll have to," she says. Marla stands in the doorway watching him sob, and Gavin thinks about how much she looks like their mother. "Look, I can't be around you right now."

Liam says something to Marla that Gavin can't catch, and she turns to him. "Sounds really bad," she says.

"I don't know," Liam says. "Last time it was really just High River."

It's only seconds before Dani is in the doorway. "Kamon," she says. "I need to go there right now."

Marla stays home to sleep, so Gavin goes with Liam and Dani to the rec centre in High River. Inside, a smattering of moms and elderly people supervise kids running between cots. Near the main entrance is a kitchen, where sandal-footed women and teens make sandwiches. A senior with a clipboard sits at a table. She squints at them and says something Gavin can't understand. No one translates.

"No," Dani says, and then a small person breaks out of the game of tag and wraps himself around Dani's legs. He is towheaded and freckled and so obviously Dani's son that Gavin's heart breaks.

"Mommy Mommy Mommy!" the boy squeals. She squeezes him, kissing him until he starts arching his back. "I can't fucking breathe!"

Dani sets him down. "Kamon, don't talk that way. Wave to my friend, Liam. This is Gavin." She catches Liam staring at her. "What? He has a problem with profanity."

Liam grins so hard all his teeth are showing. "Interesting."

"Hi ... Gavin," Kamon says, his body wagging with his wave. "Holy shit ... the water ... pick one toy..." Kamon speaks in a hurry with his head wiggling all about and his eyebrows raised as if every phrase is a question. He looks right at Gavin. "Are you ... boyfriend?"

Gavin feels the sick stab of shame. He shakes his head.

"You know ... Mommy gets all better ... with her instead ... bring your pillow, Mommy?"

"No, baby. Where's Nanny?" She takes a stick of gum from her pocket and unwraps it. Kamon grabs it.

He points to the kitchen. Another little boy runs up to him, and Kamon talks with his hands in his excitement. "My mommy's here, sucker!" He jumps on two feet all the way to the kitchen, leaving the other boy behind. Dani watches him go.

She throws the gum wrapper in the garbage can, pausing there, then suddenly shakes out her coat pockets as if they were full of sand. Pants pockets too. She dumps her pills, keeping her eyes on Gavin. He swallows a lump in his throat, and this time it feels good.

The kitchen smells like ham. A short woman with thighs that touch and a rolled-up long-sleeved shirt leaves the bread she was buttering. Dani's mom, Sandra. She's angry. "... tried to call ... Danielle."

Liam takes the slices she's buttered and lays meat on them, arranging it just so. Gavin starts washing lettuce. It puddles in the sink. He doesn't see a salad spinner, so he dries it with paper towel, which makes little white pieces of paper stick all over it.

"Sorry, Mom, I forgot my phone. We got evacuated too."

"... that business ... before."

Kamon leans in closer. "Nanny said ... welfare ... useless. You're not ... Mommy?"

Dani glances at Gavin, and he suddenly feels her fear. All the women in the kitchen are staring at her and pretending not to. Dani gets down on her knees and puts her hands on Kamon's shoulders. "Me? Useless? Never. But I did have some hard days. 'Member when we talked about hard days?"

"... lots right?"

"Yep. All hard days for a while. But not anymore." She nods to herself.

Sandra snorts. "... clean this time? ... long?"

"For good. Look, you're busy here. I'll take Kamon for a sleepover."

"Yes yes yes yes motherfuckers!" Kamon pounds his fist into the air, then whirls around the room with his lips pursed, blowing air. He bumps into a woman carrying two loaves of bread and bashes one of them to the floor by accident, where he steps on it.

Sandra narrows her eyes at him. "Get out of here, Kamon!" He rushes out, and Sandra shakes her head, arguing. Dani's mom looks old, deep crow's feet around her eyes, thin hair.

Dani takes Sandra's arm. "Listen, I'm staying at Marla's boyfriend's house." She nods at Liam. "Nothing will happen."

Sandra shakes her head like only she could have so much suffering. "... basement already flooded, you know ... really bad."

Gavin thinks of his list at home—sit ups and weight lifting and not making a baby present for his nephew because he broke it. "I could help." He signs "I" and "help", then lets his hands fall to his sides when everyone stares. This is exactly the kind of place he can't make it work.

Sandra is momentarily startled by the sound of his voice. "... earth can he do?"

Dani catches the look on Gavin's face. "Maybe he could fill

sandbags." She stage winks at him. "By the river."

Gavin cannot believe she just made a suicide joke, but he laughs, and it feels less hollow than he thought it would. This is what real people do, he thinks. They go out and make sandwiches and sandbags instead of sitting around feeling shitty.

"We have a plan," Dani says, already taking giant strides out to the open hall. She cups a hand to her mouth to call her son, but her lips don't look like English words. Gavin thinks she must be yodelling.

Whatever she said has the whole hall of kids running to her. Kamon shrieks something that looks like, "*Ariba*! *Ariba*!"

"Get your toy, little guy."

Kamon nods and pulls it out of his pocket. A green turtle. "... got it, Mommy ... I keep ... right here." He has a smile on his face that burns a hole in Gavin's heart.

At the riverbank, Gavin works through the night, his arms strong and his mind perfectly empty, his crutches abandoned in the back of someone's pickup. There is an irresistible togetherness about these people, these foothills people who Gavin had thought were too proud, too self-involved. They work together with such energy, without the grimness Gavin finds in himself. They smile at him and help him, and Gavin feels welcome.

When people leave, others come. Guys aim their headlights at the berm they're building, then work in a dirty, wet line. Everyone is ready for the roast beef buns with potato salad that older women bring at eleven o'clock. Gavin fills sandbags, passes them person to person. Some people are in knee-deep water.

The way the river moves is so convincing, like it should be washing over the road and filling up the town. He understands the water sliding under cars and around their wheels, going everywhere it can. It's how Gavin feels most of the time, if he thinks about it, worried that everything will spill over and be uncontained. Overwhelmed. But this is easy—with enough sandbags and people it might be possible to coax a broken river to be tame and quiet. Whether it works doesn't matter to Gavin. It matters that these people know exactly what to do.

Trees and garbage cans hurtle down the river, dragged downhill. That's all there really is—gravity. Inertia. The work is rewarding, but gravity is winning. At dawn, he can see that no amount of sandbagging will prevent this town from washing out. And so, Gavin paddles in a flotilla of canoes and rowboats and dinghies, rescuing people whose houses are already filling up with water. Everyone works together, stern, yet resolute. This is their town. When he feels tired, he thinks about Kamon. Dani told him everything would be all right.

Gavin gets a ride back to Calgary with a guy named Keel, which seems like a last name, although Gavin isn't sure. He has a boxy head, and he's wearing real overalls, not just ripped sweats like Gavin. He smokes in the truck with the window open.

Gavin tells Keel to drop him off in Sunnyside, which is where Keel's girlfriend's basement suite is. "Hope ... flooded ... all this shit, you wouldn't believe." Gavin nods to be polite, trying to think of what he could lose that would mean anything at all.

Keel parks in front of a pale purple house. There's water on the road now, so much that Liam's little car wouldn't have made it. The lights are out all down the street but there's a note taped to the door.

Keel rips it off, slopping through the lawn in his boots. "... gone ... school that's where people ... you're okay?"

Gavin nods, staring at Keel's girlfriend's empty house. No one lives here tonight, and maybe for a lot of nights. When Gavin turns around, Keel is gone.

Gavin wades down Memorial Drive to the bridge at Centre Street, trying to picture this water laying on the flat floodplain across the river that is downtown. Tonight, the stone lions look angry. He had read that they were copied from the lions of Trafalgar Square for the northern gateway to downtown, and that they were rumoured to wander Chinatown at night. The bridge is longer than it needed to be, crossing the river at an angle to stay on axis and make a dramatic entrance. Maybe it's hubris, not just for him, but for this whole city—nothing and no one can ceaselessly reinvent while ignoring reality. But that's unfair. No one is personally responsible for the way the river rushes, how it can't handle all the water coming down. He wishes he could hear it. It would be so much louder than the thoughts in his head.

Water sloshes against the lower bridge deck, which is now closed to traffic. Gavin walks uphill to Liam's, past the video store and the carwash and the diner. He turns right at the lights.

The door is open for him, the light on. No one is awake.

Gavin peeks in the spare room to see Dani and Marla in the early morning light, Kamon on the floor. He watches them sleeping, Dani's bare legs sticking out of the sheets, Marla's heavy belly on its side, like she ate a rock. They're safe. This is what he can't lose. He feels a terrible surge of protectiveness, wishing everything could be this simple and right forever. Dani rolls over in her sleep, then leans over the bed and pukes into a mixing bowl. Gavin steps back, conscious of his dirty clothes and bumps into the doorway. He feels too big for this space, too fucked up and messy, and goes back outside to sleep on the porch.

The morning is promising, with birds squawking and sunlight streaming in. Seems like a long time since the weather has been dry. Or hot. Marla sits up, sweaty in just a tank top and panties, peeling herself from Dani, who's curled in a ball, clammy and rank.

Marla pulls clothes on to take Dani's puke bowl to the toilet, but scrapes her bellybutton against the counter. Ouch. She remembers Dani telling her how big she would get and not believing her. No one's been pregnant forever, she tells herself, but it's hard to believe. Eight days until her due date.

Marla puts a cold cloth on Dani's head and a roll of toilet paper beside the bowl. Kamon's sleeping, his mouth open with drool hanging out. He seems like a happy enough kid, proud of his special backpack with some cartoon character on it and sleeping like a starfish. She gets that having Dani as a mom would not be awesome, but Kamon looks like any kid you'd see getting on a school bus or having a water fight. A totally normal little guy.

She makes eggs and coffee, not wanting to hear the news. It's probably fine, she tells herself. She'll go back to her regular life, and everyone who was hoping for a really big thing will be disappointed. Like making history really matters.

Liam's wearing only his robe when he appears, scrolling on his phone. "Looks like your place is in the do-not-re-enter zone. Bow River expected to crest today."

"You mean it's under water?"

"Well, the basement will be flooded." He turns on the TV, and images of cars up to their windows in water and houses washing under bridges appear. "I'm sorry."

Gavin walks through the patio door with his same dirty jeans on. He leans his crutches on the couch and watches the news. "Going back out," he says, signing. "It's bad."

"Did you sleep outside?" Liam asks, signing sleep. Gavin nods. Marla squints at him. It's hard not to be annoyed with how he's always doing something a bit bigger than anyone else. She tells herself to shake it off because Liam's standing right there. She hands Gavin a plate of eggs, wondering if he'll eat it.

He takes it with full eye contact. "Thank you, Marla," he says. He eats standing up, watching her. Waiting.

"I'm glad the sandbags are helping you," she says, but it feels really lame.

"I'm not doing it for me," he says. He scrapes his fork against his plate to get the last bits of egg.

She waits until he turns to put his plate in the dishwasher.

"I think you kind of are," she says, knowing he can't see her mouth.

"Don't," Liam says. Gavin spins around. He probably knows they're talking about him, but Marla doesn't apologize.

"Where's Zigzag?" Gavin asks.

Shit. The dog. Marla tries to remember if she left her window open. She thinks she did. "We have to go back."

"As soon as we can." Liam thanks her for breakfast. He doesn't kiss Marla goodbye, or ask if she'll be alright even though she's massively pregnant. If she needs anything, like an ice cream bar or a hug. After Liam leaves for work and Gavin leaves to be a martyr, Marla stands in the window like an old woman waiting for family to call or visit or need her somehow. Like Elise probably does. It's an ugly feeling.

Soon enough she can hear Kamon jabbering, and she feels a stab of hatred. Even Dani, stinking of withdrawal, has a kid who truly loves her. Marla abruptly steps away from the window, letting the curtains block out the sunlight.

When Marla's baby doesn't come that day or the next, they pile into the car to rescue Kamon's puppy. Gavin knows it's a distraction, one Marla needs.

Marla's street is full of brown river mud. The high-water mark is clearly visible on garage doors and telephone poles at the height of a truck's side mirror. Others have come back, and in front of their houses are piles of sodden furniture, carpet, electronics, and ripped out drywall with threads of mould. Cars full of muck, tractors pushing garbage.

They squelch up together, Kamon piggybacked by Dani and Gavin's ankle wrapped in a garbage bag. He repeats what Liam told him in his head: Marla's dealing with a lot right now. She loves you. She'll forgive you. As they get closer, Liam smiles at something.

"What did they say?" Gavin asks.

"Kamon asked if it's going to be all fucking watery."

Dani's making a sad face. "It might be yucky, too yucky to live in right now."

"Where ... water ... go?"

"Back into the river."

"But why ... come out?"

"That's how it is sometimes." She gives Kamon a little squeeze. "It's okay. You'll see."

Gavin's touched at how she speaks to him, not like he's a nuisance or an idiot. Just explaining so he can understand. Gavin feels left out somehow, like he could have known her real self, gotten under her bravado and been taken care of, but now he cannot. This way of speaking is only for her son. He resents it, then feels really good about it. She should love Kamon more than anyone else.

"You know, my mom used to swear like a sailor too," Liam says. "And look how I turned out."

Dani and Gavin laugh, but not Marla. She jiggles her key in the lock. As soon as she opens the door, Zigzag bursts out. He has his tail between his legs, pissing and whining. Kamon squeals, trying to hold him.

Marla sniffs inside. She says something to Liam.

"I'll get one," Liam says. "Flashlight," he tells Gavin. Liam walks with efficiency, even in mud. Gavin reminds himself to stand up straight. He can do this.

Dani takes Kamon to the backyard to check out river garbage, but Gavin follows Marla into the house. The basement still has water in it, and black mould climbing the walls. The wooden doorframes are warped and the whole place has a terribly earthy, filthy smell. A plastic bowl of Dani's floats near the stairwell. Upstairs, some of the chairs have tipped over, but Dani's records are safe in their crates on the counter.

Marla's in her bedroom with a black garbage bag clutched to her chest, her head bent over it. There's still some wetness on the floor. "What is it?" he asks her.

She opens it to show him a soggy mess starting to mildew.

Baby blankets. She's crying, saying words he can't understand, but he knows exactly what's happening. It's grief.

He gathers wet baby things in his arms. "I'm sorry, Marla," he says. "It's going to be okay."

"No. They're ruined," she says. "Everything's ruined."

It's gravity again, Gavin thinks. The sweet seduction of falling down and giving in. "It will be the hardest thing you've ever done." He thinks about it. "And that's saying something."

She's got her fingers laced in the smelly blankets, kneading them. "I don't want the baby to come yet," she says. She shakes, bites her lip. She closes her eyes, and tears spill down her cheeks.

"You will love him forever," Gavin tells her. "Wherever he is."

Liam nods in the doorway, flashlight in hand, his mouth opening and then closing as if he thought better of saying anything.

Marla shakes her head. She holds Gavin at arms' length, speaking deliberately. "Don't you see? That's what I thought about you, Gavin. That's how I loved you."

It's harder to get up here now. Marla leans forward on the incline, grabbing at shrubs to steady herself. Liam is behind her, his hand on her wobbling bum.

"Let's sit here," he says.

"No, I want to go to the top," she says, searching in the dark for the flat rock they always sit on when they take the path up Nose Hill from 19th Street.

When she gets there, Marla looks down at the cars on John Laurie Boulevard, picking out the obvious buildings like the university and the malls and the technical school first, then the grocery stores with their sparsely lit parking lots, the unusual buildings, like churches and fire halls, and finally the non-spaces like the river and the looping black hole that is Confederation Park. She finds Centre Street and picks out the avenue that is most likely where Liam lives, where Dani and Kamon are now. But probably not Gavin. The downtown skyline is upstaged by a searchlight swivelling, spewing random light to the sky. Far out in the distance are little farming towns where they still grow wheat and cars on fast highways that look like toys.

She looks for the pony she's sure she saw, but nothing moves. "I love Hannah and Josh," she says.

"I know."

She was waiting for him to agree, to tell her Hannah and Josh are the perfect parents. That's what he told her after they met at the restaurant, but it's harder now. She takes his hand and kneads it like she used to. "I know it's not easy for you either."

"Don't you think about changing your mind?"

This is the opening she would have jumped into headfirst a few weeks ago, like when they were in Banff and their lives were going to be lived happily ever after. "Always," she says, careful. "But this is about the baby, not me."

Liam stares at the city. "I don't know where I'll be in ten years, you know that? My hands could give out."

"I'd still love you." Marla whispers it, and the way he looks at her takes her breath away, his jaw moving a bit like he's thinking of what to say. It's going to be amazing, she thinks, all those times she expected something huge rolled into one. But it's not. He exhales through pursed lips. "You're a good person, Marla," he says finally.

Something deflates in Marla's throat. All this time she worried it was her who wasn't good enough, but he felt the same way. He flexes his hands, his back very straight, his feet together. She wants to cry, not just from the effort he puts in, but how it comes from fear. He wants to be perfect because he's afraid.

"You're my favourite person," she tells him.

There's a kick from inside, and Liam startles, then busies himself to the task of finding the baby, identifying its moving limbs. The baby is the reason they're here, why they've put so much emotion out there at each other, evading the messy crap that happens and scooping up the little moments that are worth holding onto. "We don't even have a name for him," Liam says.

"He will have a name. A beautiful name."

"Or a present."

"Maybe Gavin can fix up the crib," she says, and tips her head over her shoulder to kiss Liam.

"No," he says, pulling his head back. "We can't."

She's suddenly freezing in the summer breeze with her T-shirt and cut-offs. She stares into the night and realizes she can't see her own house. It's somewhere beyond the curve of the hill, full of black mould and river mud.

"I thought we were—"

"A couple?" He stares at her like Dave did when she broke the casserole dish. "But we hardly know what we're doing."

"That's the thing, Liam! You can't know everything—like I don't know how to have a baby. Other women are scared of that and practise stretching and opening and breathing for months."

He takes her hands. "Marla, I'm here. I will be there for the whole thing, holding your hand and stretching and opening and breathing with you. I'm not leaving."

She shakes her head, impatient. "I'm not talking about that. I'm talking about us."

The search light does its lazy rotation. "Can't we just get through one thing at a time?"

"No," she tells him. "Real life doesn't work that way. We have to stop pretending, accept that nothing's perfect."

His wraps his arms around her. "I'm not pretending." She concentrates on how warm his breath is on her neck and almost doesn't hear what he says next. "Just afraid."

Marla inhales, her whole body softening as the long grasses bend in the night breeze. To the north, silhouetted against the lights of the city, is a doe. "Me too."

Gavin was nervous at first, but finds himself enjoying his second meeting with Justin, and loses himself in signing. It's good, except Justin can't keep up, and he uses home signs Gavin doesn't recognize.

"Why so hard?"

Justin makes obvious mouth shapes. "Mainstreaming ... friend ... I ... nobody ... to sign."

"Not your family?"

He shrugs. "They ... just learning."

"Got to be other deaf people."

"You ... the first."

Gavin feels a terrible sense of loss for Justin, shouldering deafness all alone. "We'll go out, meet people." Justin nods.

"You're great with him," Justin's mom says, signing. "You ever think of working with kids?"

"I wanted to be an architect," Gavin says, remembering his other life.

"You should."

When Gavin returns, he finds Liam and Kamon on the couch with the handbook, the boy tracing pictures with his finger and rubbing his cheek on the fabric. "This is the best fucking book," he tells Gavin, "but it's kinda broken."

"You're right." Gavin gets tape and string and twisty-ties and elastic bands so Kamon can bind the book, then draws a bird singing music notes. "This is your mommy's handprint," Gavin tells Kamon, signing.

"I wanna do my foot!" So, Gavin traces it for him. When Marla brings Dani around the corner wrapped in a blanket, feverish, Gavin jumps up, but Dani shushes him.

"Keep going, Gavin. It's okay." Dani takes a lipstick tube out of her pocket and draws a smiley face on the open page.

Gavin exhales, realizing he'd been holding his breath. He knows exactly who to give the handbook to.

Weather Forecast:

Thursday, June 27
Cloudy Periods
High 23, Low 10

Friday, June 28
Mainly Sunny
High 24, Low 11

Saturday June 29
Sunny
High 25, Low 12

Sunday, June 30
Cloudy Periods
High 26, Low 13

Monday, July 1
Mainly Sunny
High 27, Low 14

Tuesday, July 2
Sunny
High 28, Low 15

Wednesday, July 3
Sunny
High 25, Low 12

Every day everyone but Marla goes to work: Gavin does cleanup, and now Dani faces cans and bottles of salad dressing at the grocery store. She's working on getting her mom's permission to have Kamon overnight once a week as soon as she gets her own place. So, each morning Marla sits alone at Liam's house which is not her house and watches the sun rise in the sky, heavy and round.

She worries the start of labour will be so small she'll miss it while she's doing dishes or cleaning the bathroom, and so she does nothing. She worries today will be the day, but still she feels nothing. When Marla can't stand the waiting anymore, she calls the only person she can think of to come pick her up.

Hannah bumps her SUV up the driveway, and Marla clutches her belly. Their house number is 455. "Are you sure this is okay?"

"Definitely. Josh took Brady to the park, so we have all morning."

There were no house numbers of any kind in the info binder, which makes sense, really. Not that Marla would just show up whenever she's lonely. She'd call first, for sure, like today. Marla loves Hannah for making this seem normal, giving Marla her number like they're friends.

Hannah seats her on a wicker chair and pours lemonade. Ice clinks in the pitcher. "How are you?"

The pretext of this meeting is to discuss Marla's latest ultra-sound, but she can't resist the openness of Hannah's face. She has these huge eyes. "Not great, actually."

Hannah leans forward, still holding the pitcher of lemonade. She looks afraid. Marla shakes her head. "Not with the baby, I mean. Everything was normal this time. He's a rock star. I was talking about me."

"Oh." Hannah sets the lemonade down on the round glass table. "Is there something I can help with?"

Marla thinks about the cigarettes she smoked with Dani. "Well, not really. The flooding and everything."

"That must be very difficult." Hannah looks at a spot be-hind Marla, then seems to interrupt herself. "But the baby's doing well?"

Didn't Marla just say that? "Yeah. Definitely fine. I asked about the gender, and they said they sometimes can't tell this far along because of the position of the baby. So, it's a surprise, but I think it's a boy."

Hannah smiles. "That's exciting. You know we will love any baby, right?"

Is Hannah trying to reassure her? Marla wants to scream, I chose you! I'm giving you my flesh! Instead, she takes another sip of lemonade. Her words feel like bricks that drop on the patio one by one. "Yeah. I'm sure you will. Look, I don't want to put my shit on you. I don't want to do that to anybody." She realizes she's come to the wrong place. "I should go."

"No. Please, stay." Hannah scooches her chair closer to Marla's.

Marla looks at Hannah's bright white slacks and her snappy bracelet and wishes someone would come in or the phone would ring. Neither happens. She shakes her head, feeling like she's going to unravel.

"You haven't had it easy, have you?"

Marla likes the way Hannah said that. It makes it sound like it's no one's fault, and it would be okay to start over, or at least start from here. And it's true. Marla pictures everyone she knows and how they get up every day and try again, even Candace.

Hannah allows Marla to cry, handing her a tissue to wipe her nose. Then she says, "I'm not perfect, you know."

"Yes, you are." Hannah is the epitome of perfection.

"No. Listen: I did drugs in high school, not just pot. I had a suicide attempt and three miscarriages. My uncle went to jail for vehicular manslaughter, and we have a huge mortgage on this house. Huge."

"Really?" Marla feels a tickle of delight, like there might be a breeze blowing. If she had any niggling doubts about Hannah being the right mother for her child, they are gone now.

"Yeah. Really. And I've spent the last ten years trying to have a baby, which seems like the simplest thing in the world until you can't do it."

Marla hadn't thought of it that way, that there are all these women out there like Hannah who are humping every night and peeing on sticks every month. "That sucks, too. I mean, it's not fair."

"No. But it's what led us here. Marla, I'm so grateful to you. More than that: I'm inspired by you."

Marla's never heard anyone say that about her in her entire life. There is something tall inside her, a feeling she hasn't had in a long time, and it's coming from the way Hannah looks at her. Marla smiles and rubs her hand on her warm belly before she remembers what it's called: pride.

17. BABY

THE PAIN IS NOTHING at first, because Marla forces herself to think about women like Hannah who will never get pregnant no matter how hard they try. But it's worse than she thought it would be. She squeezes Liam's hand at the beginning, then doesn't want anyone else touching her. Soon she can't think about the baby, because there is only searing pressure and heavy mashing muscles. When the nurse checks the baby's heartbeat, Marla remembers again how Hannah and Josh are going to be such good parents and they want a baby so bad. How someone has called them by now and they're waiting by the phone, thinking of her, waiting to hear what they're having and when they can come in their fancy car with big balloons and stuffed toys for the baby. And the pain again.

Marla thinks if she could just sleep for five minutes it would be the most amazing thing she's ever felt. Just five minutes, but then the thought is gone. It's winding up again, rushing at her, and she lets out long, low sounds she didn't realize a woman could make.

"You're doing it," Liam tells her, and his voice brings her back. He holds a straw to her lips and she sucks on it, feeling horribly vulnerable, yet all taken care of. Safe. Liam supports her under the arms, and Marla leans into him, swaying her hips like they taught her in baby class.

People move past her and touch her and Marla doesn't see them, hardly feels them. Liam is there with his hands on her back, but it's as if her body doesn't really belong to her. It's become abstract and yet perfect. Like a goddess. There is only strength and gravity now, inevitable and perfectly right. She hollers, feeling pain and pride and sheer force.

As the baby is crowning, she reaches down to touch his soft hair, then like magic, the pain is all gone.

The baby is soft and warm in Marla's arms. She shakes with shock and feels like she might throw up as nurses cover her and wrap the baby. They prod her, and something happens down there with the placenta, but none of that matters at all. There is nothing so real as this, so right, so deserved. A daughter, her black eyes open and staring. Of course. It has been this way all along.

"Can I hold her?" Liam's voice is softer than she's ever heard. His arm on her shoulder is disorienting. She had forgotten anyone else was there.

Marla nods, and Liam takes the baby awkwardly, as if he is afraid of her just a bit. He cradles the baby's legs back into her body and speaks to her as if she is a kitten. "You are a good baby," he says, stroking her. Crying.

Their daughter is weighed and checked and wiped while nurses badger Marla about eye drops, stitches, bleeding. It means nothing to her. "Give me my baby." As soon as she says the words she hears how wrong they are, even before the nurses look at her with both pity and alarm.

Baby niece. Healthy, beautiful. Here.

In the middle of the night, Gavin gets out of bed and scrubs Marla's baby things by hand, water full of vinegar and baking soda that he's crying into.

When Marla and Liam are finally alone with her, their baby is two hours old, and they have less than a day to say goodbye.

"I have to go home," Liam says.

She finds herself holding onto his shirt sleeve. "You can't stay?"

"Hospital policy," he says. "I can come back at six tomorrow morning."

Marla consults the ticking clock. "That's only three hours from now." She is thankful he doesn't ask her if she thinks everything will be alright.

"I'll see you soon." He takes the baby to kiss her, to uncurl her little fingers and smell her hair. He sets her in the bassinet, then swallows, standing up straight. And then he is gone.

Marla makes sure the door is closed and takes her daughter back into her arms. She tries not to sleep, to spend this time memorizing, to keep this image of her daughter with her kiss-shaped mouth slightly open and her black baby hair tufted and softened by vernix. She strokes every part of her baby, loving her until—

Suddenly she is awake because the baby in her arms is crying, not just whimpering, but really screaming. The door is still closed. Marla looks around like someone should be here, but she is alone. The baby arches her back, and Marla shushes her, jiggling her on her lap. The sound of her baby is tremendous, getting right inside her head. Her baby crying is the most horrible sound in the world.

Marla sticks a finger inside the baby's diaper, and yes, it is puddly, as are her clothes. She takes all of it off, not even throwing the diaper in the garbage, just letting it drop beside the bed. She wraps her daughter in a blanket, naked and screaming, and remembers what to do. She takes the baby close to her, folding the baby's body around her own and opening her gown to nurse.

It's harder than it looks. Marla tries to wait until the baby's mouth is open, but feels like she's suffocating her. How can the baby breathe with so much flesh in her face? The baby screams. Marla's breasts don't feel any different; maybe there's nothing in there. She squeezes her other nipple, just to see, and feels somehow very gross.

Nurses power in, two of them. One is releasing the brakes on the bassinet, because it apparently has wheels and is a baby transporter. The other looks at Marla with a horrified expression. "There's no need for that," she says, gesturing to Marla's open gown. She takes the squalling baby and places her gently in the bassinet, then pulls her hand back and gives Marla a dirty look. The blanket is wet. The nurse diapers the baby with brisk efficiency, talking to Marla the whole time. "Go to sleep. We'll bring her back in the morning."

Marla is sitting up, then following them to the door, her eyes on her daughter. She didn't know this is how the baby wriggled inside her, with fists waving, legs jerking. That was such a comfort, the baby growing and moving inside of her. But the sound of this baby, the horrible redness of her face, the way her cries carry down the long hallway to the nursery pulls Marla down. She sinks to the floor as her daughter turns her head from side to side, looking for Marla. Looking for a mother.

When it is light out, Marla wakes with only one thought. *I will see her again. I must see her again.*

She hurries down the hall in bare feet, worried she might be late somehow, the nursery filled with other women cuddling her baby.

Her baby is asleep. "She just took another bottle at five," the nurse tells her. "She should sleep for a few hours."

Marla reaches into the bassinet to pick her daughter up and thinks Liam is right. They absolutely should have chosen a name, because this is a person with fingernails and a ferocious amount of black hair, not just a bump that gave her heartburn and a lower centre of gravity. Hannah and Josh no doubt have their own names picked out. She clenches her jaw, and surprises herself with how much she hates them, their perfect life, and the kid they already have. Their money and their wicker furniture and their jobs.

The baby cries as Marla walks back to her room—not at

all like a grownup's wail or wet hiccup—instead, a panicked series of sharp yells with each breath. Marla smooths her hands over her baby until the screaming stops and the baby stares at Marla, taking her in. Her lips are soft and round, and Marla worries one day she'll have a boyfriend who will dump her or the people she thought were her friends will laugh at her. How can she stomach her baby out in the world without her?

A nurse brings her a note. "Phone message for you."

"You guys still do that?" Marla asks, glancing at the phone on the bedside table.

"It's from last night. Breakfast is in an hour."

Marla folds the note in her hand, knowing what it says. She strokes her baby's face, her soft, downy cheeks. There's a tiny blister on her lip from where she took the bottle. A bubble of spit at the corner of her perfect mouth. Marla feels like the luckiest person in the world holding the only miracle that could ever happen, and she doesn't want to be alone. Everyone should be here.

She calls Liam. "We're awake."

"I'm just parking right now. I'll be right up." His voice fills her with relief. As an afterthought, he asks, "Did you sleep?"

"Sort of. You?"

"No."

"Please hurry." She strokes the baby's face, the same arch as Liam's eyebrows, his earlobes. Perfection.

"I will." There's a staticy space. Then: "I love you, Marla."

In this moment, those words lift her, envelope her in ways she didn't know possible. "I love you, too," she says, trying it on again because it's something they can both hold onto.

The note says Hannah and Josh would like her to call them when she can, and so Marla does.

Hannah answers right away. "Marla," she says. "How are you?"

Marla blinks. "Fine, I'm fine."

"No, tell me everything."

Marla does, about the back labour and being afraid to go poo. About the baby peeing on the scale when the nurse weighed her and about Liam crying. About being afraid. "I'm holding her right now," Marla whispers.

Hannah is calm, an ocean. "What would you like from us today?"

The baby sighs in her sleep, and Marla feels a jagged feeling in her stomach: ripping love. "Please come in the afternoon. Like we said. I think that would be best."

"Of course. We'll be there whenever you like."

Gavin carries a bouquet, not sure how he feels. He makes a list in the elevator, the feelings like spokes on a wheel, melting into each other in the middle.

- afraid of hating Marla for this
- nervous about holding a baby or (worse) not being asked to
- off-balanced by the antiseptic smell of this place
- hungry because couldn't eat this morning
- worried that now there's no reason to be here and Liam will produce a plane ticket to Toronto

He reads over them. None are happy feelings, so he adds:

- honoured to meet my niece

Fifth floor. Liam is there to greet him and gives Gavin a big hug. "This way."

The little room is full of people, but all Gavin sees is Marla, Marla and a baby. "It's a girl," Marla says. Her cheeks are flushed, and, except for her red eyes, she looks radiant. Beautiful.

Gavin leans his crutches against the wall and lays the flowers beside her. He can tell she doesn't know what to say. He steps back, but she pats the bed for him to sit beside her.

When she looks at him he can feel all of her, the anger and the shame, but also older emotions, stronger ones like courage and love. Things they have shared for a long time. "Thank you for coming," she says.

"Of course," he says, signing, "I love you." She signs back to him.

Gavin's niece is the softest person he has ever seen. Tufts of black hair, little nostrils that flare while she sleeps. Perfect skin. Gavin strokes the curl of her ear, and she looks at him. "Hello, lovely," he says. "We've been waiting for you."

Marla puts the baby in his arms, and it's as if the world starts over again. He looks at his niece, and then his sister, and knows that everything will get better if he lets it.

Marla watches her daughter sleep in Gavin's arms and thinks it is the most bittersweet happiness. Her brother has his head up, strong and proud, crying.

Elise pokes her head around the doorframe. "Marla?" she asks, as if Marla might be someone else. She looks out of place, and suddenly small.

Dave is behind her, carrying takeout bags. "We brought burgers and fries because we know you hate hospital food," he says, trying to smile, but he has to set the bags down and squeeze Elise's shoulder. She's frozen in the doorway, pressing her fingers over her mouth like she will scream.

"I'm glad you came," Marla says, reaching for Elise. And she really is glad. This woman who used to fashionably rip Marla's jeans and then sew the frayed bits so the pants would last longer and still look cool is absolutely her mother. They hold onto each other, and Marla wants it to last all day.

But of course, they don't have all day. As Gavin hands Elise the baby, her eyes flutter open, and Elise draws a finger across her eyebrows, coaxing her back to sleep. Marla is amazed to see Elise do the same thing she's been doing, memorizing the baby's face. It must be a mom thing. "She has your ears, Liam, and Marla's little chin."

"She's perfect," Liam says.

"Yes," Elise agrees, never taking her eyes from the baby.

In the hall, two voices belt out an inappropriate set of limericks. Dani's here. "Okay, be quiet now," she tells Kamon, the door opening. He stands in the doorway while Dani wraps her arms around Marla. "You look bitchin' for a girl who just gave birth. Sorry we couldn't get here sooner—we missed the bus."

"You should have phoned," Liam says. "I would have come to get you."

"You're not staying at Liam's?" Marla asks.

"No. We're at your place, fixing the shit out of it. Literally, I think." She and Kamon both make gross-out faces on cue, and Marla feels tired. Your place.

Dani edges up close. "I'm sorry, I had to bring him. Do you want me to take him downstairs?"

Marla shakes her head, glancing at Kamon, the sweetest boy in the world, who's mesmerized by the baby in Elise's arms. He reaches out one finger to touch her. "She's got white shit on her," he says, and Elise startles.

"White stuff. You did too, buddy." Dani reaches for the baby, and Elise gives her up, reluctantly. Dani sits on the bed with Marla to hold the baby and nods, swallowing. "She is fucking amazing, Marla. I mean it."

Dave clears his throat and opens the takeout bag. "We might as well tuck into this, hey? Lots for everybody."

Everyone eats except Marla. Her burger is greasy and thick and full of relish. Yesterday she would have eaten two.

"What's wrong, honey?" Dave asks.

"Are you going to be sick?" Liam asks.

"No," she says.

"Look at me," Dave says, and Marla does. "I'm so proud of you."

Marla shakes her head. "They're coming this afternoon. I'm scared."

"You will nail this," Dani tells her. She puts the baby in Marla's arms. "You're strong as hell."

Elise holds her knees. "You can still change your mind," she says, and Gavin almost nods.

"Oh, no," Dani says, shaking her head. "Don't start."

"I just never thought you would have a baby, honey," Elise says. "What if you don't have another?"

"What kind of comment is that?" Dave asks her.

Liam gives Marla the eyeball, the one that asks if he should get everyone out of here. She shakes her head. No.

Everyone talks at once but it is easy to ignore them with her baby in her arms, a baby who will grow and who Marla will visit once a month so she can hear about new words and be given sloppy kisses and macaroni birthday cards, and then be sympathetic about the bossy friends or the annoying brother, and much later, be worried but proud at the decisions this woman will make about where to go and who to be with and how to live her life. The baby stirs in Marla's arms, opening her soft lips, and she is so right and beautiful that Marla feels inside herself a surge of confidence that everything is going to be just fine.

Everyone else is struggling: she sees grief, people poised on the cusp of huge emotions. She can help them. "I'm glad you're all here. We need your support."

Dani nods. Elise starts to interject, but Dave hushes her.

"Our baby has a beautiful family." Marla bites her lip and keeps her eyes on her daughter. "She's going to meet them today," she whispers.

It's Gavin who starts it, snapping his fingers repeatedly like the kids at the open mic. Dani does it too.

"What are we doing?" Dave whispers to Elise.

"Quiet clapping," she tells him, tears in her eyes. "For our daughter who's doing a courageous thing."

Everyone reaches their hand out to Marla, on her shoulder or her head or her leg. Marla feels their warmth, the bones in their hands, and the weight of their arms. She leans her head down onto her baby's and sends all the tender feelings she can summon into the little person in her arms, wrapping her in an invisible blanket of love.

When Cynthia arrives, Marla sends everyone away to the cafeteria. Gavin knows it's half an hour before Hannah and Josh are supposed to be there.

"Are you sure?" Dani asks.

Marla nods. "Just me and Liam, okay?" She repositions her daughter in her arms, taking the little knitted hat off so her entire face is visible. Then she shuts the door.

In the elevator, Gavin feels hot air on his back. Dave and Elise look alarmed, and Gavin turns around suddenly, dropping his crutches, worried there's a fire.

Inexplicably, Kamon is yelling, his face strained and red. Dani laughs. "We're doing an experiment. Kamon, it's true! He couldn't hear you at all!"

Gavin feels like he might cry. "You're a great mom," he says. "He's lucky to have you."

Dani shakes her head. "No. I'm lucky to have him."

Gavin nods, his throat tight. Even Dave and Elise look impressed, but the fragility is overwhelming. "Let's get Kamon some pop," Dani says, and everyone nods, grateful.

They sit at a plastic table in the cafeteria. Gavin wonders if other people would be able to guess how they know each other, or why they're here.

"Are you staying around town?" Dave asks Gavin.

"Yeah. I think so. I'm meeting some deaf people, volunteering." His time with Justin feels silly and far away now.

"Super," Dani says.

"What about you, Dani?" Elise asks.

Kamon pulls on her arm. "I'm done, Mommy. I want a donut."

Dani shakes her head, then rolls her eyes as Kamon glues himself to the display case with the baked goods inside. "I have Kamon with me two afternoons a week unsupervised now. Maybe I can have him overnight when I get my own place."

"That's so good," Gavin says, but it feels hollow. Everyone jumps. Kamon has knocked over the post and chain that shows people where to line up to pay.

Dani touches Gavin's arm, and he feels his heartbeat quicken. "I have to take him outside. Come and get us after, okay?"

Gavin nods, deflated, watching her walk out the door. Dave sips coffee, and Elise fiddles with her phone. Gavin's glad they can't see the elevators here, or the doors, because two people are going to walk into this building with an empty car seat and leave with Marla's baby.

Hannah and Josh are exactly on time. She's wearing a print dress, nothing fancy, just summery and comfortable, not showing too much skin. Josh's wearing belted black shorts and a fitted golf shirt, carrying a bouquet of flowers. Not an overly big showy bouquet like Marla hates, but a nice, appropriate bunch of flowers. Hannah has a diaper bag.

"Marla, honey, you look beautiful." Hannah smiles, her arms open in a hug aimed at Marla before she sees the baby. "Oh," she says, clasping her hands to her heart. "Oh."

Marla holds her daughter tight, and Liam leans down to whisper in her ear. "It's okay, however you want to do this." Cynthia stands beside the bed, with perfect posture, like a sentinel. Everyone is looking at Marla.

Josh puts his hand on Hannah's back, and they stand like a couple getting married who were just told no one could find the music for their first dance. Stalled.

Marla thinks of Kamon and Cynthia and Gavin. Foster families she had and packing up her stuff in grocery bags. Dave being proud of her. The teary smile breaking out on Hannah's face and the way her shoulders settle as her whole body moves forward. Marla's arms shake. Her child is the heaviest thing she has ever held out to someone else, and when Hannah takes her daughter in her arms, Marla becomes weightless.

"She's amazing," Josh whispers. He strokes the baby's head with his fingertips. Hannah's tears roll down her face and puddle into the receiving blanket. She tries to speak and can't, and Marla's heart surges. These people love her baby just as much as she does.

Liam gets Hannah the chair, and the baby starts to whimper. Hannah shushes her, patting her over a shoulder in a practised way, but the baby fusses, her fists clenched. She stands up, jiggling. "Shhhh, honey. It's okay. I'm here." She glances at Marla and stops. "We're all here."

Marla's body seems to grow smaller with each breath, as if her ribs are caving in. She forces herself to inhale, be open to this moment, because she wants to remember it forever. She smiles, and it hurts. "What will you call her?" she says, just to hear words come out.

Hannah smiles like only new mothers can. "Beatrice," she says, her eyes on Josh. "Beatrice Angel."

"Beatrice," Marla says, trying it out. The name feels stiff and old.

Hannah looks upset. "You don't like it?"

Marla wants to like it. She wants Hannah and Josh to know she is going to be a great birth mom and not a pain in the ass. She swallows. "I love it. It really suits her."

Hannah reaches for Marla's hand and squeezes. As she leans forward, baby Beatrice audibly fills her diaper. Everyone laughs, and Marla starts breathing normally again.

It takes all four of them to coordinate the wiping and positioning and repositioning necessary to change the diaper. Marla keeps her hand on Beatrice's head, looking in her eyes as she kicks her chubby legs. Then Liam picks her up.

Cynthia clasps her hands, the room suddenly all business. "I'm so glad she's awake for this moment." She nods at Liam.

Marla feels her stomach hit the floor. She watches Liam's Adam's apple move as he swallows, the look in his eyes as he holds his daughter in his arms. "I'm glad to be a part of your life," he tells her. "I promise to do my best." She blinks at him, and he smooths the black hair on her head, lost in emotion. He passes their baby to Marla and sits on the bed beside her, curling around her. "I hate goodbyes," he says, his voice breaking.

Cynthia says things about adoption being the most beautiful gift and how strong everyone is and how thankful, but Marla stops hearing her. It feels like time has ended. Marla holds her daughter's soft weight to her chest, feeling her breathe. It is the simplest thing. Everything from two people in one embrace. "There's no one I love more than you," she whispers. Her ears hurt from holding the tears back, so she lets them go. "I'm keeping this moment forever," Marla says, and taps her heart. "Right here." It's sweet and horrible and perfect. Marla realizes their daughter won't remember any of it.

She stands with her baby, Liam with his hand on her shoulder, and Cynthia nodding. I can do this, Marla tells herself, kissing her daughter on the forehead. And she can. Marla sets baby Beatrice in Hannah's arms, telling herself it's going to be okay. Everything will be okay. "I know you'll take care of her." Marla's nose drips, and she wipes at it with her arm.

Hannah passes the baby to Josh and holds onto Marla like they are the only two people in the world. "I promise," she whispers. "Thank you, Marla. She means everything to us." Marla hugs Hannah for a long time.

Josh brings in a car seat they had the foresight to leave in the hall. As he buckles the baby in, Hannah gives Marla a little box. Inside are two silver chains, each with a heart. "One for each of you," Hannah says. Marla kneels to put the tiny chain around her baby's neck. She kicks her little feet, oblivious. Happy.

Marla takes Gavin's handbook from her bag. "This is for Beatrice," she says. "We all worked on it."

Hannah takes it with reverence. Liam and Josh are shaking hands, and Marla knows it's almost over. Cynthia passes around papers to sign.

The proud parents stand at the door, smiling down at the car seat. Marla can't see her baby's face anymore.

"Goodbye," Marla says, and they nod and smile and walk out the door.

18. SHRINKING

MARLA GIVES THEM a twenty-minute head start, then packs her bag.

"What are you doing?" Liam asks.

"Going home. I can't be here now." She feels dead, as if everyone predicted the world would end, and then it really did, but just for them. There are diapers on the windowsill and flowers to pack up, useless stuff. In the bathroom, she takes a handful of pads, the squeezy bottle they gave her, and an extra pair of panty-hose underwear. And some soap. She stuffs it all in her purse, which she drags down the hall to the nurses' desk, Liam following.

Marla's name is on the big white board. In the second column where the nurses have written the names of the babies born, the space next to Marla's name is blank. She takes the cap off the marker and writes, Beatrice Angel. "That's her name," Marla says to the shocked nurses. "I'm leaving."

They tell her several things about hospital policy and discharge times and postpartum depression and liability, and Liam sighs, holding her bag. "I'll let you know if there's any crying or whatnot," he says, his voice falsely upbeat. She squeezes his hand, proud that he can take insensitive bullshit and make it okay, even today.

A nurse offers to wheel Marla out of the hospital. "No thank you," Marla says, thinking that she already looks wrong not carrying a baby on her lap. Her baby's in a car going home.

She doesn't even know what her baby's bedroom looks like, what colour crib or cradle she has. Marla hits the elevator button and tries not to be weak. Liam says nothing, which is exactly what she needs.

Downstairs, everyone is waiting in the cafeteria. They stand up abruptly, not moving, no one smiling, like a doctor just told them Marla didn't make it. Everyone's eyeing her bag.

"I'm going home," Marla says, and they all talk at once.

"But you're so pale."

"Are you feeling okay?"

"You should be lying down."

Marla can't seem to take her eyes off a stack of plastic trays on a table. "Look, I'm glad you're all here, but I'm done."

"Do you want us to come over?" Elise asks.

Marla shakes her head. She doesn't want to talk at all.

"I'll drive you home," Liam says, and Dave and Elise nod.

In the car with Dani and Kamon in the backseat, Liam admits that he can't stay. "I've got my students tonight."

Marla nods, staring out the window. So it's over. She doesn't have the energy to protest.

"Do you want me to come back later?" Liam asks, and she wants very badly to say yes, as if she could have Liam and only Liam for whole days without interruption while she gets used to the hole inside her.

"Are you going to move in with her?" Dani asks.

The reality is messier, much more. Marla is tired of hearing so many voices. "I'll be fine. Just take me home."

At home, Dani makes Marla tea and takes Kamon with his dog to the park. Marla sits by herself in her empty house. Dani's done a good job of cleaning up, but it still smells kind of soppy. The basement is now off limits, so Kamon and Dani are sleeping in the living room. The landlord said he couldn't get any contractors in until next month at the earliest.

Marla looks in her closet and finds all her baby gifts stacked beautifully and smelling brand new. Every good and right thing.

Marla howls, clutching the baby things to her and yet dropping them in her haste, her hands over her ears as if she could put all that noise back into her head.

Marla's made a horrible mistake. She picks up the phone and dials.

Cynthia answers right away. "I thought you might call."

"I can't do this," Marla says, out of breath.

"Remember what we talked about? It's time to be strong."

Strong. Marla hates that word, and hates Cynthia for saying it. Like she should just fall out of love because anyone can decide to do that. Cynthia tells her all the things she said she would, about how prepared Marla is and how she chose Hannah and Josh because she had faith in them. She tells Marla to surround herself with people. Marla hears about half of it. Cynthia makes an appointment for Marla to come in next week. Fucking Cynthia.

Marla collapses on her bed, pounding her fists into the pillow. She screams into its softness, feeling her hot breath come back at her. It hits her that she's laying on her stomach again. Because there's nothing in there at all.

angry
Marla, honey, we couldn't be prouder of you.
hard to feel anything good
You are generous and strong and we love you
thanks for being there
Always

That night, Gavin dreams the room is flooding, only it's not an ordinary room. There's asphalt where the floor should be, and Gavin can't be certain it's not a mall parking lot. Water laps at the bedframe, and Gavin knows it will not float. He glimpses a concrete island with brambly bushes growing into the water, but it is hazy like there is too much cloud cover. Through the wispy wet, Gavin can see Marla there, with her baby, but he's too far away to collect what she says. Gavin steps off the bed and can't touch bottom. It's like before. He holds his breath until he breaks the surface, swimming.

In the middle of the night afterpains twist and rip through Marla's belly. Dani rubs Marla's back, but it aches like the baby's coming all over again. The puppy whines, and Marla wakes up Kamon with her groaning. He wanders over from the couch rubbing his face and trailing his blankie. "Mommy," he says.

Dani takes him in her arms. "Kamon, Marla's sad and her tummy hurts."

Kamon's round blue eyes are full of sympathy as he wraps his arms around her. "Don't cry, Marla. Don't be sad." Little boy arms and little boy smell.

"Do you want me to call him?" Dani asks.

Marla feels a wave of relief. "No. Just give me the phone."

Liam answers on the second ring. He's been crying too. "Marla, I can be there in ten minutes. Do you need anything?"

"Why are we crying without each other?"

It takes him a second to answer. "I don't know, babe. I'm coming now."

"Bring Gavin, please. I need everybody."

Nose Hill bouquet:
horsetail
fairy bells
yellow lady's slipper
prairie crocus
buffalo beans
northern buttercup
wild blue flax
silverweed

Found wet newspaper to wrap flowers in. Nicest ones by water. Lots of nodding thistle on south side, waving five/six feet tall. Three dog walkers: two black labs, one Shepherd cross, and a greyhound. Orioles and kestrels. Sky clear.

Liam stays to make tea, bring Marla her slippers, and cook tortellini. While Liam is at work, Gavin plays Scrabble with her. He takes walks when she naps and brings her wildflowers.

When she wakes on the third day, her breasts feel like rocks. They hurt, and they're leaking.

She runs a bath and sits there, dripping. Crying.

The door opens, and Liam enters. "Look—porn star boobs," she says.

"You're beautiful, Marla. Can I come in?"

She nods. He just saw her give birth, after all.

"Do you think this happens to women who have a stillbirth?"

Liam sits on the edge of the tub and strokes her hair. "Probably."

"Do you miss her?"

"Of course."

Marla wants to ask if Liam misses the two of them together, if he misses Marla. "What should we do?"

"That's what I wanted to ask, about us. When Gavin was talking to Dani the night of the flood, it made me think about you, and how you've always believed in me, how you've helped me."

"I care about you."

"Me too. Can we try again? I finally understand what you were saying when Gavin was in the hospital, about not having to be perfect. I'm hopelessly imperfect."

"Me too," Marla says. "Come in here."

He takes his shirt off and his belt, folding his clothes before he sits down in the water behind her so she can lean back on him.

"I want more you. I'd love to try again."

Liam trails a finger down her stomach, down into the soapy water. She can feel that he's hard, and she laughs, leaning forward, holding the edge of the tub to get up. Water runs off her body. "I just had a baby," Marla says. She wraps a towel around herself, feeling kinda fat.

"Like I said, truly imperfect."

"It's a deal." Marla smiles, then hurries to get dressed. As she bends to pick up her clothes, her milk lets down again, dripping on the floor. Such a waste.

Liam gets her a plastic sandwich bag from the kitchen, and she sits on her bed squeezing breast milk into it. The puppy yips at her feet. When she can't stand it anymore, she tries the other side. The bag sloshes, a significant amount. Marla zips it shut and writes the date with permanent marker, then puts it in the freezer. It feels good to be doing something right.

Marla's been purposely not calling them, not after the last time when she revealed herself to be not tough and kind of annoying. But when she sees the flowers on the doorstep on the fifth day, she picks up the phone.

"How are you, Marla?" Hannah says. "We've been thinking about you so much."

"I've got all this frozen breast milk," Marla says. "I can bring it over in a cooler."

"Oh, honey," Hannah says, and Marla can't tell if Hannah's mortified or full of pity. "That is such a generous thing to do." Hannah starts crying. "We would *love* to have that."

Marla braces herself against the wall. She's going to see her baby. She takes the phone with her to the freezer to look at the heap of bags, then to the spare room to find the cooler, which is under the new notebooks Dave and Elise bought her. "It's good for only so long in the freezer, and once you heat it, you can't reuse it."

"Marla, thank you. I'm so happy you thought of this. Maybe we could get together on the weekend and you can tell us all about it."

Marla's heart hits the floor. "The weekend?"

"Sure. Or next week sometime? It's just that we have company right now, and then Beatrice's doctor's appointment tomorrow. Things are very busy."

They don't want it. Her baby has other plans. Hannah's baby, Marla reminds herself. Not hers.

Marla hangs up the phone without really saying goodbye, just sort of grunting out a small ball of emotion that could very easily lead to something bigger. Now she wants the feelings, refuses to pretend it's easy to give someone else a human being she made from her own meat.

She takes the baby things out of her closet one by one. The little onesies make her stomach squeeze up. They are impossibly small now, not just cute. Something her baby could wear this week and next, but not her baby: someone else's baby. She was so excited when she opened them at the diner. How naïve. She throws the 'Baby's First Handprint' kit at the wall, where it punches a triangular hole in the drywall. These are the kind of memories birth moms have, she thinks. Angry ones.

"Marla," Gavin says behind her, and she clutches the baby bathtub to her chest as if he might take it away. He runs a finger down her back, tentative, then lays his hands on her shoulders, feeding strength into her with his touch. "I'm here," he says, and it is enough.

Marla cries at the absurdity of clinging to a baby bathtub, at the awkwardness of its plastic contours and how unhuggable such a thing really is. It's her baby she should be holding, and for a second she forgets and thinks perhaps her baby has died and she is alone. And then she remembers her baby is probably sleeping in a room full of brand-new furniture amidst a houseful of hushed grandparents and aunties and uncles bearing baby presents that are expensive and trendy and not at all like this box-store plastic bath tub. And Marla holds the tub a bit tighter, as if it had feelings of not being quite good enough either.

Gavin hugs her and the bathtub, keeping it with her as he leads her away from the baby things and into her bed, tucking the covers around her. He hums to her as she sobs, and she thinks it is probably the most mournful sound in the world, a deaf person singing. She loves Gavin even more for it.

"I'm getting milk on you," she says.

"I don't care."

"Is it always going to be like this?" she asks, meaning crying in bed leaking milk. Holding the bathtub.

"Maybe," Gavin tells her. "But we'll always have each other."

Marla does something she should have done years ago. She calls and talks for a long time. She takes the bus with Gavin, lets him lead her there. They knock on the door together.

Candace takes one look at Marla and falls into her arms. "It's too late," she wails. "Your baby's gone."

Marla holds on to Candace as tight as she can. She smells like cheap perfume and mint gum. Marla's touched her mom planned to smell nice, that she wanted people to know she tried. "Mom," she says, and finds herself crying. "I'm having a shitty day."

"I know, baby. I tried to see you sooner, to tell you to keep him, but now it's done."

Marla wipes her eyes with the neck of her shirt. "Her. It's a girl. Actually, they don't file the papers until tomorrow."

Candace pulls back and holds Marla by the shoulders, shaking her. "Then what are you doing, girl? Go get your baby."

Marla glances at Gavin. Strong. "I'm not going to do that."

"Then you're going to spend your whole life crying, just like I did."

Gavin's voice fills the room. "I've never seen you cry."

Candace looks at the floor. "I lost my children too," she says. "I came to visit you in those supervised rooms and brought you candy and they threw it out." She looks at Marla, then Gavin, her face pleading. "I always brushed your teeth, both of you. You know that, right?"

Marla tries to remember being eight in a supervised visit with

Gavin. It's easier to recall foster homes, and later Candace, who was always messed up and forgetting to send birthday cards. She remembers explaining to other kids that she didn't have a real mom. "That was a long time ago," Marla says.

"Not for me. I live with that right here," Candace says, thumping her fist on her breastbone. It makes a thunking sound. There are tears in her eyes. "What you feel now, I feel it every day."

Marla tells herself she did not make the wrong choice. Her baby is fine, happy, and being held, but she has a paralyzing thought—what if something goes wrong? What if it's SIDS, and no one knows until morning, or she drowns when Hannah is answering the phone or someone else is looking after her or they're on vacation? She looks at Candace. What if her baby hates her for her whole life, the same horrible pity-hate balling up in Marla's stomach right now?

"If you knew what to do, why didn't you do it?" Marla shouts, her face too close to Candace's, but Marla doesn't care. She pushes closer. "Why couldn't you be there?"

Candace nods. "Tell it to me," she says. "Get mad, baby." She points her chin up like she's expecting Marla to hit her, and then Marla does remember: late at night, crawling into Gavin's bed because of the yelling. Wet thuds, a sort of barking cry. Sick moaning, the furniture being slammed around. Her mother being beat. Marla remembers wanting to rip whoever it was this time apart or run away or do anything except hide with her sleeping brother who couldn't hear a thing.

"Mom, no. I don't want to be mad at you. I'm working on forgiving you."

Candace shakes her hair off her face. "You're better than me, Marla. Having a kid? You could do it."

"I am doing it," Marla says. It's true. She's been doing it for days, making breakfast and taking phone calls and making sure she has clean clothes.

"Don't be like me," she says, but Gavin shakes his head,

signs *strong*. Candace makes the same sign back, tentative. "What's it mean?"

"It means it's okay, Mom. It's going to be okay." Marla thinks about the last time she came to her mom, when she was a teenager living on the street and fucked up on meth. Candace took one look at her and called the cops to take her home, back to Dave and Elise's. "Here," she says, and hands a photo to Candace.

Candace strokes it, tracing the baby's cheeks and nose. "Beautiful," she says, and hugs her, pulling Gavin in too. "I love you guys."

Marla exhales a breath she realizes she was holding for most of her life. "I love you too, Mom."

EPILOGUE: **LATER**

THEY LOOK NERVOUS for sure. Liam's wearing cufflinks for breakfast. "Do I look good?" Liam's signs are so much cleaner now. He's really picked it up fast.

"Top notch," Gavin says.

Marla pulls him aside. "You sure you don't mind babysitting Kamon today?"

"Of course not—it's Saturday. I don't have to work."

"I'm glad you're talking to Dani."

He is too. His counsellor has been helping him with the anger and his need for control, but it's Dani he talks to more. They've been meeting for coffee after work, getting feelings out and sharing successes and failures. He's realizing it's a life project, not a checking it off a list thing, but a gradually doing things better most of the time thing. They encourage each other.

"Marla, let's go." Liam straightens his tie in the mirror.

"We'll be early," she says, and Gavin sees a hint of a different Marla. A more confident Marla.

"It's okay," Liam tells her. "Everything's okay." He takes Marla in his arms, drifting her into a slow waltz. They lean close, and Liam whispers into her ear until her body softens and a smile begins.

It's monthly visit time, baby Beatrice is waiting, and so they go, waving to Gavin as they close the door. Gavin sits down and whistles with Kamon, teaching the little guy how.

ACKNOWLEDGEMENTS

I wish to express my gratitude to the staff and students of the University of British Columbia Creative Writing MFA program, especially Joseph Boyden, Gail Anderson-Dargatz, Annabel Lyon, Sara Graefe, and Merilyn Simonds. I learned not to be comfortable, and to ask better questions. Your voices inspire me daily.

Thank you to the tireless staff at Inanna Publications, who are kind and have incredible attention to detail.

I am lucky to have had many thoughtful readers, including Kim McCullough, Katie Wagner, and Christina Sheppard. Special thanks to Heidi Grogan, who opened my heart.

Thank you to all the birth and adoptive parents who shared their stories. You are incredible.

A round of appreciation for the ladies of the Husky Energy Land Department of 2002, who allowed me to be their pet and were tickled pink when I told them I would be a writer.

Much love to my family, who is always there for me, and my daughters, who write fiercely too. Lastly, James, who is everything from a creator of calming jingles to my soulmate.

Jennifer Spruit was born in Lloydminster, AB/SK, and now lives in Courtenay, B.C. She attended the Creative Writing MFA program at the University of British Columbia. Jennifer enjoys teaching kids, playing music, and paddling a blue canoe. Her work has appeared in *Arc, The Antigonish Review, Prairie Fire Magazine*, and *Event Magazine*, among others. This is her first novel.